DEADLY VERDICT

A DETECTIVE EMILY TIZZANO VIGILANTE JUSTICE THRILLER

KJ KALIS

This is a work of fiction. Names, characters, places, and incidents either are the products of the author's imagination or are used fictitiously. Any resemblance to actual persons, living or dead, or locales is entirely coincidental.

Copyright © 2024 KJ Kalis, BDM LLC
eISBN 978-1-955990-57-8
ISBN 978-1-955990-58-5
All rights reserved

Without limiting the rights under copyright reserved, no part of the publication may be reproduced, stored in or introduced into a retrieval system or transmitted in any form or by any means (electronic, mechanical, photocopying, recording, or otherwise including technology to be yet released), without the written permission of both the copyright owner and the above publisher of the book. The content is not to be used for AI training without permission.

The scanning, uploading, and distribution of this book via the Internet or via any other means without the permission of the publisher is illegal and punishable by law. Please purchase only authorized electronic editions, and do not participate in or encourage electronic piracy of copyrighted materials. Your support of the author's rights is appreciated.

Published by:
BDM, LLC

ALSO BY K.J. KALIS:

New titles released regularly!

If you'd like to join my mailing list and be the first to get updates on new books and exclusive sales, giveaways, and releases, click here!

I'll send you a prequel to the next series FREE!

OR

Visit my Amazon page to see a full list of current titles.

OR

Take a peek at my website to see a full list of available books.

www.kjkalis.com

1

Chicago PD cold case detective Lou Gonzalez was in the middle of what he decided was a long morning. He checked his watch, the engraved gold Bulova his wife had given him for their anniversary five years before and nearly groaned out loud. It wasn't even seven AM yet.

He sighed, then took a sip of the lukewarm cup of coffee he'd snagged on his way to the crime scene. He'd paid five bucks for the cup. *They couldn't make it hot?* He shook his head. Some lawyer somewhere must be worried about lawsuits. He took a sip, wrinkling his nose. It wasn't even good coffee. Having a cup with him usually boosted his mood, but unfortunately, it was doing nothing to help him at that moment.

Lou took another sip and returned the coffee to the cup holder in the blue sedan the department had been letting him keep at home to use for occasions like this. He slammed the car door and walked from where he'd parked the car down to the beach. He stopped for a second, wondering if he had everything he needed. He wasn't sure. "It's too early for this," he muttered under his breath and then turned back to the car.

He opened the door, rummaged around in the back seat

and pulled out a notebook and a pen. Many of the detectives just took their notes on their phone, then somehow transferred them directly into the file. Lou wasn't quite that tech savvy. He'd been with the department for long enough that he was almost halfway to retirement. He shook his head at the thought as he slammed the car door again and strode off towards the beach. How was it possible that he'd been with the department for twenty years?

He didn't have a chance to consider the answer to that question. An officer passed him as he was on his way down to the beach, doing nothing more than giving him a nod. He remembered the feeling of being sent away or restricted by what he was allowed to do. He used to show up at a scene all decked out in his uniform, call for the detectives and just stand by until they arrived, waiting for them to bark out the same order over and over again. "Step back and secure the scene." He'd always had the urge to roll his eyes and say, "I know. *I know...*"

Now, it was his turn.

Luckily, by the time he made it down to the beach, he didn't have to issue the order. The scene had been secured. Two newly minted patrolmen — Lou could tell by their shiny work boots — were standing by. Neither of them was looking at the body. In fact, the pair had stepped a distance away from it, notably upwind. After surveying the scene, he couldn't blame them.

The department had gotten a call an hour before from a frantic woman. She'd been walking her dog at Scenic View Park, aptly named with its view of Lake Michigan. From a distance, she thought yet another log had rolled up on the beach. Upon closer inspection, it was a man. A very dead one.

Lake Michigan coughing up her latest victim was never Lou's favorite way to start the day. Drowning victims were some of the worst, their bodies usually bloated and nibbled by all sorts of creatures he'd rather not think about lurking in the water. In his career, he'd seen all sorts of dead bodies — people who had been stabbed, shocked, hung, run over by a car, and even a guy that had gotten caught up in a machine at a meat packing plant.

That had been a grizzly one.

But the bloated ones were somehow some of the most unsettling for him. Why, he wasn't sure. They were grotesque, like something from an artist's wicked imagination.

Lou spotted the location where the body was, but he didn't look at it. Not yet. Instead, he surveyed the scene. Cook County's park management system did a good job of making sure that the debris that got kicked up every winter onto the beach was cleared away, leaving a path for people who wanted to walk, run or picnic nearby. Some people even swam in the water. Lou did not.

The beach itself was covered in a wide band of pale sand studded with rocks and deadwood, the lake's newest deposit after a storm that had kicked up big waves a few days before. Off in the distance, he could see what looked like the trunk of a tree, the bark and branches stripped off of it by the water, nothing but the core of the tree left intact. He shook his head. If his buddy Stan, an avid walleye fisherman, had been there, he would have commented about how logs like those floating in the lake caused all sorts of trouble for boaters. "Those dead heads," Lou heard Stan's voice in his head. "Got my props hung up on one of those one time. Cost me seven grand to get the shaft and propeller fixed." Lou couldn't count the number of times Stan had made the comment. At least that was one good thing — the body they'd found hadn't gotten caught up in propellers.

Unable to avoid it any longer, Lou stopped about five feet from the body and pulled his notebook out of his pocket. There wasn't a lot he could do until the coroner arrived. She was new. A real stickler for maintaining the scene until she got there. He looked over his shoulder wondering what was taking so long. Then again, the traffic in Chicago was notoriously bad, and the coroner, although she moved faster than the last guy they'd had in the county, still seemed to take her time getting to scenes. Thinking about it, he wasn't sure exactly what the hurry was. Though he didn't want to be stuck there all morning, the reality was that by the time the coroner was called, the damage had already been done.

Lou cocked his head to the side and stared at the body. He glanced back at his notebook, flipping the cover open and clicking the tip of the pen out of the casing. In the background, he could hear the lapping of the water as small waves from the lake rolled gently up on shore. He stared at the body, watching it move slightly, the sand underneath getting pulled back into the lake. He jotted a couple of notes. Male. Late twenties, early thirties? The man's skin was pale from lack of circulation, gray from the water, but Lou could tell he was of Latin origin, or at least he looked to be. Lou moved around the body. From the knees on down, the corpse was still partially in the water. Lou added a few more notes on the page he'd started, including the date and the time and the location — for which he used his phone to pull a precise GPS pin. Though he wasn't very comfortable with tech, he had learned how to text coordinates to himself. Finally, he added some general notes about what he saw, what the man was wearing, and how he'd been advised of the case, all things that were likely to get lost in the shuffle if he were to get another call and have to run.

This was Chicago, after all.

Lou tugged on the collar of his T-shirt. Although detectives were supposed to dress the part, they'd called him out so early that he hadn't had time to iron his pants. He'd thrown on a CPD T-shirt and a pair of jeans, adding his holster to his waistband with his department-issued 9mm pistol and his badge. The T-shirt, one he'd gotten for the annual baseball game between CPD and Chicago's Fire Department, was one that had never fit him quite well enough. The neck always seemed to be a shade too tight. He was feeling it now.

Staring at the body, he went through the same mental checklist he'd used since he was a rookie, designed to keep him solidly focused on the facts — body position, notable injuries, questions, observations. It was a list he was familiar with, one he'd used so many times in the past it was hard to remember when precisely he'd started, though he always thought it was when he'd seen his first dead body at a scene. It had become so ingrained in him that he'd even used it when he was with the Cold Case Division. Details were details. Time might change things, but the same type of evidence caught criminals over and over again.

Lou sighed and stared at the body again, feeling like he'd lost his train of thought. He started with the things that were blatantly obvious. The body was male, resting on his right side, wearing a pair of jeans, dark wash, not unlike the ones Lou himself was wearing. He had no belt, only one sock and no shoes, a red T-shirt with a wide yellow stripe running vertically from the shoulder to the waistband. His face was pale and puffy, the lips blue and the skin splotchy, the man's eyes were open, staring blindly into the distance. Lou made his way around the body to the back. From the lump in the man's back pocket, it looked like there was a wallet in it, though Lou refrained from pulling it out. There was no reason to draw the ire of the new coroner. He circled the body again, fighting off the urge to pull the guy's wallet. The new medical examiner was a little pickier than their past coroner. She didn't want anyone to do anything other than check for a pulse until she arrived. Given the way the body looked there was no reason. As far as Lou was concerned, her insistence on keeping CPD at bay was nothing more than a turf war. If the coroner wanted to be in control, she could have it.

Lou scanned the man's pockets for any other obvious lumps. There were none. He looked down at a page in his notebook that was rapidly filling with comments and wrote, "Cell phone?" Everyone carried a cell phone with them, didn't they?

Just then he heard a voice behind him. "Hey, partner. What we got?"

Courtney Green appeared on the scene. She'd been assigned by Captain Ingram as his new partner, one he didn't want, two months before. Braylon hadn't given him a choice. "We don't work solo, Gonzalez," he'd grunted, handing Lou the paperwork.

Lou glanced at Courtney, fighting off irritation at her tardiness. She was wearing a pair of jeans and a blue T-shirt just like he was, though her badge was on a chain dangling around her neck, her strawberry blonde hair up in a ponytail.

"What took you so long?"

Courtney shrugged. "I was in the shower when the phone rang. Just got back from my run. Add that to the commute in and it took me a while. Sorry about that."

The excuse seemed plausible enough. Lou knew that Courtney lived forty-five minutes outside of the city. Why so far away, he had no idea. What he did know was that it had made her late on more than one occasion, something their captain had commented on and told Lou to keep an eye on. "The last thing I need is somebody who's habitually late," Braylon had grumbled at Lou a couple weeks before.

Lou glanced at Courtney. At least she'd shown up. He wasn't the kind of guy to turn her in, even if that's what Captain Ingram wanted.

Courtney circled the body, her expression tense. She was new to the Homicide Division, still excited by catching a new case. Lou could only hope it wore off soon. "What do you think happened to this guy?"

"Not sure yet. What do you see?" Maybe it was a good time

to test his young detective and see how her powers of observation were.

Unlike the patrolman who had walked away from the body, Courtney didn't seem to be nervous about facing the dead body at all. If anything, her bright eyes told Lou that she was interested in what had happened. Her focus reminded him a bit of himself, even if it had been from years past. From her pocket, she produced a pair of blue plastic gloves.

Lou held a hand up. "Remember, the coroner doesn't want us touching the body till she gets here."

Courtney nodded. "I know, I know. I just put them on in case."

Lou held his hands up. *What?* New detectives were a strange bunch. "In case of what? The guy gets up and walks away? By the way he looks, the odds aren't good of that happening."

Courtney grimaced. "Cute, Gonzalez. Real cute." She surveyed the body. "Well, looks like we have a male, approximate age mid-to-late twenties. By the lump in the back pocket, I guess he still has his wallet. We'll see what's in it when we pull it out."

"The fact that he has it means —?"

"Nothing. All it means is that he has it. There might be stuff in it, or it could be completely empty. No assumptions."

Lou nodded in appreciation. "Correct. All we know is it looks like he has a wallet in his back pocket. What else?"

"Well, he's missing his shoes and one of his socks. I'm guessing that could be from the water?"

"Maybe. He also could have lost them in a struggle."

Courtney conceded the point. "Right. We'll have to wait and see on that." She stood up and walked towards the man's face, leaning close. "By the looks of his facial features, I would guess he's of some sort of Latin or Spanish descent. Doesn't look like there's any bruising, though it's hard to tell with his skin so mottled."

"You'll have to ask the coroner, but I think that's called vascular marbling."

Courtney stood up, stared at the body for a minute, then looked out at the lake. She turned to Lou. "I'm guessing suicide. What do you think?"

Lou stared at his notes for a moment, then looked at the body. How had she come to that conclusion so fast? "I'm not sure."

Courtney's eyes got wide as if she couldn't believe that he was disagreeing with her. "Well, I know we have to wait for the coroner, but there's no bruising that I can see, the skin on his hands is intact, so it's not like he has any defensive wounds. There are no holes in his clothes that look like he's been stabbed or shot. What else could it be?"

"Um, I don't know, maybe an accident?"

"Oh, come on Lou. An accident? Where's his cell phone? Everyone carries their cell phone with them."

Lou scowled. He had wondered the same thing. "What does that have to do with anything?"

"Well, if he fell in the water, wouldn't he have his cell phone with him?"

Lou shook his head. "It could have fallen out." Lou paused. "Or, the cell phone could be in this guy's house, in his car or at the bottom of Lake Michigan for all we know. Haven't you learned anything yet? We don't know anything until we know something for sure."

To his relief, that quieted Courtney. Lou took a couple steps to the side, looking at the body again, wondering why he hadn't told Captain Ingram he still didn't want a partner. Maybe he could have held off the inevitable pairing a little longer. He appreciated Courtney's enthusiasm, but jumping to a conclusion so fast made him a little nervous. Was it possible she was right? Absolutely. Was it also possible she was wrong? Absolutely.

Lou knew the biggest mistakes he'd made as a detective was to make assumptions too fast. It was one of the things that he'd appreciated about being part of the Cold Case Division. He was missing it now. He'd been transferred out of there the year before when he discovered he couldn't get along with the new captain that was put in charge. It was surprising. He'd had little to no flak from anyone he'd worked with in the past. Lou was known to be a good collaborator.

But not in this case.

The solution was that the department had slid him over to an open position in Homicide, which was how he ended up where he was at that moment, paired with Courtney. He liked Braylon. The captain was, for the most part, a straight shooter. He'd been patient with Lou about not wanting a partner but had finally put his foot down. But working live cases were different than cold ones. At least with cold cases, there was plenty of time to review the evidence. The dust had already settled. There was a lot of space for interpretation, for new theories, for really studying the details of a case. A new case, however, was completely different. There was immense pressure from the brass and the family to find out what had happened and get justice. But justice didn't work like that. Lou had learned that he had to slow things down and take his time. Sometimes the littlest detail would be the one that would lead them in a completely different direction. If they missed it, the case might end up where no one wanted it to.

Cold.

2
―――――

Emily scowled, realized it and tried to relax her face. It was hard. She felt the grip of frustration in her gut. "Come on, Martina," she groaned over the bass thump of music the guys were playing at the other end of the gym. The sour smell of sweat hung in the air. "We just have a couple of minutes left."

The woman in front of her stopped, bent over and put her hands on her knees, her chest heaving, sweat dripping off of her forehead onto the stained canvas of the boxing ring floor. "Emily. I can't —"

Emily shook her head, dropping the cracked vinyl hand pads covering her palms to her sides. She'd been working with Martina for the last three weeks, helping Clarence out at the gym, covering some of his private lessons while he was busy getting some new members started. Apparently, Martina wasn't as used to as hard of a workout as Clarence had suggested when he asked Emily for the favor. From over her shoulder, Emily heard a voice. "What seems to be the problem here?"

Clarence wandered next to the ring where Emily and Martina were working out. Martina hadn't moved, her chest still heaving. Drops of sweat were running off of her forehead, leaving a puddle on the boxing ring floor. Emily glanced at Clarence. "She said *it*."

Clarence arched an eyebrow. "You mean, *it*?"

Emily nodded. "Sorry to turn you in, Martina. The truth is the truth."

Martina looked at Clarence and then at the ground.

Clarence shook his head. "We don't say 'I can't' in my gym, Martina. I told you that on the first day. I don't allow anyone to say that. 'I can't' is for babies and whiners. If that's who you wanna be then walk out the door and don't come back. If that was just a mistake and you feel bad, give me ten push-ups and then finish your dang lesson."

Clarence stomped away. Martina gave Emily the side eye. Emily just shrugged. She wasn't gonna lie for anyone, especially someone who was willing to flake out on the last five minutes of their workout.

Grunting, Martina got down on the floor, gave Emily ten push-ups and then stood up.

The whole interaction had put Emily in a mood. She knew not everyone was tuned up like her, but why not at least try to give it everything you've got? Emily slipped her hand back into the hand pads, slapped them together and held them up, calling out combinations. She pushed Martina to run through a fast combination of punches, crosses, and footwork, calling out the names of the pads faster than Martina could even hit the targets. "One, one-two, two-two, two-one, one-one"

By the time Martina was finished with the final five minutes of her private workout with Emily, the only thing she could do was drop to her knees. Emily stood, watching her for a second. She knew what Martina wanted. She wanted Emily to walk over, tell her what an amazing job she'd done, and be sympathetic to what she'd been through. Martina wanted to be coddled, begged to come back to the gym the following week to repeat the process.

But Emily wasn't like that.

She pulled the hand targets off, tossing them on the floor where Martina was still sitting on her knees. Her face was red and splotchy, the sweat glistening on her forehead, running down the sides of her face. Emily stood and looked at her for a second, giving Martina a chance to do or say something that showed she had some fight in her. Anything at all.

Nothing.

After counting to ten in her head, Emily ran out of patience. She sighed. "Clean up the gloves and targets before you leave. There's a mop in the corner so you can sanitize the ring for the next student."

Emily walked away.

Climbing out of the ring, Emily stepped down onto the gym floor, hearing the thump of the bass from the music playing at the other end of the gym. Clarence didn't care what the kids put on to listen to as long as it didn't have any foul language, which limited many of the artists that the boxers wanted to listen to. He was a stickler about that. Real old school. Still went to church every single Sunday and refused to have the gym open. Emily liked that about him. Clarence stuck to his guns. She did too.

The noise of boxing gloves hitting bags echoed off the unfinished ceilings of the gym. Emily could hear the slap of legs hitting bags as well. While Clarence's gym had started off as a boxing only kind of place, over the last few years people had begun bringing in some other styles, more MMA, with kicking and knee strikes in addition to old-fashioned Sugar Ray Leonard type of boxing. Clarence had objected for all of about thirty seconds and then allowed it as long as people were under control.

Emily picked up her duffle bag from where it had been

stowed in the corner, took it with her to the other end of the gym, where no one else was working, dragging a kickboxing bag out from the wall. She put in a set of earbuds and pulled on a set of shin guards and boxing gloves.

Over the next hour, Emily did the workout that Martina refused to do — a pretty much nonstop assault on the punching bag in front of her, not caring how much she sweated, not paying any attention to the burning of her muscles or her lungs. She went through combinations, attacks, defenses, every kind of kick she could think of, and even managed to include some elbow strikes and knee strikes as well. On the few breaks she took, she did a combination of burpees, sit-ups, and push-ups. Out of the corner of her eye, she saw a few people walk by, including Martina, who eyed her. No one ever said anything to her, just giving the woman beating the tar out of the kickboxing bag plenty of space.

She liked it that way.

An hour later, Emily was drenched. Her hair was soaked, her shirt clinging to her skin. Even the bike shorts she wore were covered in sweat. From inside her bag, Emily pulled out a dry T-shirt, tugging it on over her head, and added a pair of loose shorts. There was already a towel covering the seat of her pickup truck to protect it from the daily dose of sweat, but she knew from experience she needed an extra layer.

After spraying down the kickboxing bag with disinfectant and putting her gear away, she pulled on a baseball cap. She heard a voice over her shoulder. "You working off something we need to talk about?"

Emily glanced over her shoulder to see Clarence standing nearby, his hands shoved in the pockets of his track pants. For an older guy, he was in good shape, his arms and shoulders showing off the hours of work that he still put in at the gym. His only nod to age was a slight bit of silver at his temples. The rest of his hair was jet black, nearly matching his skin.

"No. I don't think so."

It was a lie.

There was a lot for them to talk about. But Emily didn't feel like talking. She never did. She looked away, feeling Clarence's eyes still on her. *Did you want me to tell you about the people I've killed? How the last case I was on nearly left me buried alive?*

"You sure?"

"No. I'm good."

Clarence shook his head slowly. "So you say. That bag might tell another story."

Emily glanced at the kickboxing bag. There were still some dents in it where the foam was trying to recover. She reached into her bag, pulled out a fresh towel and wiped her face. "It'll be fine."

"And you?"

"There's nothing going on with me that a good workout won't fix."

Clarence didn't respond. She didn't give him a chance to. Picking up her bag, she strode out of the gym and headed for her truck.

3

Lou took another walk around the body and then stopped at the man's feet. He knelt down, pulling his cell phone out of his back pocket and turning on the flashlight app. He pointed it at the toes of the man who was lying on the beach. "Courtney? Come here."

"What did you find?"

Lou shot her a look. She needed to relax. Breaking in a detective was like having a new puppy, filled with energy. A few years before, he might have been happy to do it. Now, twenty years into his career, he was tired of having to train people over and over again. On the good side, at least she didn't pee everywhere. "I don't know. Why don't you tell me?"

Courtney frowned and then looked at the man's feet. She reached her hand out as if she wanted to pull the man's toes apart and then stopped, her hand hanging in midair. "Are those puncture wounds between his toes?"

Lou snapped a couple of pictures. There were a series of tiny red and black dots between the man's toes. "Could be. Also could be animal or bug damage. He was in the water, after all."

"They look too regular to be from an animal, don't you think?"

He didn't know. That was the point. "Possibly. We're gonna have to wait and see what the coroner says."

Courtney stood up and stripped off her gloves, turning them inside out and shoving them into her pocket. Her expression hardened. "I think it's a suicide. Either that or an overdose. Not much more to tell here."

Without another word, Courtney started walking towards the parking lot. What exactly she was doing, Lou had no idea. As she walked up the beach, she passed the medical examiner. Elena waved. Courtney did not. Lou stayed where he was by the body. Maybe it was good she left. Fewer cooks to ruin the soup, or something like that.

"Morning, Elena."

"Morning, Lou. What's up with her?"

Lou grimaced. He hated having to answer for other detectives. "No idea. Probably interrupted her morning ritual or something."

Elena shrugged. "Whadda we got?"

"Best as I can tell, male, mid-to-late twenties, maybe early thirties, found in this spot about an hour to an hour and a half ago by a lady walking her dog."

Elena knelt next to the body, pulling on a set of blue gloves and pressing on the man's neck. "She move the body?"

"According to her statement, no. Said she was so freaked out she didn't know what to do other than call 911. Apparently, her dog just kept barking."

"Typical. My dog does the same thing when it sees something it doesn't understand."

Elena McMillan, the Coroner for Cook County, was a studious type in Lou's mind, the kind of personality that was a perfect fit for her job. She had medium brown hair, wore no makeup, and hid a set of brilliant green eyes behind a pair of glasses. She had a slight frame. Her assistant, an average-sized guy named Miguel who had worked for the Medical Examiner's office for at least a dozen years, came charging out onto the sand, carrying a duffel bag filled with equipment. He had as much energy as Courtney, but at least he knew what he was doing. He looked at Lou. "*Hola.*"

Lou nodded. "*Hola*, Miguel."

Miguel set the bag down and pulled on a pair of gloves. As Lou wondered how many pairs of gloves he and Elena went through in a year, he heard Miguel suck in a breath. "Oh my God. Is that —?" He didn't finish his sentence.

Both Elena and Lou looked at Miguel. "Is that who?"

Miguel moved closer, leaning over the body, grabbing the man's chin and rotating it toward Miguel's face. "Yes. I'm sure of it. This is Ander Sabate." Miguel stood up, shaking his head. "Oh, man. Oh, this isn't good."

Lou cocked his head to the side. They hadn't even moved the body yet and there was already a twist. Where was Courtney? "What are you talking about? Do you know this person?"

Miguel's face drooped. "And you don't? I think this is Ander Sabate. He's from Portugal. Great soccer player. Best forward in the country right now. He's been on the Chicago Fire. You know, the pro team."

Lou pressed his lips together. "No, I don't know. Don't follow soccer. Is this guy a big name?"

Miguel nodded enthusiastically. "The biggest! He's like the face of the team, dude." Miguel looked at Elena. "What happened to him?"

"Other than taking a really long swim in the lake? Not sure." Elena was huddled over the body. She glanced up at Lou. "Did you spot anything I should know about?"

Lou paused. Elena was testing him. "Looks like there's a wallet in the left back pocket, no defensive wounds or marbling that I could spot, though you have a better eye for that. There might be some puncture wounds between his toes, but again, not sure. Could be critter damage. You have an idea how long he's been in the water?"

"Given the slight vascular marbling and lack of bloating? Probably less than forty-eight hours. If I had to guess, it's likely closer to twenty-four. You can do some digging on your end about that. It's not likely I'm gonna be able to give you an exact time of death given the fact that he was in the water. It messes with the body temperature too much. Summer water temps are about seventy. It's not like a body on land. Ambient air prevents the body from cooling too fast. The water acts like a refrigerator. If he was bloated, then I'd be able to say it's closer to two to three days. Without that, like I said, I think we're closer to twenty-four hours."

Elena's expression became grim. She stood up and walked toward the back of the man Miguel thought was Ander Sabate, digging out his wallet and handing it to Lou. "Here, have a look at this while I check out his feet."

Lou flipped the wallet open. Miguel was right. There was a State of Illinois driver's license for Ander in it. Newly issued. Behind it, there was another driver's license from a city in Portugal that Lou wasn't familiar with called Silves. There was cash and cards still in the wallet. "Well, this wasn't a robbery. All his money is still in here."

Elena was hunched over Ander's feet. She frowned. "I'm glad you pointed out his feet. This is problematic."

"What do you mean?" Courtney had rejoined them on the beach. She shot Lou a "told-you-so" look.

"He has track marks between his toes."

"Aren't soccer players tested for drugs like every other professional athlete?" Lou asked.

Miguel, who had been rummaging in the duffel bag he'd dragged down to the beach, looked up. "Yeah. They are. More than one soccer player has gotten suspended from the MLS because of it."

Lou could only guess that the MLS was Major League Soccer. Seemed logical, at least.

Elena shook her head. "Well, I can tell you that I've never seen any medical procedures that offer shots between the toes except for a nerve block or anti-inflammatories. That's pretty rare, though. Usually when I see this, it's some sort of drug issue, something that someone wants to hide."

"That's a powerful motive for suicide," Courtney offered.

Lou shot her a look. One of the most dangerous things a detective could do was make a ton of assumptions before all of the evidence had come in. More cases than not had been left in CPD's cold case files because some close-minded detective had decided that it wasn't worth pursuing a case when the motive, or the method, or the opportunity seemed obvious and they got off track, wasting time, allowing leads to cool and wasting taxpayer dollars. Assumptions weren't a safe way to work in their line of business. "Courtney, we don't know that yet."

"What else could it be? It fits. He's a pro athlete. They're known to be temperamental. He's probably having money problems. Maybe he was worried that he'd get caught since he's clearly taking drugs. Probably took a big dose and walked himself right out into the lake and here we are. Seems pretty open and shut to me." Courtney stared at Lou. "I have my laptop in the car. I'll go get the paperwork started." She started to walk off and then stopped, staring at her phone.

Lou looked at her. "Everything all right?"

Courtney blinked. "The captain just texted me. Wants me to go to some strategy meeting."

"Really?" Lou had been with the department for years. He'd never been asked to go to any strategy meetings.

"Yeah, something about women in law enforcement. Some new task force." She stared at Lou, her mouth slightly open.

"He knows about Ander. I texted him when we found the ID. Thought he should know since this guy's a bigwig. He said they will contact the team and send a liaison over." She glanced at her phone again. "There he is again. Gotta go."

Lou was a little surprised by the way that Courtney was acting. Something was off. A liaison was doing the notification? He wasn't doing it? Why hadn't he gotten a text from the Captain about it? Lou frowned. Then again, telling someone a person they loved was dead was no fun. But why the liaison? Didn't Captain Ingram trust him? That left more questions than answers. He glanced at his own phone. No messages. *Strange.* "Good luck," he managed to mutter as Courtney walked away.

Elena frowned at Lou. "She's new, right?"

Wasn't that obvious? "Yes. Opinionated, too."

Elena's expression darkened. "You might want to remind her that four years of undergraduate work, four years of medical school, and then four years of residency, plus two fellowships, would be the reason that I get to make the call on cause of death, not her."

"Copy that." There was no point in arguing. Elena was right. Lou closed his notebook after making a few more notes in it. "Other than Courtney's *theory*, is there anything else that you want me to know?" He was careful to stress the word theory. The last thing he wanted to do was to alienate Elena. He needed the medical examiner on his side.

Elena stood up, waving for Miguel to bring the body bag over toward them. "Nothing at the moment. I'm not going to rule on this until I get the tox screen back. We'll get Mr. Sabate packed up and into cold storage. Once I do the exam I'll have more information for you." She looked around. "I notice his shoes and one sock are missing. Did you happen to find them?"

Lou shook his head. "No. Why do you ask?"

Elena shrugged. "Usually they wash up with the body. I'll be in touch."

4

Emily pulled into the driveway of her house, slowing the truck long enough for the garage door to open. She pulled it inside, slipped out, dragging her workout bag with her and shut the garage door. From the direction of the house, she could already hear Miner yipping inside. "Hold on, hold on," she called. Miner, her Australian Cattle Dog, had radar instead of hearing. She swore he could hear a pin drop in the next county.

Making her way to the back door, Emily unlocked the deadbolt and the handset and stepped inside, quickly keying in the code for the back door. Her tech guy, Mike, had recently upgraded her security system, even putting an app on her phone where she could arm and disarm not only the system from her phone, but adjust about a million different things — everything from the code she used to the volume of the alarm should it go off. He'd added cameras inside and out, plus motion-sensitive lights around the exterior of the house. When she asked him why he was doing it, he'd commented, "Can't ever be too safe." Emily had tried to object, but Mike stood his ground. It all seemed to be overkill. She lived in a nice area of

Chicago, the epitome of the suburbs, with nicely manicured lawns and what she imagined were friendly neighbors, though she didn't really know them. It didn't matter what she said, though. Mike upgraded it anyway. He refused to be paid for the installation or the upgrade, which she felt she owed him. After all, he worked for her. But then again, they'd worked together for so long that they were practically siblings.

But they weren't.

Emily dropped her bag just inside the door, knelt down and rubbed Miner behind the ears. He smiled up at her, his tail wagging, his eyes bright. She looked over at the dish of water and food she'd left out for him before she left for her workout. For the most part, it looked untouched. "On a hunger strike this morning?" Cattle dogs were known to be particularly fussy eaters. Miner was no exception, happily forgoing his food until she added something he deemed to be delicious on top of it, whether that was yogurt, some bites of turkey, rice or the salmon oil that their veterinarian had prescribed.

Miner stared at her, seemingly nonplussed by her observation. She stood up and walked across the kitchen, dragging her workout bag with her, the exertion of her workout catching up with her. She stopped at the washing machine, stripping off the shorts and T-shirt she'd put on over her sweaty workout clothes and tossing them, plus her workout towel, into the washing machine. She headed upstairs, the jingle of Miner's collar trailing her as she went into the bathroom. That's the one thing about cattle dogs Emily had learned. They were glued to their owners.

Coming out of that bathroom, Emily scooped up her sweaty clothes and started a load of laundry. She stopped, just outside the laundry room and looked around. An eerie feeling enveloped her. She lived in the same small brick house in Chicago that she and Luca had purchased when they were married fifteen years before. That was before their divorce and before his OD. She hadn't changed any of the decor after he'd left her. Instead of their marriage, he'd chosen a life of women and drugs rather than a wife. The same cabinets were in the kitchen, the same worn wood floors ran through the space. Emily thought for a minute about how many times she'd walked in after a case, the familiar surroundings a comfort to her.

But looking at them now, she wondered whether they still were or not.

Emily stopped for a second, pushing the thought away. It wasn't the time for being sentimental. Pulling a bottle of water out of the refrigerator, she took a swig. Since she got home from her last case, her life had taken on a predictable rhythm — workouts, walking Miner, figuring out what to have for dinner. It had been a nice respite for a month or so, but now things felt dry and boring. There was a resistance in her soul to moving forward though, one she couldn't really explain. She hadn't bothered to check her e-mail to see if there were cases available. There were always cases out there. Her reputation as someone who could get justice when other people couldn't had gotten her national attention.

It wasn't the kind of attention she'd wanted.

Emily walked into her office. Against the back wall were banker's boxes filled with emails she'd printed off from people that had found her on social media sites for missing people, cold cases that had gone unsolved, even sites where lovers had disappeared. She used to print off their requests, filter through them and then choose a case to work on, something to keep her mind busy after she was fired from the Chicago PD.

Looking at the boxes, Emily frowned. Lately, the cases had been choosing her. She stared at the boxes and then opened the lid of the first one. There were piles of invitations to help inside, the weight of people's expectations landing heavily on her. She closed the lid, picked up the first box and carried it to the kitchen, stopping to grab a butane lighter stick, one she had in the drawer for her grill in the backyard. She walked outside to the fire pit, a circle she'd made with rocks just off of her deck, tossing the box in the middle of it. From a cabinet near her grill, she found an old bottle of lighter fluid. She doused the box and lit it on fire. Standing nearby, she watched the flames lick at it. The hopes and dreams of people who wanted justice were being destroyed right in front of her. She wanted to feel bad, but she didn't. She was one person. Only one. She couldn't possibly fix everyone's life. Heck, she wasn't sure she could fix her own.

Emily went back inside, leaving the crackling fire, gathering up the rest of the boxes. It took her a couple of trips. There was half a dozen or more stacked in her office. She heard the hiss of the flames as they lifted higher, quickly eating away at the emails she had kept for years.

She stared at the fire, her gut tightening. Something was changing. She just didn't know what.

5

Lou stayed with the body of who they now knew was the recently dead Ander Sabate as Miguel and the coroner got him ready for transport. Miguel put bags over Ander's hands and feet, securing them with rubber bands. It was a standard practice to protect any evidence that might have gotten caught under fingernails, particularly skin cells that could have been transferred during a struggle. Miguel glanced up at Lou as he finished the bagging procedure. "Not sure we'll find anything since he's been soaking, but you never know."

The fact that Ander wasn't wearing any shoes explained why Miguel had bagged his feet as well, one sodden sock immediately soaking the paper bag, leaving dark marks behind. Lou watched as Elena walked down to the edge of the water, scanning up and down the beach as if she was trying to figure out how Ander had gotten there in the first place, as if the answer might rise up out of the water. It didn't. He had often wondered if medical examiners, people who saw death every single day, experienced any sort of trauma. Did they become jaded, each body no different than a slab of meat at a butcher shop? Did it give her bad dreams? Was Elena the kind of person who'd become compulsive about things she could control — cleaning or exercise, or what she would eat — in order to get control over her life and the things that she saw every single day?

When Elena walked back to the body, she motioned for Miguel to lay out the body bag. "Let's get him out of here and back to the office."

Lou waved to the two patrol officers who had been protecting the perimeter of the crime scene, preventing beachgoers from tromping through the area while they worked, letting them know it was time to help. Elena and Miguel got Ander situated in the black bag, carefully arranging his arms across his chest, Elena gently closing his eyes, then tugging on the heavy-duty zipper.

As soon as the bag was closed, Miguel motioned for the two patrol officers to take one end of the body. He and Lou grabbed the other end, the four of them lifting the dead athlete within this black bag.

As they trudged up the beach toward the parking lot, Lou's boots sank into the sand. Ander Sabate was heavier than Lou thought he would be. The man's dead weight made it hard to maneuver, a sheen of sweat quickly forming on his forehead. He made a mental note to get the clothes off of the treadmill in the extra bedroom and try using it.

At the edge of the parking lot, Lou spotted the gurney. Elena had gone ahead of them, opened the van and pulled it out of the back. The four men angled for it, gently setting Ander's body down on top of it. Miguel expertly tied it down with what looked to be seatbelts over the legs and chest, securing the body to the bed. He offered a friendly wave over his shoulder as he pushed the gurney into the back of the van. A moment later, both Ander and Miguel disappeared inside.

Lou spotted Courtney sitting in her vehicle, her head

bowed over the glow of a computer screen. He narrowed his eyes. Things had changed vastly in the last five years. It used to be CPD rookies were almost too gung-ho to get into the field. Their training officers had to hold them back. Now their rookies had one look at the scene, made a hunch of assumptions and ran back to go and play with their computers and write reports. They were looking for a tech-driven solution to a problem that was distinctly human. The answers weren't in a laptop. They were out at the scene. Death wasn't something that could be quantified by an algorithm, AI, or social media. Death had its own rules and in order to solve cases, you had to play by them.

Lou ignored Courtney and went back down to the beach to look around one last time as the two patrol cars pulled out of the lot. Out of the corner of his eye, he saw Elena's van disappear as well, Miguel behind the wheel. Lou turned toward the water, hearing the waves crashing on the shore. He felt a nagging in his gut, as if he was missing something.

Despite the vast span of beach, it wasn't hard to figure out where Ander's body had been. There were heavy footprints in the sand from where the four men had carried the body bag out. Down at the water line, Lou stopped. He looked right and left, roughly east and west from where he was standing on the southern shore of Lake Michigan, wondering how someone like Ander Sabate had ended up dead on the beach that morning. The smell of the lake filled his nostrils — the faint scent of water, the sour smell of a dead fish nearby. He bent over and ran his finger through the sand. Though there was an impression of where Ander's body had washed up, some of it had already washed away as the waves continued to roll in. If a storm blew up, as frequently happened on the Great Lakes, the impression in the sand would disappear underneath the rolling tide within minutes. Lou stared up at the sky. The morning was cloudless, though there was a little bit of wind. Lou stared at the sand again, not seeing anything out of the ordinary. He stood up and then looked to his right, seeing a piece of deadwood about twenty feet from where Ander's body had been resting. Seeing a glimmer of something red nearby, he walked over cocking his head to the side. Was he seeing things?

As he approached the piece of deadwood, he realized his eyes weren't playing tricks on him. There was a thin strip of something red underneath the wood that had washed up on shore. He pushed the branch aside with the sole of his shoe. From his pocket he pulled a set of gloves. Lou bent over and dug around in the sand, tugging at what was underneath.

A minute later, he pulled a shoe out of the sand. It was red, an Adidas model that he hadn't seen before. He blinked, wondering if it was just coincidence, until he looked at the back of the shoe. There was a flame embroidered on the back. Miguel had said that Ander Sabate had played for the Chicago Fire soccer team. Lou stood up, the shoe dangling from one of his hands. He looked back at the spot where the body had laid. Elena had been right. The shoes did want to come up with the body. He stared at it for a second, then frowned. There seemed to be something sticky on the side of the shoe, some sort of residue he couldn't explain. Even with the gloves on he could tell it was something that didn't belong there. He rubbed his fingers together. It felt like adhesive, like the underside of some sort of tape. His heart skipped a beat. Maybe it was from the manufacturing of the shoes themselves? Some sort of glue that had softened when the shoes were soaked in the water for so long? It was possible, but something didn't seem right to Lou. Frowning, he looked around for another minute. Something wasn't right. There shouldn't be adhesive on the outside of the shoe. He grabbed it with a gloved hand wondering what it meant, and then headed for the path back to the parking lot.

By the time he made it back to the parking lot, everyone was gone, including Courtney. Knowing her, she was probably halfway back to the station by now, happily getting ready to make her way into the Homicide division, declaring that Ander Sabate had committed suicide. *The world according to Courtney.* Lou opened the trunk to his cruiser, pulled out an evidence bag and slid the shoe inside, then sealed it, signed it, and dated it. He'd drop it at Elena's office.

Lou got in his car and sat for a minute, staring at the water just beyond the edge of the parking lot. Business at Scenic View Park was back to normal. A runner passed by the spot where Ander had been found just a few hours before, followed by a woman walking her dog. A car pulled in two spaces down from where Lou was parked, a man and a woman getting out, both of them with exercise clothes on as if they were planning on either walking or running the beach that morning before work. It was amazing how quickly things returned to regular business. "Nature abhors a vacuum," he muttered under his breath. Lou stared out at the glimmering water. It was quite a way to start the day, wasn't it? Bad coffee, dead body, stubborn rookie.

Couldn't get much worse from there.

As he started the car, he thought about what Courtney had said. She had been so sure that Ander's death was a suicide. But why? What made her so sure?

As Lou pulled out of the parking lot, his mind wandered. Courtney's comments rang hollow in his mind. His gut told him something didn't fit. Courtney was a little too eager to call Ander's death a suicide. Was she somehow connected to him? Or was she just so new she didn't know better?

Lou struggled with both of the questions. There was something about her dogged insistence that Ander had killed himself that tugged at a well of suspicion inside of him. She was almost defiant, as if she'd made up her mind before she'd ever gotten to the scene. He shook his head as he drove. It was more than that, though. The way she'd challenged him and refused to listen seemed strange for someone so new. She hadn't been that way when they started. It was only in the last few weeks that she had become difficult to manage. Lou scowled. It took brass ones to go against a veteran detective. The act would require backup from elsewhere.

A shiver ran down Lou's spine. He realized he wasn't just worried about Courtney assigning the cause of death to Ander Sabate too fast, it was something else. There was something in the way she'd handled herself that made him wonder what she was really up to. There had been other candidates for the opening in Homicide, but somehow, she'd been chosen, though she had far less experience. Lou had just chalked it up to politics at the time, but was it? He gripped the steering wheel a little harder. Maybe he'd just been in the department for too long. Maybe he'd seen too many police officers get targeted by their own leaders, even somebody with a stellar reputation like Emily Tizzano.

Was he next?

6

After the early morning trip to the crime scene, Lou decided to swing home and get better prepared for his day. The couple hours before his shift started should earn him some flexibility, he decided. It was one of the privileges of seniority, or at least one he was planning on taking advantage of whether anyone liked it or not.

The entire way home, he kept thinking about the body they'd found. That wasn't normal for him. He was usually pretty good about going to a scene and then leaving work at work. The exceptions were the kinds of cases that tugged at his heartstrings, like the death of a five-year-old little boy in a drive by shooting six months before. But there was something about the body he'd seen on the beach that was hanging with him.

Worse yet, Courtney wasn't helping the situation. The idea that she was so focused on her own assessment scared him in a way. Detectives had one job — and that was to look at the facts. They couldn't make up their mind ahead of time about where the information was taking them. In Lou's mind, that practice had led to more people being falsely jailed, cases going cold, and good leads being wasted than anything else. He'd seen

Courtney do just that with the body they had found on the beach.

Lou shifted in his seat as he got off the freeway heading toward his house. There could be a million reasons that the body ended up on the beach. Heck, the coroner hadn't even determined if the guy had drowned or been dead when he hit the water. What was Courtney thinking?

He smiled just a little. *Oh yeah, it's gotta be a rookie thing.*

But the nagging in his gut lingered.

Pushing the thought away as he arrived home, Lou pulled in the driveway of his bungalow in the Bridgeport neighborhood of Chicago, where he'd lived for years. The house was quiet when he got there. The smell of last night's dinner hung in the air, plus the smell of coffee, the remnants of what he'd brewed the day before. Lou tossed his keys and phone on the counter, walked over to the coffee maker and pulled it toward him. Coffee — good coffee — would be the best way to restart his day. The glass pot was tinged with brown. Frowning, he turned on the water in the sink, gave it an aggressive scrub with a sponge that was sitting nearby and refilled the carafe with water.

Setting up the coffee to brew, he went into the shower, got cleaned up, shaking sand caught in his socks into a wastebasket nearby and changed into more proper detective clothes — a pair of black pants and a dark purple shirt. He pulled on a matching black belt around his waist, clipped his badge and gun to it and looked into his closet for a tie. Curling his fists, he decided to forgo a tie. It was too hot.

His mind circled back to Ander Sabate. He'd have paperwork to do when he got back to the office. He stopped for a second, sitting on the edge of the bed and sliding his feet into a pair of dress shoes with thick soles. He'd seen dozens of other bodies throughout his career. Forget that, it was probably more like hundreds, maybe even a thousand. Being a detective in

Chicago meant that he saw dead bodies all the time. There was no shortage of them. Just the week before, he'd dealt with a case of three bodies all at once, the result of a drug war. The young men had all managed to shoot each other in front of a grocery store. Only later, after interviewing the store manager, did he figure out that it was over some girl. Two of the guys interested in her were from rival gangs. The other guy got caught in the crossfire.

It was senseless and yet Lou hadn't given it a thought.

But there was something about this case, something he couldn't put his finger on that was sticking with him. He picked up his keys and cell phone to walk out the door and then stopped. He pulled his notebook out of his pocket and walked into what he called his home office, a converted bedroom, quickly making copies of it. From the laptop in his office, he accessed his work database, quickly forwarding the pictures that the coroner had already loaded into the case file to his personal account, then sending them to the printer. Lou furrowed his eyebrows. He could see that Courtney had already added them to the case database. As he looked at her work, Lou heard the whirr of the printer start from behind him as he stood up from his desk. He stood, watching as the first picture rolled off the printer, and Ander Sabate's face gray and still emerged, his eyes unfocused.

Lou picked up the picture and stared at it for a second, a chill running down his spine. It was as if he was looking at his own future, but he had no idea why.

7

Lou spent the rest of the day cycling through paperwork that needed his attention, everything from a vacation request for a weekend getaway to Canada that Captain Ingram had denied, to file updates that needed to be handled on their online system. Courtney, who had been at the office by the time he'd gotten there, had forwarded him the file on the Ander Sabate case and promptly disappeared, saying she was going to follow up with a witness for one of their other cases.

That was fine with Lou.

Lou sat at his desk and spun his chair back and forth a few times, thinking. He stared at his computer and then pulled up the information that Courtney had already constructed on Ander. As he stared at the screen, he had to admit she'd done a good job. All of the information was in the correct fields, the time, date, and GPS location of the body had been added correctly so it was displaying as a map. It was the description that gave him pause. He frowned as he read the words:

"Body of Ander Sabate found this morning by a woman walking the beach near the Scenic View Park beach access. No obvious signs

of blunt force trauma, gunshot wounds, stab wounds to account for the state of the deceased. Puncture marks found between his toes suggesting illicit drugs, possible overdose. Waiting on ME determination, but likely cause is suicide."

Really, Courtney? Lou shook his head. She just couldn't let it go. The fact that she had the nerve to go over his head was one thing. The fact that she had the stones to even mention suicide before Elena even had a chance to take a peek at his body was something else. He chewed his lip. Courtney wouldn't be spending much time as a detective if she didn't start to listen to him. Lou looked around the office. There were a handful of other detectives working at their desks, two off to his left, leaning over a computer, another one filling his coffee, and Rebecca Carner, who he'd known for years, hunched over her desk, staring at some paperwork.

Where are you, Courtney?

It wasn't as if Lou really wanted the answer to the question. The whole situation was strange to him. Lou glanced at Captain Ingram's office door. It was closed as tight as a steel drum.

Something strange was going on.

Lou focused on his computer. There were always office politics with the CPD. He'd managed to last as long as he did by ignoring most of what was going on and doing his job. He shied away from gossip and kept his opinions, for the most part, to himself.

He was a survivor.

But in his gut, he knew there was something going on that he couldn't see, like a shadow that was threatening to catch up with him. Lou leaned over his desk, rubbing his chin. He focused on the open file on his screen. He needed more information.

Lou spent the next two hours working on notes about the Sabate case. At one point, Rebecca Garner wandered over to his desk, leaning against the edge, her curly hair forming a frame around her face. "What are you working on?"

"Background," he answered, suddenly glad the department had installed privacy screens on all of the computers. They said it was to protect victims' identities. Lou thought it was just as helpful to protect them from each other. He looked up at her. "You taking a break?"

She nodded, suddenly looking discouraged. "Yeah. The captain put me on a theft ring, but I'm not making much progress. Have tracked them back to some junkyard on the far side of town but keep running into roadblocks."

"That happens."

She looked away. "I heard you pulled the Sabate case." Her voice was strained.

So that's why you are hanging out at my desk? "Yeah."

"Courtney told us all about it this morning when she got back from the scene. Was all excited that it's somebody high profile." Rebecca scowled. "Not sure a soccer guy qualifies."

Lou tried not to laugh. Chicago sports were all about two things — the Bears and, for the smart ones, the Cubs. The folks that liked the White Sox, well, that was another matter entirely. Ander Sabate might be a big deal to someone who grew up outside of Chicago, but until that morning, Lou had no idea Chicago even had a major-league soccer team. "Agreed."

"How's the case coming? Courtney seemed to think it was an open and closed case."

"I'm not so sure about that."

Rebecca nodded. "She's definitely green. That's for sure." Rebecca tapped her fingers on the desk. "You gotta hear this. A friend of mine turned me on to this new tool. It's a website that collects information about a single place or a single person, but without all the garbage ads and info we usually get."

That sounded promising. "All right. Send it over."

Rebecca stepped away. "Will do."

A second later, Lou's email chirped. It was a link to a website from Rebecca. He clicked on it. As it loaded, the banner was all Lou needed to see. *BioFinder. Find anyone. Fast.* "We'll see about that," Lou muttered under his breath. He typed in Ander Sabate's name and waited.

Within a moment, the screen populated with five pages of information. There were the basic pieces — where he was born, where he went to school, and then there were more personal items Lou was almost startled to see. Almost. Things like what he ordered at the last place he had breakfast and what time he normally arrived at work.

Creepy.

Lou fought off the urge to look up his own name. He was a nobody, just a cop from Chicago, a kid from the neighborhood who was trying to get through the day. No one would care where he was or what he was doing. But Ander Sabate? Someone might definitely care.

He spent the next hour scouring the information on the BioFinder website. He saw pictures of Ander out walking with his wife, Ana, the two of them staring into a stroller, loving expressions on their faces. There were more pictures, too, of Ander laughing during a recent soccer match, of him out with a buddy at a coffee shop, and even at a Cubs game with some of his teammates. The pictures were recent, within the last few weeks. Lou frowned, then scrolled down, looking for medical information.

There wasn't any.

Lou bit his lip. What he really needed was a sense of whether or not Ander had seen a psychologist or was taking any anti-depressants. There was nothing wrong with either in his mind. What he was wondering was if Ander had recently been diagnosed with anything that would support Courtney's theory. Other than a lot of paperwork that would run him smack dab into HIPPA privacy regulations territory, it would be hard to get what he needed, unless...

Lou picked up his phone.

"Yes?"

"Can you get medical information for me?"

"Depends."

Every detective had their sources. It just happened that one of Lou's favorites was a woman that worked at the largest healthcare billing agency in the country. She had access to more medical information than anyone he'd ever met. They'd met when her mother's house had been broken into. Lou had handled the case, retrieved the stolen items, made the arrests, and even took the time to help the woman, an 86-year-old long time Chicago resident, to install new deadbolts on her doors. The daughter, whose name was Donna, handed him her card. "You've done a lot for us. If I can ever repay the favor, let me know."

From that time on, Donna had become an informant for Lou, a good one.

"I'm trying to see if Ander Sabate was seen by any doctors recently."

"Oh gosh, I thought you were gonna ask me something hard."

Lou relayed the correct spelling of Ander's name and his date of birth. A second later, Donna came back on the line. "Nothing. I've got nothing. Last time he was at the doctor was two years ago for a sinus infection."

"No trips to a psychologist or filled any prescriptions?"

"No. He's as squeaky clean as they get."

Interesting. "Okay, thanks."

Lou felt his entire back tense. There was no record of Ander getting psychiatric care. In fact, from everything Lou could see, he had everything to live for — a beautiful wife, a gorgeous new baby, a promising career. Lou frowned. Maybe this case wasn't as simple as Courtney had made it out to be after all.

Staring at Captain Ingram's door, Lou wondered what was really going on. He grabbed his keys and his phone, nodding to Rebecca, who was still at her desk. Suddenly, what had become home — the CPD — didn't feel so friendly anymore. Something was going on. He could feel it in his bones.

He just didn't know what.

8

"Hold on there, buddy. I gotta dry you off before you can go free."

Emily was attempting to dry Miner from the bath she'd just given him, the leggy cattle dog running around the house frantically afterwards, trying to get the water off of him, shaking and dropping to the floor and rolling on the carpet in the living room. Emily grinned at his antics. "You're such a baby. How many baths have you had in your life? It's just water."

Emily whistled to him and he trotted over, allowing her to rub a giant soft bath towel against his fur, the dog diving his head into the fabric as if it was the only thing that would save him from the terrors of soap and water. As she stood up, watching him leave little wet paw prints all over the wood floors of her kitchen, her phone rang. Frowning, she walked over to it, staring at the screen. She wrinkled her nose, tempted to let it go to voicemail, then decided to pick it up.

"Lou?"

"Hey, Emily. Did I catch you at a bad time?"

She looked at Miner. He gave her the side eye from where

he'd positioned himself on his dog bed in the kitchen and began to lick his front legs, as if somehow that would remove the horror of the bath he'd just experienced. "I guess not. What's going on?"

Emily furrowed her eyebrows while she waited for him to answer. Lou sounded distant.

"I was wondering if I could get your take on a case."

Emily walked over to the window that faced out into the backyard. She and Lou had become acquaintances again when she'd needed his help with a case, but it was a relationship — more accurately a friendship — that Emily still wasn't sure about. "My take on a case? I'm not a cop anymore, Lou. Haven't been for a long time in case you forgot."

As soon as the words came out of her mouth, she knew Lou would take them as a dig. She didn't care. Lou had been the one who had fastened the handcuffs around her wrists on the day she got arrested. The department hadn't even had the decency to do it in private. No, they made a full spectacle of it with the chief and the media standing outside of her front door, taking her completely unaware. Even all of these years later, many of those when she didn't talk to Lou, she was still a little bitter. That she was innocent had been proven beyond a shadow of a doubt, thanks to the help of her former father-in-law, Anthony Tizzano. They'd gotten her a hefty settlement and an offer to come back to CPD, but she didn't. She'd been on her own ever since. "Don't you have a partner for that?"

"She's green."

"That's not my problem. I gotta go, Lou." Emily started to pull the phone away from her ear to hang up when she heard Lou suck in a sharp breath.

"Wait!"

"What? I said I have to go."

"It's just, the guy that died, he's kinda high profile. There's something about the case. It doesn't feel right."

Emily's stomach clenched. She'd spent years trying to stay off the radar of the Chicago Police Department and everyone else and now Lou wanted her to look at a case that was high profile? "No thanks. If the brass is sniffing around you, I don't need them turning their attention on me."

There was a pause, as if the weight of the words unsaid had dropped down between them. She and Lou had never talked about how she felt betrayed by him. One time he had told her he was sorry. The effort was barely notable in her book. Honestly, she hadn't been sure at the time if he actually was or if he just felt like he had to apologize. That brief interaction was the beginning, middle, and end of their conversation around her arrest. That was fine with her. Emily wasn't the kind of person that needed to talk through things. She had a far simpler solution... she just walked away.

But now Lou was back and asking for help. She glanced at the ceiling, seeing a cobweb she needed to get rid of. From the small black flecks in the nearly clear threads, she could tell some bugs had gotten stuck in it. It had been their last trip. They'd gotten caught in a web and died.

Emily had no interest in having the same experience.

"Good luck with the case, Lou," she said.

"I wouldn't ask if I didn't really need your help." The words came out nearly in a whisper. "There's something going on, something I can't see. Things don't seem right." He paused. "I'm not asking as your former partner, Emily. I'm asking as your friend."

9

Emily sucked in a breath. Her gut was throwing a red flag at Lou's request for her help, but her mouth moved before the feeling landed. "All right. No promises. Why don't you tell me what you're thinking?"

Lou spent the next couple minutes explaining what he and Courtney had found on the beach that morning. "The thing is, the victim just signed a huge new soccer contract and an endorsement agreement with Nike. Why would he kill himself when he landed a deal that could set him up for the rest of his life?"

"How do you know that?"

"I've been doing some snooping around."

Emily raised her eyebrows. This wasn't the Lou she'd worked with — the strait-laced, by-the-book-kind of detective who wanted every "I" dotted, and every "t" crossed, the one who arrived at work at least an hour early every morning and stayed late, even though he had a wife at home. No, this was a new Lou.

"Maybe he didn't do it intentionally. Maybe it's like your new partner said. Maybe it's an overdose. He got the news about the new contract, bought some product so he could have his own private party, and things got a little out of hand."

"Then how did he end up in the water? I mean, a lot of these guys party, but I'd really expect that at some fancy hotel downtown. That's where all those athletes hang out. How did he end up on a beach, especially a beach on Lake Michigan? Miami, maybe. Here? I don't know…"

Emily started pacing. She could hear the indecisiveness in Lou's voice. "I just don't think this is that big of a deal, Lou. There are a million possible explanations. Maybe the guy has a buddy who's got a boat. They went out. They decided to party, and your victim went overboard. So they didn't call it in. So what? That's happened a ton of times." Emily frowned. Lou was too experienced of a detective to be calling her for this. There was something else. There had to be.

Lou paused. Emily waited, remembering that this had been one of his habits when they worked together. It was as if he needed a minute for his brain to catch up with what his gut was telling him.

"Lou? Is there something else?" Emily was getting impatient. She glanced at Miner. He groaned and adjusted himself on his dog bed.

"Yeah, I found a shoe that looked like it probably belonged to him nearby. There was something on it. A sticky substance. Things don't add up."

"What do you think it is?"

"No idea. It was clear. Only found out when I grabbed the shoe. Maybe adhesive?"

Emily licked her bottom lip. That was strange. If it was adhesive, that pointed to some sort of binding. Definitely not the mark of a suicide.

"And the other thing I thought was strange is the puncture marks between his toes."

Emily shook her head. "What's so weird about that?"

"Nothing on the face of it except for the fact that these guys, pro athletes, I mean, are usually really worried about their bodies. Sure, a lot of them have drug issues, but it's usually some sort of performance-enhancing drugs, the kind you take with pills or a shot in the thigh, not the kind you'd inject between your toes. These guys get tested regularly. The MLS doesn't play when it comes to drug usage. He could have lost everything. That's a lot to risk when you have a wife, a new baby, and a huge endorsement contract."

Emily knew that people who had a drug habit, like her ex-husband Luca, had all sorts of interesting ways to get the high they wanted — everything from snorting things up their nose to soaking tampons in alcohol and liquified fentanyl. It was amazing the number of people who would do whatever they had to do in order to get a fix. Just thinking about it made her stomach turn. She never wanted to be the kind of person who had that scary, desperate kind of need.

"So you're saying you just don't buy the illegal drug part of it?"

"Nope. I don't buy the suicide either, at least not yet. That's why I want your help. I need fresh eyes."

Emily chastised herself. She had gotten caught up in Lou's request and hadn't stopped when she should have. His concern about the case was separate from her involvement. "I don't know, Lou."

Lou sucked in a sharp breath again. "Listen, Emily. I get it. I understand why you probably wouldn't want to help the CPD with anything, let alone help me, but something isn't right here." He paused. "There's more, but I can't talk about it right now."

Emily threw her hands in the air. "You can't talk about it? So, you bring me a case on a silver platter that's going to have all eyes on it, and you won't give me all the information? I'm not so sure about this, Lou. You took the job. You carry the badge. I don't. If I get exposed, no one is gonna back me." Lou started to object. Emily stopped him, feeling a knot in her gut. "Don't waste your breath, Lou. I know no one will back me. I've lived through it."

There was silence on the other end of the phone as if Lou was silently acknowledging the fact that he, along with dozens of other cops who had been Emily's friends, had turned their back on her when she had gotten arrested. "Just think about it, okay? Let me know. If you don't want to, I'll understand. The thing is, it's one thing if Ander Sabate killed himself. It's something completely different if he didn't. This wasn't an obvious kind of death, Emily. If someone killed him, they were careful, very careful."

Emily paused, thinking for a moment. "If that's the case, then you have a killer on the loose."

Lou's voice got serious. "And, if I'm right, one that my gut is telling me is highly sophisticated, something we haven't seen in a while."

Emily narrowed her eyes. She'd think about it, but she was pretty sure that helping Lou on a high-profile case was probably not the direction she wanted to go. Lately, her cases had been choosing her, not the other way around. It was a dangerous precedent. She needed time to think. "I'll text you in the morning."

10

As Emily hung up the phone after her conversation with Lou, she realized her mouth was dry. She walked into her family room, made sure the front drapes were pulled closed tightly and sat down. A second later, Miner, still damp and annoyed because of his bath, came to join her, flopping himself down on the corner of the rug that was closest to where she was sitting. Emily stared at a spot on the wall and then looked down at her phone. Part of her wanted to call Lou back and tell him off. How dare he reach out and ask for help after everything they'd been through?

She winced. Then again, she'd done the same thing the year before and he'd shown up, rescuing her from the same guy who'd tried to kidnap her in the middle of a case. In her book, loyalty meant something.

But was this loyalty or just a foolish risk getting involved with CPD again?

Thoughts thundered through her mind. Was she expecting too much? Was she expecting him to be perfect?

Her stomach soured. No, then and now, she'd expected him to be on her side, to mind the thin blue line that police officers were taught would protect them in the line of fire. He hadn't. He'd hung her out to dry.

Frustrated, she picked up her phone and dialed Mike.

"I was just about to call and see how you like the upgrades on your security system."

"It's like living in Fort Knox." Emily snorted.

"Actually, your security is probably better than what they have at Fort Knox. I read online recently that there's no actual gold left in Fort Knox. The government moved it out of there about a decade ago. No one knows exactly where it went, but there's a theory that they might have moved it to Area 51."

"With the aliens?" Part of Emily couldn't believe she was actually following Mike's conspiracy-laden commentary with a question.

"Yeah. They may have given some of the gold in trade when they made first contact with a new species." He paused, as if waiting to see what Emily would say. He continued. "It doesn't matter anyways, the paper dollar is likely to fail any day now. There's not enough gold to back up the economy anyways. Alice and I were just taking care of business at our cabin over the weekend. Getting it ready. You know, just in case."

Emily scowled. "Aren't you afraid to say all of this over an open line?"

"You're assuming it's open."

Mike and his tech strikes again. "Touché." Emily decided it was time to change the subject. "Hey, listen, I just got a call from Lou."

"Like Lou Gonzalez, the former partner that betrayed you, Lou Gonzalez?" His tone was dry, bordering on obvious disrespect.

Emily rolled her eyes. "Yes. That Lou. Remember, he did help us out. He's the one that put Richard Henry away when he kidnapped me."

"Yes, and he's also the one that betrayed you."

"Can I just get to the point here?"

"What did he want."

"My help."

Mike laughed. "You're kidding, right? What could he possibly need your help with?"

Emily was convinced that the only person on the face of the planet who was more suspicious than she was, was Mike. Mike, with all of his tech genius, had used a large portion of his brain power to engage in conspiracy theories, including believing that the moon landing was faked and that aliens had infiltrated Earth and were roaming about in disguise. Most of the time Emily thought he was wrong about his suspicions. At one point he even worried that Carl, the guy that ran the meat market where Emily bought dinner nearly every single day, was fronting for some sort of illegal organization. Which one, Emily couldn't remember. That said, it was highly unlikely that if he was, it was anything but the Mafia. Anthony Tizzano had bought the building where Carl's store was. If Carl wasn't clean, then he was with Anthony's organization.

"A case."

Mike snorted again. "What, the mighty Chicago PD doesn't have enough assets to handle business on their own?"

"That's not exactly it." Emily took a minute and explained Lou's suspicions about Ander Sabate's death — his new contract, the puncture marks between his toes, and the adhesive on his shoe. "He said the department thinks this is a suicide. He's not so sure. He's concerned there's more that's being covered up."

"Who does?"

"Apparently his partner."

"He has a new partner. Isn't that rich?" Mike's voice dripped with sarcasm.

Emily was starting to lose her patience. "Listen, how about

if you dial back the sarcasm just slightly? I've moved on from what happened. Maybe you should too."

There was silence for a second. "Fine. Why are you telling me this?"

"I was hoping you could engage that big brain of yours and tell me something helpful."

"I have only one thought."

"What's that?"

"Don't do it. Don't get involved."

"How original. You're going to have to do a little bit better than that." The fact that Mike couldn't give her any actual information beyond his emotions wasn't helping the situation at all. Emily needed to make a decision based on what *she* thought, not Mike's opinion. She was fully able to defend herself. She'd done it before Mike was around. She'd do it after.

"I mean, why should you? Yeah, Lou helped us out a bit. He helped with a search and gave you a little backup. Okay, great. He owed you at least that, if not a lot more. Your debt has been paid. You don't owe him anything. And now he comes crawling back because he has a partner he doesn't like or agree with? That's his problem. Not yours. And you know the minute that anybody at CPD gets wind that you're involved, it's going to paint a target on your back."

Emily stiffened. "They can't do anything to me."

"Really? You sure about that? Because this time you don't have a badge."

The way that Mike said it punched Emily in the gut.

Mike continued. "I still don't see exactly what Lou thinks the big deal about this case is. These highly paid, high-profile people die every day. Who cares?"

Emily sat back for a second. It was as if all of the information she had was coming together. If she had been in Lou's shoes, she'd be suspicious too. And he was right, if Ander had been killed, then whoever had done it was likely more dangerous than anyone Chicago had seen for a while. "There *is* something more going on here, Mike. I don't know exactly what it is, but Lou is unnerved. That's not like him." That single fact was enough to sway her decision-making.

Mike grunted. "Well, do what you want. You're gonna do it anyways, no matter what I say. Just watch your back."

Emily nodded to herself. He was right on all counts. She was going to do exactly what she wanted to do. Mike worked for her. It wasn't the other way around. "Copy that. I'll be in touch."

11

Judge James Conklin fiddled with the glossy black Mont Blanc pen on the desk of his home office. Like everything else in his home, it was of the highest quality. He'd worked hard over the years, harder than his peers. That's why he had the life — and the career — that he did.

He stared at it for a second. It had been a gift from his wife Janice ten years before when he'd gotten elected to the bench. At the time, it had been an extravagant gift. Now, with his investments and his salary, it almost looked ordinary. He tapped it twice on the leather desk pad that covered the massive mahogany wooden desk in his office and then looked up.

Seated across from him was Layla Riley, an elegant-looking dark-haired woman in her early forties. Judge Conklin knew her age from the resume she'd sent him after a few of his donors had recommended her for the job of his next campaign manager.

Layla recrossed the set of long, toned legs that were sticking out of the hem of a professionally appropriate length skirt in front of his desk, moving them slowly in a way that he was sure was meant for him to notice. "Your Honor, I understand what you want to accomplish with your campaign, but we have a problem."

He narrowed his eyes. "Lemme guess. We need more money."

Layla nodded, then steepled her fingers in front of her face. "That and more backers. Making the jump to governor of Illinois is a big one, especially from your current position. The truth is, it would be easier if you were currently a state senator or congressman — even the mayor of Chicago. Honestly, the governor is the big league. Once you are there, it's not that hard to become vice president or even president. It's just the getting there is hard."

Layla, for all her fancy education and recommendations, wasn't telling him anything he didn't already know. The problem was Judge Conklin didn't want to hear about the difficulty of the situation. He felt blood rush to his face. He looked down for a second. His wife always told him that with his fair, Irish skin, his irritation showed up in the flaming of the blood vessels in his cheeks. Layla had a grave expression on her face. She knew things were serious and about to get more so.

He narrowed his eyes. "Layla, I am paying you a good sum of money to handle problems for me, not to tell me what the problems are. I spend all day long dealing with issues and people's bad decisions. The last thing I need are more obstacles in my way. I want that governorship."

She shifted in her seat as if she'd felt a poke to her backside. "That's understandable, Your Honor. But —"

Judge Conklin held up a hand. He hated the fact that she kept calling him "Your Honor." It was probably a reflex given her background. Layla had been an attorney before she got into the political world. It was one of the reasons he'd hired her. He was counting on her contacts within the legal and business community, in addition to his own, to get his campaign moving.

"I need solutions. Do you have those? Because if you don't, I can find someone who does."

Layla's expression stiffened. "I have solutions. That's what you hired me to do."

Judge Conklin looked away for a moment as Layla outlined a new fundraising strategy, aligning himself with some of the unions and businesses throughout the state who shared some of the same vision that he did. He frowned. Unions and big business weren't normally on the same side of the voting booth. It was an innovative solution. "You think that could work?"

"I do. If there's anyone that can bridge the gap, it's you. You have the background to do it. A partnership between business and unions could be lucrative for the campaign and good for the people of Illinois."

He scratched his chin. It was worth considering.

Before he could comment, she continued. "There *is* something we haven't talked about that we need to deal with."

"What's that?"

"There are some people that would prefer to see you stay in your current position." She looked away as she delivered the news, picking at a single, perfectly manicured fingernail.

Judge Conklin's face reddened again. People were always blocking his plans. *Always.* He knitted his fingers together and then looked up at Layla. His words came out slowly and measured. "Is there anyone in particular that I should be aware of?"

It took Layla a moment to respond, as if saying the words were challenging. "Well, it's unfortunate, Your Honor, but it's come to my attention that Eric Atkins isn't supporting you."

Judge Conklin shot up out of his seat, as if his chair had suddenly launched him to standing. He walked to the window in his office that faced Bridger Avenue, an affluent area just on the outskirts of downtown Chicago, lined with rows of brick townhomes. Outside, he saw a well-dressed couple with an even better-dressed Yorkie walking past. Judge Conklin looked back at Layla. "Eric Atkins isn't supporting me?"

"No, sir. There has been nothing official, of course," she held up a hand, "but my sources are telling me he's going to back Liv Gardner."

"Liv Gardner?" he spat. "Of all people! She's an idiot."

Layla held a hand up. "Unfortunately, she has the support of quite a few of the state senators and congresspeople. I guess her legislation in reforming the education system in the state of Illinois has become very popular. People like her ideas. They see her becoming the next governor."

"And the fact that she's a woman helps things along, doesn't it?"

"It does, sir." She looked at her lap, as if letting the news sink in. "There's more. I heard on my way here that Eric Atkins is also looking for a promotion."

Judge Conklin narrowed his eyes. "Really?"

Layla nodded. "He wants Senate President as soon as he's reelected."

Judge Conklin gripped his hand into a fist. Atkins wanted it all. He wanted his person in the Governor's Mansion, and he wanted the highest seat of power in Springfield, other than the governor herself. What a nightmare. "So what do we do? What solutions do you have?"

"Like I said, I think partnering with the unions might be helpful. The unions hold a lot of power, but they also hold a lot of influence."

Judge Conklin nodded. And they had a lot of money. "What's the ramification once I get elected." He decided to speak in the positive, although his gut was telling him things had just gotten much more difficult.

Layla arched her eyebrow. "Yes, *when* you get elected..."

James gave a single nod, conceding the point.

"*When* you get elected," she stressed. "There will be people who are looking for favors. I don't want to lie to you. The unions will come calling — labor, the Teamsters, the police unions. Anyone who thinks that this is a clean process is kidding themselves. Politics are as messy as they have ever been. They are going to have asks — projects they want funded, people they want helped, favors they want done. They will come in the dark of the night and in the bright light of the morning. There's no shame anymore."

Judge Conklin pressed his thin lips together. It wasn't much different from the legal world that he was operating in. Being an elected judge came with a lot of perks, including an excellent salary, a visible position, and more interesting, high-profile cases than the ones he had experienced when he was first elected to the bench. But he'd quickly learned that everyone had an agenda, including the county district attorney, the mayor of Chicago, and even the attorney general. At one point or another, they'd all come calling, and he'd had to deal with them. He was tired of it. He wanted more, to be a visible figure, a person of real power on a more national stage. "Doesn't seem much different than how we do business now."

She shrugged. "If you can stomach it, sir, I can make some calls and see if we can get the unions on board."

Judge Conklin looked away for a second. "And if they won't play ball?"

He saw a small twitch near the corner of her eye. It was almost imperceptible, but years of watching people testify had honed his skills at observation. "Let's not go there, Your Honor."

12

The rest of the day, Emily went about her business like she normally did, the conversations she'd had with Lou and Mike lurking in the back of her mind. She took Miner for his afternoon walk, taking him over to Sammy's Meat Market, where they slid in through the back door. Miner knew that if he went and laid down underneath Carl's desk that within a minute or so Carl would show up with some sort of a delicious treat for him. Today it was homemade chicken jerky.

After a brief chat with Carl, Emily picked up some of Carl's homemade meatballs, two for her plus a few for the freezer, and headed home. When she was on a case, it could be days or weeks before she'd have a regular schedule. But when she wasn't, life just sort of stretched out in front of her, empty and formless except for her walks with Miner and her training at Clarence's gym. For the most part, she liked it that way, but lately she'd been feeling restless, as if she needed something more.

As she walked, she thought about what Lou had said about the case in front of him. She still had questions in her mind about why Lou wanted her to be part of it at all. But she also knew him well enough to know that if he was feeling squirrely, he likely had a good reason for it.

As Emily rounded the corner from the shopping district back into the residential area near where her home was, she passed a couple of boys who were laughing loudly and poking at each other, the way kids do. She saw Miner tense and quickly guided him off the sidewalk and onto the grass, putting him in a sit using a hand signal. The boys, probably middle schoolers, seemed to pay no attention. But Emily was paying attention to them, especially given the fact that one of them had on a red T-shirt that said Chicago Fire on it. And it didn't mean the Fire Department. It was the soccer team, the same one that Ander Sabate had played for. Did anyone even know he was dead yet?

Emily held her phone up to her mouth as soon as the boys passed, starting a voice search. "Ander Sabate death," she said slowly. A second later, the results came back.

There was nothing.

She shoved her phone in her back pocket, silently chiding herself for not paying attention to where she was or what was going on. Some people might think she was paranoid, but situational awareness was one of the things that had kept her alive and out of trouble since she'd been kicked out of the department. Playing with her phone while she was away from the house was a distinct no-no in her world. Even a second of distraction could be fatal. It might not happen while she was on her walk, but technically, it could. This was Chicago, after all.

Emily sighed and moved her hand back to her side where her pistol was hidden, holding the bag with the food and Miner's leash in the other hand. She tugged her shirt down, making sure it was hidden, the weight of the gun on her hip reminding her that she always needed to be aware.

The boys well past her, Emily's mind started to drift again, thinking about the conversation she'd had with Lou. It was interesting to her that Ander Sabate's death hadn't been leaked, at least not yet. Whether the press people at the Chicago Fire soccer team were trying to figure out how to best release the sad news to their fans or his wife had asked for a reprieve before it was made public, Emily had no idea.

She frowned. Or maybe there was something more, something that they were hiding.

As soon as Emily got back to the house, she unclipped the leash from Miner's collar. He gratefully trotted inside the cool house after walking in the heat, making his way to his water bowl and lapping up half of it before throwing himself down on his bed in the kitchen. Emily put the bag of food in the refrigerator and paused. She felt caught between two different tensions — Lou's request for help and Mike's fear about exactly what that help might do to her.

And they were both right.

The rest of the evening went by quietly. Emily made two meatballs, a small salad, and pasta. She almost texted Mike and invited him to come and eat, but looking at the calendar, Emily realized it was one of their gaming nights and not a night Alice was working late. She ate her dinner sitting at the kitchen table, scrolling through her phone. When she was done, she dumped the rest of the spaghetti and meatballs on top of Miner's food. He gobbled down the leftovers happily and then sat by the door, asking to go outside. Emily followed, spending the rest of the evening watching him wander around the yard, sniffing for chipmunks, pouncing on a few bugs. At one point, she wandered out to the back fence line where her tomatoes were growing, pinching a few suckers off between stems that were threatening to take the life away from the tomatoes that were growing. But most of the time she just sat on the chair in her backyard and stared, thinking. Wondering.

It had been months since her last case. She was feeling restless. But there was no part of her that was interested in any of the other cases that had come in recently. She glanced at the ash pile where she had burned the boxes filled with e-mail requests she'd eliminated a few days before.

The itching in her gut told her it was time to shift gears, to work on a case. Walking Miner, going to Carl's for their daily dinner, even helping out Clarence at the gym wasn't enough. She needed more. She knew she was built to solve cases.

It was time to get to work.

13

The next morning, Emily was still in bed when her phone rang. It wasn't as though she was lying around. It was barely six AM. Her alarm was due to go off in fifteen minutes so she could head to the gym. She rolled over and grunted, wondering if it was Lou trying to put another layer of pressure on her about the case.

It wasn't.

"I'm not calling too early, am I?" Angelica said in a sing-song voice.

"No. I was just about to get up."

"I was just about to get up too."

Emily frowned. Her sister Angelica lived in Rome. If it was six AM in Chicago, then it was probably two in the afternoon in Italy. "Did you have a busy night or something?"

Angelica was living in Rome under the protection of Dominic Andriano, a notorious mob boss, the head of the Mafia in New York City. Like all good mafiosos, he had ties to Italy. Dominic's men kept a watchful eye on her after she was kidnapped by billionairess Vasso Stamatea.

The courtesy didn't go just one way, though. Dominic had

done the favor not just for Angelica, who was a trained medical doctor. He had done it for Emily too, based on her relationship with Anthony Tizzano, her former father-in-law, a higher-up in the Chicago Office, the euphemistic name for the Chicago branch of the Italian Mafia. It had been called that since the time of Al Capone. And like all good things that had to do with the Mafia, they didn't feel there was any need to change the name.

"Last night was the same as usual. A couple of Dominic's guys needed to be stitched up after a tumultuous evening. Then I headed to the Jewish quarter and helped a family with three cute kids. Two of them had strep throat."

Emily shook her head. After medical school and her residency, Angelica had turned down a lucrative offer to work in Chicago. She darted off to Europe, quickly finding her calling by becoming something of a Robin Hood type of character. She'd treat anyone who needed help. No questions asked. Sometimes they paid, sometimes they didn't. Sometimes a family would offer her a freshly baked loaf of bread, which she accepted with as much gratefulness as Emily knew she did a stack of cash. Emily had witnessed it on several occasions.

"What are you doing today?" Angelica asked.

"Nothing much. Heading to the gym."

"How's subbing for Clarence going?"

Emily sat up on the edge of her bed and ran her hand through her dark hair. She recently had it cut off just above her shoulders. She was still surprised every time she felt the back of her neck and touched skin and not hair. "Okay."

There was a pause on the other end of the line. "Emily?"

Emily rubbed her chin. "What?"

"What's going on? There's something you're not telling me."

Emily pictured Angelica in her mind, her fiery red curly hair, a gift from their Italian grandmother. Angelica had the disposition to match. She was also strangely able to read between the lines. Whether that was because of her medical training or something else, Emily had no idea. Maybe it was because they were the only family each other had anymore. Their parents were gone, and their brother was someone they didn't have contact with.

"There might be a case."

Unlike many of the other people in Emily's life, Angelica wasn't one who would try to convince Emily one way or another. In the past she had, but after Emily had rescued Angelica from Vasso, Angelica had apparently developed a new appreciation for what Emily did.

"Why do you sound unsure? Or is it just you because you are just waking up?"

Emily blankly stared at a spot on the floor. She felt Miner rustle near the spot where he'd curled up by her feet. "You know how it is. It always takes me a little time to decide whether I wanna take the case or not."

"But that's not it. I hear something else in your voice."

Emily stood up and started pacing. There was no point in lying to Angelica. Angelica was the kind of person that would figure it out. And Emily quickly reasoned, if she expected Angelica to be honest with her, she needed to be honest with Angelica. "It's just that there's more risk than usual."

"Meaning?"

"Meaning that I'm not sure I wanna get dragged in."

Angelica huffed on the other end of the line. "Emily, for God's sake. Just tell me what's going on."

"All right, all right. I got a call from Lou Gonzalez yesterday."

"Like your ex-partner Lou?" Her voice was breathy, as if she couldn't believe what she was hearing.

"That would be the one. He needs help with a case."

"You've got to be kidding me! He has a lot of nerve calling

you. Do you want me to call Dominic? I can get some guys to talk to him."

Emily fought off the urge to roll her eyes. It was cute that Angelica was offering to rescue her, but Emily could handle herself. "No. I've got this."

"Well, what are you gonna do? I mean, this is the guy that put the handcuffs on you. I know he's helped you out a bit, but seriously, how can you even consider helping him?"

"That sounds a little hypocritical coming from somebody who treats mafia thugs, drug dealers, thieves, murderers —"

"And small children with strep throat," Angelica answered calmly. "What's the case?"

"A supposed suicide of a pro soccer player here in Chicago. Lou has some concerns."

"A soccer player? From what team?"

"What does that matter?"

"I might know him."

"How?"

"Well, when I was in Chicago, I treated some of the players from the team. And Emily, come on, soccer is the most popular sport in the world. Everybody watches soccer."

Emily raised her eyebrows and stopped moving. The only football she liked to watch was the Chicago Bears. She had no use for the sport that was called football around the rest of the globe. She'd tried watching it one time. The players had run back and forth on the field, spread out like tiny ants. After ninety minutes no one had scored a goal, and everyone went home. It was useless in her mind. "It was a guy named Ander Sabate. Lou said he played for the Chicago Fire."

Angelica swore in Italian under her breath. "Mother of God. Are you kidding me? Sabate was their star! I haven't seen this in the news. It hasn't been released yet?"

Emily balanced the phone on her shoulder as she pulled on

a pair of shorts. "No. I guess not. The team and the family are probably figuring out the PR end of it."

Angelica made a pfft noise. "Why does everything have to be about PR? Social media has ruined us all." There was a pause. "What are you gonna do?"

"About what?" Emily asked as she tugged on a pair of socks. Angelica or no Angelica, she had a workout to get to.

"The case."

"I don't know," Emily said, shaking her head.

"I think you should help Lou."

Emily froze. "Didn't you just remind me two minutes ago that he was the one that put the handcuffs on me?"

"Well, I've had a change of heart."

"Huh?"

"Everyone deserves a second chance, Emily. And this is Ander Sabate. Everyone deserves justice, even if it involves the CPD. I think you should help Lou. Make things right for his family."

14

Emily put her conversation with Angelica out of her mind until after her time at the gym. She guided Martina through another hour-long workout, only having to yell at her to keep going once.

That was an improvement.

Clarence came to the boxing ring after and put Emily through her paces, leaving her out of breath, sweating, her chest heaving by the time he was done with her. Whether it was a comeuppance for what she'd been doing to Martina or just Clarence trying to see where she was with her own skills, she had no idea. Clarence walked off at the end of their workout with a nod, pointing to the puddle of sweat that she left on the floor of the boxing ring. She knew the drill.

After mopping the floor, Emily pulled on a dry T-shirt, mopping her face with a towel. She walked out to her truck and got inside, sitting for a second, taking a long drink out of a bottle of water she had in her bag. The conversation with Angelica came rattling back into her mind. She picked up her phone, scrolled through her contacts and placed a call.

"Does this mean we have a case?" Mike asked.

Emily shrugged. There was no hello, no how are you. Just straight to business. That was fine with her. "Maybe. I want to take a look at the information Lou has. Wondering if there's a safe way to do that."

"I hope you look good in orange," Mike muttered under his breath.

Emily felt the back of her neck prickle. "Don't do that. What you do for me is voluntary. If you're not up to it that's fine. I'll find someone else."

"You'll never find anyone as good as me."

"Probably not," Emily answered as she pulled her truck away from the curb.

"Aren't you worried they're gonna try to nail you?"

"It's been a long time since I was with CPD, Mike. And Richard Henry isn't even in the picture anymore."

"Oh yeah, I forgot about that guy."

Emily hadn't. Richard Henry had been the head of the Internal Affairs Bureau for the Chicago Police Department, the key figure in the accusations against her. He'd been so annoyed when his plan hadn't worked that he had stalked Emily without her knowing for years, finally showing his hand a few months before when he tracked her down in the middle of a case at a college campus. He'd kidnapped her and held her at gunpoint, babbling about how she'd ruined his life. He'd completely lost his mind. The last time she had heard, her old IAB nemesis was spending time in jail, on a heavy dose of drugs to keep him calm. Her last update had been three months prior. She made a mental note to find out his status again. "Is there a way to get access to the files?"

"Has Lou put his report in the CPD database yet?" Among other things, Mike was a skilled hacker. He'd managed to work his way into all sorts of different databases, including leaving himself a back door to the FBI.

"I don't know."

"Give me a sec."

Emily heard typing in the background. It seemed that wherever Mike was, there was a computer. "Okay, there's not a ton in the database about this yet, except for a case number and a couple of pictures and some basics, like time and place. Looks like they were submitted by somebody named Courtney. Are they trying to keep the death quiet?"

"Probably. Lou has a new partner. She probably is the one that submitted the pictures."

"Do you think that Lou has more information?"

"I'm sure he does."

"All right. When you get home, check your phone. I'll set up an e-mail for him to use. It won't track back to you. That way you can have a look, but if anyone's watching, they won't have any idea where the data went."

Emily shook her head. The fact that Mike knew where she was at that moment was no surprise. He'd put tracking equipment and software on her phone and on her truck. She winced, feeling resolute. Mike was determined. Probably just as determined as she was. There was no point in kidding herself. There were probably tracking tags in at least a half a dozen other places she had no idea about. *At least someone knows where I am.* "Okay, thanks."

15

As Emily pulled into the driveway at her house, she heard her phone ping. It was Mike, sending her the dummy e-mail address she could use to get information from Lou. Emily put her truck in park, quickly copied the e-mail address and penned a quick text to him. "Send me everything you've got." She pasted the e-mail address Mike had sent her.

Now all she could do was wait.

An hour later, after taking Miner for a walk, coming home and hitting the shower, Emily was just coming downstairs when she heard the back door rattle. Miner charged at the door, barking, paused, then sat and whined. In two steps, Emily moved quickly to the kitchen drawer that held the nine-millimeter pistol she carried with her, sliding it open. She waited, her hand on the grip, her body tense. The door pushed open.

"Hey, Miner," Mike said.

Emily took her hand off the gun and closed the drawer.

Mike smirked. "Thanks for not shooting me."

"This time," Emily grumbled. "Maybe give me a heads up when you are planning on showing up."

Her comment went unnoticed. "Maybe this will improve your mood."

Mike shrugged off his backpack and set a lumpy duffel bag down on the floor of Emily's kitchen, then set a white bakery box in the center of the counter. "There's a new bakery near my apartment. They have the best crumb cake I've ever eaten. Figured after you worked out for three hours this morning you might need a snack."

"It was only two and a half. A whole hour of that was just training Martina."

"How's that going?"

Emily shrugged. She flipped the top of the box open, looking at what Mike had brought. The smell of sugar and cinnamon filled her nostrils. With all of her workouts, Emily's body had turned into not much else but muscle and bone. She knew she could afford to eat whatever she wanted. Heck, if Angelica was here, she'd probably take one look at Emily and promptly make a batch of their mother's manicotti and sauce to fatten her up. Some people might say the training was too much. For her, it was a lifeline, both mentally and physically. Emily never knew what she'd come up against next. She had to be prepared.

She turned away, walking over to the coffee pot, quickly filling it with grounds and water and setting it to brew. From a cabinet nearby, she grabbed paper plates and a few napkins, setting them on the table. "It's going okay. When are you gonna let me train you?"

Mike held his hands up making fists, feigning a serious look on his face. "Train me? Seriously? I'm ready to go. I don't need no training."

"Hardly."

He plopped down at the table. "You don't need to train me, Emily. I'm a ninja already, just with tech."

A slight smile tugged at her cheek. "True enough."

By the time the coffee brewed and she set a cup in front of Mike and poured one for herself, Mike had already gotten his computer plugged in and set up in her kitchen. Emily stared at her phone, taking a sip of coffee. She winced at how hot it was. "I didn't hear from Lou. yet"

"Yes, you did."

"I did?"

Mike nodded. "Yeah. He just sent a file over with a short message."

"What does it say?" Emily asked as she picked up one of the crumb cakes from the box and peeled the paper away from the edge. She broke off a bite with her fingers and put it in her mouth. She nodded, the sugar, cinnamon, and butter filling her mouth. He was right. It was good.

As she chewed, she stared at the box and then at Mike. Lots of things about him hadn't changed since they'd met during Emily's first case after she'd left CPD — his overly skinny frame, his floppy brown hair that usually covered at least half of his face, and his nearly consistent wardrobe of either a T-shirt and sweatpants, a T-shirt and jeans that were three sizes too big, or on exceptionally hot days, a T-shirt and shorts. Of course, in the winter, he added one of what looked to be about a million hoodies. At least his taste in food had improved since she met him. When they started working together, he seemed to live on a diet of chips — particularly Funyuns — and whatever soda he could find. Emily being Italian, started feeding him things like lasagna, chicken cutlets, and Italian sausage. Taking another bite of the crumb cake, she nodded once more. She could appreciate why he liked it. His taste was improving.

She decided she could take credit for the improvement.

Mike grabbed the plate and a crumb cake out of the box

without ever taking his eyes off his computer screen. He broke a chunk of the crumb cake off, nearly half, shoving it in his mouth, wiping his powdered sugar-coated fingers on his jeans before putting them back on the keyboard. Emily shoved a napkin toward him. "I do have napkins."

Mike looked up. "Yeah," he answered.

Emily shook her head. When Mike got focused on his computer, trying to communicate with him was like trying to drive a wedge between a mother grizzly bear and one of her cubs. His attention was completely focused on the technology in front of him. It got even worse the deeper they got into a case. But then again, Mike's singular focus had saved her bacon on more than one occasion. "What's in the file?"

Mike's expression changed from one of focus to one of confusion. "Not much, to be honest. Just a single picture of the body."

Emily frowned as Mike slid the computer towards her. She leaned forward, staring at the image Mike had retrieved from Lou's message. The corpse had dark hair, his eyes open and lifeless, his skin gray and pallid from soaking in the waters of Lake Michigan. His lips were blue, his mouth slightly open as if he was about ready to say something but hadn't had a chance before he was killed. "Lou didn't send any other notes over?"

"No. He didn't."

Emily held her hands up. *What kind of game are we playing here, Lou?* "I need to get a better look at the body than this."

"On it. Already have a program running."

Emily shook her head. "What does that mean?"

Mike looked up and grinned. "I've been working on a program for Alice. You know, she's still doing genetic testing. The thing is, she's been having trouble visualizing the DNA strands with their current technology. Needed a program to help do 3D modeling. I'm running it on this picture. It should give you a better idea of what the body actually looks like

IRL." Mike glanced up. "That's 'in real life' in case you didn't know."

Emily grunted. Alice was Mike's girlfriend. They lived together. Emily wondered why they just didn't get married. Her family had been old-school Italian. Anything that wasn't approved by the Catholic church was forbidden, including living together before marriage. But then again, she didn't really care what Mike did and, more importantly, no one had asked her opinion. She shrugged to herself. More accurately, she didn't really care what most people did.

A second later, Mike spun the computer back toward her. "Is that better?"

Emily stared at the screen then cocked her head to the side. What had come over as a two-dimensional image of a dead body on a beach was now defined enough that she felt like she could reach out and touch it. The background had been stripped away, the body floating in space. Mike pointed at the screen. "You can spin the picture by drawing your finger left and right. You can zoom in too." He took a second to show her how to manipulate the image and then pushed the computer toward her, shoving another big chunk of crumb cake in his mouth.

Emily pulled his computer closer to her. She looked down at the keyboard. It seemed to be new. Then again, Mike always seemed to have a new tech toy he was playing with. He had an entire stable of clients that he helped with all sorts of tech issues. Not the kind that anyone would admit to, of course. His own business now funded his hobbies. The last time they talked about it, Mike had told Emily that he had just finished dealing with a case of corporate espionage and was working on a new way to track ransomware demands and reclaim the funds. It was a product he hoped to launch to the black market, giving some of his black hat friends a way to fight back against the tech gangs located in Russia.

Emily stared at the image and then started zooming in and rotating it. The first thing she noticed was that the eyes did not appear bloodshot which was one of the grossly visible manifestations of petechial hemorrhaging, a common occurrence in victims of strangulation. When normally circulating blood is prevented from leaving the head due to hands or a cord wrapped tightly around the neck, the smaller, more fragile blood vessels rupture leaving behind tiny red spots in the eyes, on the neck, face or scalp which are called petechial hemorrhages. She checked the image around where his neck was. No marks there, either. What the effect would be on a body that had spent a lot of time in the water, she wasn't exactly sure. It wasn't something she'd run into with the bodies on the last case that involved water death — the torso killer in Tifton, Louisiana. He'd just chopped them into chunks and tossed them away. That was something to check into. Emily rotated the image and checked both of his arms, as best she could with the limited information she had. There were no marks, nothing on his hands that indicated he'd been in a fight, nothing like split skin on his knuckles or a dislocated finger. His body looked to be intact, no broken bones, no open lacerations.

After staring at the screen for a few minutes, she furrowed her eyebrows. "I'm not seeing anything here that doesn't scream suicide."

Mike was just finishing his second crumb cake when he pulled the computer back toward him. "I'm running a second program in the background to look for anomalies in the skin, things like cuts or bruises. I can let you know about that. But honestly, I don't see anything either."

He frowned at the screen for a second and then leveled his gaze at Emily. "I don't know, Emily. This feels funny. Lou sends you a single picture? He would have taken more, wouldn't he? And why does he think that this is something other than a suicide? I mean, I read about these high-profile guys all the time. They get involved in drugs or women or gambling, then decide they're in too deep and take their life. They don't want to deal with the bad PR."

Emily had exactly the same questions. What was Lou seeing that she wasn't? If he wanted her to help, he'd have to give her more — a lot more.

"I don't know."

16

Their weekly meeting over, Judge Conklin walked his campaign manager to the door, passing through the living room appointed with heavy leather furniture, noticing one of the heavy books on the architecture of Frank Lloyd Wright had been moved. He shot his wife a look. She was sitting at the breakfast room table with his two children, James Junior and Lisa, as they worked on their homework. It was the first week of school, so he was sure they wouldn't be at it for very long. Janice gave James a thin smile as he passed by with Layla. Janice, knowing her place wasn't to interfere in his business dealings, did nothing more than offer Layla a simple wave. The kids looked up, registering the fact that their dad was having a meeting, then went right back to work, their heads ducked down over the papers in front of them as if their completion meant a release from jail.

As soon as the door clicked closed and James turned, he found Janice, standing right in front of him. She blinked with watery eyes, somehow crossing the room without him hearing her. "How did it go, James?"

"Fine. Fine," he lied. His stomach was in knots.

As he turned to walk away, she called behind him. "Honey, it doesn't seem like you are fine. Are you okay? Did something go wrong?" Janice had vacillated between spending hours pinning decorating ideas to online mood boards for the Governor's Mansion and telling James it was a horrible idea, one that would put all of them under a spotlight that none of them wanted. The two of them still hadn't finished wrestling with how to resolve the issue. James was matter of fact about it and his word was final. If he won, Janice and the kids would adapt. If he didn't, Janice and the kids would adapt. He was the one providing the money and the life they all loved. Janice liked her nice car and beautiful purses. If she wanted to keep that up, then she'd have to give him the freedom to do what he thought was right. He was the man, after all. It was his home and his career. Janice and the kids were just along for the ride. He knew it wasn't a modern or popular idea, but he didn't care. It was a simple *quid pro quo* — they provided the allure of a stable, happy family and he provided a nice place for them to live and pretty much whatever they wanted. In his mind, it was ideal.

"No. Everything is fine. Stop asking me that," he answered sharply.

James stomped off, headed to the bedroom he sometimes shared with his wife. More and more, she had retreated to the guest bedroom, spending the night upstairs. She said it was to be near the kids, but he knew it was because of him. Their relationship, which had started out as a romance, after bumping its way through pregnancies, babies, challenges with work and finances, had become more of a business partnership than anything else. Sometimes it wasn't even a friendly business partnership. James paused as he walked into the bedroom. At that moment, James wasn't even sure he could say that Janice was his friend. She took care of the kids, made sure there was food available and that the house was clean and presentable.

She was perfectly appropriate at professional events and when they went to Westwood Country Club, but that was about it.

James pushed that thought away as he walked into their spacious closet. He undid the zipper to his pressed khaki pants and tossed them in the hamper, pulling on a pair of running shorts. He replaced his starched buttoned-down shirt with a T-shirt, pulled on a pair of bright yellow Hoka running shoes, and grabbed his earbuds from the charging station as he walked out the door.

James didn't say anything as he left the house, sending a gentle glare in Janice's direction as she stirred something on the stove. She knew where he was going. He did the same thing every night he was free. After trotting down the steps to the curb, he did a few cursory stretches and then began to run.

James hadn't started to run until he was in law school. The stress of the classes, the workload and the classmates, each of them eager to scrape their way to the top of the heap, had stressed him out. One night, after putting a hole in the wall of the bedroom of the small apartment he shared with his roommate just off campus at the University of Chicago, his roommate suggested that James go out for a run. The first run was excruciating. The high from the endorphins after was not. Since James was never one to shy away from hard work, he kept at it. He never looked back.

As he ran, his thoughts wandered, the rhythm of his body pounding the pavement almost sending him into a meditative state. His mind stopped for a moment on Layla Hadley. In his mind, she was like the harbinger of doom, or at least she'd become that way over the last several weeks. She'd been highly recommended to him, but it seemed over the last few months she wasn't performing the way he expected. The number of fundraisers had dwindled, so had calls from people who wanted to support him. By now he had fully anticipated leading in the polls for the governor's race. At that moment, in initial polling, he was ten points behind the leader, a man named Mark Banovich. And that said nothing about what might happen to the race if Liv Gardner decided to get involved.

James pushed the thought away as a hot bloom of anger rose in his chest. It felt like getting seared with a poker. He couldn't afford to get angry. His father used to get angry. It had been a scary kind of anger. He'd never laid a hand on James or the rest of the family, but it had been clear that disobedience, or worse, disappointment, would carry serious consequences.

He thought about Janice and how she was likely home feeding the kids, probably humming under her breath, waiting for him to come back again so they could talk. Why did she have to ask him so many questions? Couldn't she see that he just wanted to be left alone?

There were times he wanted to do nothing more than make her shut up.

The thought was so dangerous that James nearly came to a standstill during his run. Sucking in a sharp breath, he charged ahead, swinging his arms even more aggressively, feeling his lungs burn. No, he couldn't afford that kind of thought. His father had been an angry man, angry enough that he punished the family nearly every night when he got home, frustrated over his construction job, the people he worked with, and even his family.

No. James couldn't afford to get that angry. He knew what would happen if he did.

As he ran, he changed the music on his phone, listening to some cheery Motown, the voice of Marvin Gaye singing about no mountain being high enough. He tried mouthing the words, but that never went very well. His daughter, Lisa, had commented on more than one occasion that he had no rhythm. He checked his watch. He was running at about an eight-minute-per-mile pace. That meant it would take him just over an hour to complete his run. That was fine. The last thing he wanted to do at that moment was be home with Janice and the kids.

During the last mile of his run, James's mind flickered over to Eric Atkins, the senator vying for the Senate President role. Why wasn't Eric supporting James? Why was he so interested in Liv Gardner? James frowned as he ran. He and Eric met on several occasions, part of the handshaking that Layla and his other campaign managers had managed to put together. Their agendas, on the face of it, seemed to align. Eric had been a prosecutor before he'd run for office. James was a judge. It seemed to James that they were a good fit. But Layla's words echoed in his mind.

Eric Atkins isn't supporting you.

James broke down to a walk as he hit their block, looking at the wide concrete planters of white flowers that had been planted by the city near the edge of the street. The arching streetlights had just flickered on, casting a pale golden glow over the red brick sidewalks. On the other side of the street, a young woman walked a German Shepherd, the two of them heading in the direction of the park. James admired the woman. She had to be strong and determined if she owned that kind of dog.

He put his hands on his hips and waited for his breathing to slow, feeling perspiration cluster on his forehead. He walked slowly back to his townhome, walking up the steep steps and turning the polished brass knob to go in the front door, using a key he carried with him. He looked around. Janice and the kids had disappeared, probably retreating upstairs after dinner. Given the way things had been going, it wasn't likely that he would see any of them for the rest of the evening.

That was okay. He wasn't in the mood to chat with anyone, especially Janice.

James took a hot shower, pulled on a comfortable pair of

shorts and T-shirt that he'd gotten at his last half marathon, and walked into his office. There was work to be done, not just for the campaign, but also for his legal career. He stood in the doorway for a second, his head cocked to the side, his thoughts swirling. Eric Atkins should support him. His endorsement would be key to winning the governor's race. What was the problem?

Striding toward the spot where he'd left his phone to charge before he took a shower, James picked it up and sent a text to Layla. She responded immediately, providing him with Eric's private cell phone number. "Be careful," she warned. "We really need him."

James scowled. Who did Layla think she was dealing with? The warning wasn't necessary. He needed to try to win Eric over, not make him defensive. James sucked in a deep breath and then tapped on the number Layla had sent.

Eric picked up a second later, James forcing himself to smile. Maybe that would make him feel more cheerful about the predicament he was in. "Eric!" James said enthusiastically. "This is James Conklin."

There was a pause at the other end of the line as if Eric needed a minute to register who it was. Heat rose to James's cheeks.

"James. Nice to hear from you."

James sat down in his leather chair, spinning it so he had a view outside. The sun had gone down, the cars passing his townhome using their headlights to navigate. "Listen, I just wanted to touch base with you," he said casually, "With the upcoming election, I was thinking that you and I are pretty well aligned on the issues that are important to us, don't you?"

James winced as the words came out of his mouth. He wondered if he'd said too much right off the bat, possibly overplaying his hand.

More silence. "Sure, I think there are some areas where we

definitely do overlap, but then again, I don't know much about the platform that you're running on."

So that was the problem. A lack of information could be fixed. Hadn't Layla communicated with his office, even asked for his support? He felt his stomach tighten. Maybe Layla wasn't all she'd been made out to be after all.

He smiled again. "Well, that's an easy enough problem to fix. I'd be more than happy to grab a time to meet with you. Let me take you to lunch. I'd like to share my vision with you. Will you be back in Chicago again sometime soon?"

Another round of silence. "Yeah. We can do lunch sometime. My schedule's packed for the next few weeks, but why don't you have your assistant call my office and we'll see if we can't get something on the calendar."

James frowned. Eric sounded bored and not the least bit interested. The fact that he'd play James off, telling him he was too busy to meet anytime soon wasn't a good sign. By the time they did meet, it would be too late.

"I have to be honest, Eric. I feel like this is an urgent issue. You know how it is. People are starting to decide who they're going to back. I'd like you to back my run for governor. I think we could make things happen. I know my campaign manager, Layla —"

"Yeah, I saw the information she sent over. Like I said, I've been busy. Haven't had a chance to look at it. Lots of people are looking for my support."

What you are saying is that you haven't made time to look at it. "You are an up-and-coming power in Illinois. I can see that. That's why I'd like your support." James tried to sound enthusiastic, though he wasn't exactly feeling that way.

Eric cleared his throat and deflected. "Like I said, James, my schedule's pretty packed. I have no problem meeting with you, but you might have to be patient. I have been meeting with other people too. Have to do what's best for my office.

Politics isn't like the law. Things don't happen just because you say so."

James's stomach clenched. It was a clear shot. Was Eric resentful of the fact that James was a judge and he wasn't?

"Of course, of course." James forced his tone to be conciliatory though everything in him wanted to take his phone and aim it at the window. "I understand. I'll have my office call yours."

"That would be great," Eric said flatly.

As James hung up, his skin prickled. How dare Eric treat him that way? Who did Eric think he was? James wasn't just a nobody running for governor. He was a judge. A long-standing one with a stellar career. He set his jaw then stood up and started pacing. Part of him wanted to call Layla Hadley and read her the riot act, but that wouldn't help. She couldn't control Eric's reaction. James bit the inside of his lip, replaying the conversation in his head, feeling Eric's disdain deep in his gut. If this was James's courtroom, he could have thrown Eric in jail on some trumped-up charge of contempt.

But he couldn't. Not if he wanted to become the next governor of the state of Illinois. This was real life.

James looked away, then rubbed his palms together. Solving the problem of Eric Atkins might require another strategy, something a little more nontraditional.

17

Emily had studied the single image that Detective Lou Gonzalez had provided to her of the suicide of Ander Sabate for what felt like hours. In reality, she and Mike had only spent an hour on it. It was only one image, after all. It wasn't like he'd sent over the full jacket, which would have made her life easier. Why that wasn't the case, she still wasn't sure.

She spent the rest of the afternoon doing the things she normally did — going to Carl's to get something for dinner, taking Miner for another walk, and tending to her tomato plants. But in her mind, she kept going back to the image that Lou had sent her. Something didn't make sense. If it was so obviously a suicide, why was Lou fixated on the fact that maybe it wasn't?

Finally, after making dinner — stuffed pork chops, a side of pasta, and Caesar salad — Emily sent Mike on his way and picked up her phone. Lou answered after the first ring.

"Where are you?" she asked.

"Home. Sorry for the radio silence. It's been a busy day." He sounded slightly out of breath, as if he was busy mowing the lawn or something, though she didn't hear anything in the background.

Emily pressed her lips together. "I need to ask you about that image you sent me." "Yeah. What about it?"

Emily raised her eyebrows. For someone who had asked for her help, he seemed quite blasé, but there was something more to the way he said it, an edge to his voice that she couldn't quite identify.

"Is that all you have? One image? I feel like you're wasting my time." It was blunt, but to the point.

There was a heavy silence for a moment. "I think it's better if we meet in person." Lou said the words quietly.

The comment got Emily's attention. "All right. What do you have in mind?"

"Why don't you stop at the house? I have some stuff I wanted to give you anyway."

The conversation had changed direction in a way Emily hadn't expected. She hadn't been over to Lou's house since she was with CPD. Her stomach fluttered. "When are you thinking?"

"Now."

By the time Emily left her house, it was dark. The streetlights had flickered on, the roads around Chicago filled with people who were traveling home from a long day at work or headed out for a late dinner. The traffic, by Chicago standards, was manageable.

As she drove, Emily hummed under her breath, thinking about where she was going. He hadn't bothered to send her the address. He didn't need to. Emily could see his house in her mind — the small brown brick bungalow, nothing more than a square box he and his wife lived in. If she remembered correctly, he had a narrow, detached garage that could hold two cars at the back of the property, just barely. It wasn't big, even by Chicago's overcrowded standards. Like Emily, who also lived in a modest home, Lou and his wife had bought what they could afford. Things had changed for Emily after she'd left the department. While her cases didn't pay her — she had never, in fact, asked to be paid for what she did — a thick envelope with cash still appeared in her mailbox on the first of every month, courtesy of her former father-in-law, Anthony Tizzano. They never talked about it. Never. But even with the change in her financial situation with the settlement from the city and her monthly stipend from Anthony, Emily had stayed in the house where she and Luca had started.

Why, she wasn't sure.

From the back seat, Emily heard a noise. She glanced in the rearview mirror. Miner's pointed ears were standing straight up, his mouth open, his pink tongue hanging out. "How're you doing back there, buddy?" she asked.

The smile on Miner's face told her everything she needed to know. Miner loved going for car rides. She normally didn't take him to other people's homes, but something in her told her to take him with to Lou's. He was protective of her. It wasn't as though she needed to defend herself against Lou. Or did she? Something about how the day had gone down was niggling at her gut. She shifted in her seat, feeling the weight of the gun concealed at her side. It was just Lou, wasn't it? Her old partner. Someone she'd trusted with her life.

Until he betrayed her.

As soon as she got to Lou's house, she surveyed the streets. They were quiet, many of the houses dark. A single sedan passed her driving the other direction, driven from what she could see, by a woman who didn't bother looking in Emily's direction.

Getting out of her truck, she slammed the driver's side door, adjusting the oversized T-shirt she'd pulled on over her gun. She tugged down the brim of her baseball cap and opened the back door, clipping a leash to Miner's collar. Realistically, she didn't need it to control him. A quick whistle and he was by her side. Like most Australian cattle dogs, Miner was like glue. Shadow dogs, they were called. Miner was one of them. "Come on, boy. Let's go see Lou." He looked up at her as if asking what she meant and then trotted happily along by her side as she walked toward the house locking the truck with her key fob.

Lou met her in the driveway, the storm door creaking as it closed automatically behind him. He didn't meet her eyes. If Emily remembered correctly, the door he'd emerged from led directly to the kitchen. He had a five o'clock shadow across his chin and was wearing basically the same outfit as Emily — worn jeans and an oversized T-shirt. He had flip-flops on his feet. "Thanks for coming over," he said, his eyes grazing her face. He looked down. "I didn't know you were bringing Miner."

"I thought he might like the car ride."

Lou bent over and made eye contact with Miner, holding his hands out. Miner gave a single bark as if he wasn't sure it was a good idea for Lou to get that close to him and then moved in closer, allowing Lou to scratch his back. Lou stood up. "Let's go this way." He pointed toward the garage.

Looking around, Emily noticed only his car was in the driveway. Maybe his wife was out for the night? Was that why they were meeting at his house? Why was he leading her into the garage?

Lou led the way to the garage door, his flip-flops making a slapping noise as they hit the back of his heels. Emily followed, holding Miner's leash lightly. As Lou got to the garage door, he flipped open a keypad mounted on the trim and typed in what looked to be a numeric code. How long it was, Emily couldn't tell. She raised her eyebrows. If Mike was there, he would have been able to replicate it in the space of about ten seconds.

As the garage door clattered open from its closed position, Lou stepped into the darkness, reaching around the side and flipping on a light. Emily paused in the driveway, scanning the scene, her skin tingling. She didn't see anyone. She glanced down at Miner. His body language was relaxed. That was a good sign. No ambush, at least at the moment.

Am I really afraid of Lou?

The question thundered through her mind. Was she that mistrustful of him? She shook off the thought and followed Lou into the garage. He pressed a button on the wall and lowered the garage door. Emily narrowed her eyes. *Why close the garage door?* As she looked around, Lou went to a side door and opened it up, quickly flipping on a large fan. "Sorry," he apologized. "it's a little warm in here, but I don't want to leave the garage door open. The neighbors might be watching. I swear the old lady across the street has binoculars."

Emily winced. The neighbors were watching? What did that mean? Immediately, she started looking around to see what it was that Lou didn't want the neighbors to see. The garage was relatively standard. There was a cluster of tools against one side, a rusted shovel, a couple of rakes, and a fishing pole with a cobweb dangling off of it. A mower was pushed off to the side. On the side of the garage where Lou was standing, it was largely empty. On the other side, a plastic folding table had been set out in the center of where a car would usually be parked. A few old, rusted car parts sat on top of it along with a smattering of tools. Emily frowned. Something felt off, as if the garage had been partially abandoned.

As Lou strode to the back of the garage, Emily called after him, her tone intentionally casual. "You guys storing your cars outside? That might be a pain in the winter." Chicago's winters were notoriously brutal, the wind howling off Lake Michigan for what seemed to be months at a time, powerful squalls blowing out of Canada, dumping snow on the city and the suburbs, burying them in piles of ice and dirty slush.

"No, I'll get my car back in here for the winter." He looked over his shoulder at Emily, his expression flickering. "I'm divorced now. Wife left me."

Emily furrowed her eyebrows. "When did that happen?"

"About a year ago. She got tired of the job. Tired of the fact I was gone all the time and kept getting called out. Said she wanted something else. Something more stable."

"You didn't say anything. I just saw you just a few months back." Emily quickly calculated in her head. The last time she had seen Lou, he was arresting Richard Henry after pointing a gun at Emily and putting her in handcuffs.

Lou shrugged. "It wasn't exactly the time or place to chitchat about my personal woes."

An uncomfortable silence settled over them, but only lasted for a second. If there was one thing that police officers were good about, it was compartmentalizing bad news. They could carry a body bag out with a dead person in it and five minutes later be talking about what they wanted to have for lunch that day. Emily had been gone from the department for a long time, but the skills remained.

Lou pulled a whiteboard out from the back wall of the garage and turned it around. Emily frowned. "Where did you get that?"

"Had it delivered. Got it a few months back when I had a case I couldn't quite figure out. Wasn't sleeping much anyways." He looked down. "You know, with the divorce and all that."

As he turned it around, Emily saw that he had put pictures of Ander Sabate on the board. "That's a few more pictures than the ones that you sent me," she grumbled.

Lou's shoulders tensed. "Yeah. Sorry about that. I think I'm getting paranoid in my old age. I have this new partner. She's a little too fast to make decisions about how the case should be handled. There's something about her that's giving me the creeps, like she's watching me."

"She a rookie?"

"Sort of. Courtney's been with the department for, I don't know, say three or four years, but she's new to the homicide unit. Only been working with her for a month or so. It was kind of strange the whole way she got promoted. There were several people that were ahead of her that I was pretty sure would make it into the unit, but then again —" He shrugged. "You never know what's going on with the brass."

"That's what all of the secrecy is about?"

Lou ran his hand through his hair. "Yeah, I guess. Maybe? I don't know. There's something about this case and the way that Courtney is behaving that doesn't ring true, if you know what I mean." He looked away. "Like I said, maybe I'm being paranoid, but there's something about Courtney. It's like someone or something is pulling some strings that I can't see. I feel like people are whispering behind my back. Makes the hair on my neck stand up."

Emily nodded. She understood what Lou was saying. She'd felt the same way in the weeks before her arrest. "Any idea what's going on?"

"No. But I don't trust her as far as I can throw her."

So that was the reason that Lou had only emailed one image of Ander Sabate and had insisted on Emily coming to his house. It also explained the murder board in front of her. Emily folded her arms across her chest. She stared at the whiteboard in front of her. "So, if you don't think Ander Sabate committed suicide, what do you think?"

Lou shook his head. "That's what I'm hoping you can help me with."

18

Emily paused. Lou's sadness was etched all over his face. Part of her wondered how much of it was from the divorce and how much of it was from the stress of work. Emily knew how the Chicago Police Department was. Once you got on their radar, it was nearly impossible to get the target off your back. If Lou was right and they were after him, it wasn't a good situation, that was for sure. The fact that Lou had assembled what amounted to a murder board in his garage, plus the fact that he'd called Emily in to help, told her that he was suspicious. Whether it was only about the fact that he needed something else to focus on other than the fact that he was now alone or whether it was because he was worried about his future with CPD and the whispers he thought he was hearing, Emily wasn't sure.

She knew how he felt. Emily's own husband, Luca Tizzano, had left her after her arrest, more interested in the drug habit and a lustful taste for prostitutes he'd developed after she got arrested. He had no interest in trying to help her navigate through what ended up being a traumatic experience that radically changed who she was. A few years later, he'd died in an overdose, the drugs taking over. The unfairness of it all was likely what drove his father, Anthony, to still continue to deliver envelopes of cash anonymously to Emily's mailbox every single month.

Emily set her jaw. As sorry as she was that these things had happened to Lou, she wasn't about to get herself sucked into anything other than giving the case a look. This was professional courtesy, that was all. He was the one that had put the handcuffs on her. And Lou, like most of the other officers she'd served with, turned their backs on her when she'd been arrested.

Unfortunately for them, Emily wasn't the kind that forgot.

The reality was that the thin blue line was very thin, especially for those who wore badges but were deemed a liability to the department. Heck, it was nonexistent in some cases. People did what benefited them. That was the truth.

Emily shifted her weight to one hip. Enough with the secrecy. "You don't think it's a suicide. You're a smart detective. Why am I here?"

Lou stared at the murder board for a moment and then glanced at Emily. "I already got a call from the captain of the homicide division about the case. They want it solved quickly and quietly. I guess it's because Ander Sabate is a public figure. Or was…"

Emily shook her head. Politics and the CPD worked hand in hand. They might as well just move the mayor into police headquarters for all she cared. At least that way they'd be honest about it. "Do you follow soccer?"

"Are you kidding? No. I didn't even realize Chicago had a professional soccer team until this morning."

"So this has become news, then? Somebody leak it?"

Lou nodded. "Maybe?" He rubbed the back of his neck. "I don't know. Maybe they are trying to avoid bad news, spin it the way it's best for the team. Definitely feels that way."

Emily furrowed her eyebrows. "Some of the bigwigs have ties to the case?"

"Yep. The captain said the chief, for some reason, wants this kept quiet. How far it goes above that, I have no idea."

Emily became immediately suspicious. Anytime there were political motivations, the investigation itself got pushed to the back burner. It seemed the priorities of the living were more critical than honoring the dead, or even the truth. "So what are you asking me to do, exactly?"

Lou sighed. "I don't know. I know that something doesn't seem right. I know that my new partner is gonna be of no help. I also know that there's nobody better at putting together the pieces of the case than you. I swear, it's a gift from God."

Emily winced. All the flattery was making her nervous. "Lou, if you think —"

He held his hands up before she could even finish her sentence. "Listen. I get it. I'm probably the last person you want to help. The department did you dirty. I get that. I get why you have been off the radar for so long. I also understand why you want to stay that way. But at the same time, my gut tells me there's something going on here. And if there is, Ander Sabate deserves justice, just like the rest of us."

Emily narrowed her eyes. "Even if that justice comes from a source that doesn't necessarily follow all the rules?"

Lou straightened. "That's getting to be my favorite kind."

19

Detective Courtney Green pulled up in front of Lou Gonzalez's house as two people disappeared inside of Lou's garage, the garage door cryptically sliding closed behind them. Courtney had only caught a glance of the silhouettes of the people as they walked inside. One of them was clearly Lou. She could tell by his shape and the way he ambled when he walked. She felt her stomach tighten. The visitor could be something, or it could be nothing. Which one it was, she had no idea. Only time would tell. She narrowed her eyes. The other person looked like a woman. She had a dog with her.

Curious.

Courtney drove around the block, turned around and came back, parking around the corner, out of the direct line of sight of Lou's house and the truck parked in front. Where she stopped, she had an angle where she could see movement through his neighbor's backyard. As she passed, she had taken a photo of the pickup truck in the driveway. It was newer, red, and spotlessly clean, as if someone either had enough money to hire a detailing service or spent a lot of time scrubbing it, given the tumultuous weather in Chicago.

Courtney leaned back in the seat of her car sliding down to make it harder to spot her. It was her personal vehicle, a newer white Ford Focus sedan. It looked the same as a million other vehicles on the road, giving her a bit of anonymity. Frowning, she slid down in the seat a little bit more and pulled up the picture she'd taken of the pickup truck as she'd driven by. Who was in the garage with Lou? And why had they closed the garage door? She had no personal issue with Lou other than he was in the way of her getting what she wanted. She wrinkled her nose. He'd lost his energy for the job. Cops like him should retire.

Stil frowning, Courtney enlarged the picture, getting a good look at the license plate. It was an Illinois plate. She tapped her screen and dialed a friend she had that worked at dispatch.

"Courtney! What's up, girl?"

"Same old, same old, Tanya." Tanya and Courtney had gone through the police academy together. But Tanya had taken a different path. She'd blown out her knee during one of the arrest training scenarios at the Academy and had been unable to finish. The department had quickly offered her a position in dispatch after she'd recovered from her surgery. It wasn't on the road where she wanted to be, but the structural damage to her knee made it impossible for her to complete the police physical.

"Do me a solid and run a plate for me?"

"Sure. You want me to tag this with a case ID?"

Courtney paused. Technically, she was in violation of department standards if she ran a plate without being on a case.

But then again, she was. Sort of.

She cleared her throat. "If you can keep this one off the

books for now, I'd appreciate it. I can go back later and tag it in the system at my end."

"Oh, it's one of those kinds of cases. Yeah, no problem. I do it all the time."

Courtney shook her head. She was glad she had called Tanya on her personal phone and not through the department. Tanya could lose her job for giving out that information without a formal case number. So could Courtney, for that matter. Dispatch recorded everything that was said. At least Courtney had some cover from her contacts that could help her out. She blinked, wondering if push came to shove, if they would. She shook her head. She had a job to do. One that she'd been told would earn her some goodwill with people up the chain when it came to promotions. *Gotta take a risk to get the reward.* Courtney read off the combination of letters and numbers to Tanya.

"Give me a sec. Computer is slow today."

"Isn't it always?"

"You don't have to tell me about that."

There was a pause. "All right. The plate comes back to an Emily Tizzano." Tanya read off the address.

Courtney frowned. "Isn't that on the other side of town?"

"Hold on. Let me check."

A second later she came back. "Well, I guess it depends on where you are, but from where you live, yeah. Probably about a half hour drive or so." There was a pause, as if Tanya was already becoming a little suspicious. "You need backup, Courtney? I've got cars in the area."

"No, no. It's nothing like that. Just doing some follow-up on a case. You know." She adopted a relaxed tone. Courtney didn't need Tanya asking too many questions.

Tanya snorted. "Yeah, I heard you made detective. You're a big shot now. We're going to have to get together sometime soon. I wanna hear all about it."

"Yeah. Let's do that." Her answer was intentionally vague. Maybe she would. Maybe she wouldn't.

As Courtney hung up, she started wondering about who it was that was visiting Lou Gonzalez. Who was Emily Tizzano? A girlfriend? A friend? A relative?

It seemed obvious, but one of the easiest ways to identify someone was by using a search engine, the same kind people used to find a recipe for apple pie, a sale on tennis shoes or a new book. Now coupled with the rise of AI technology, people's privacy was nearly gone, unless someone had no social media profiles, didn't have an e-mail address, and only used cash.

Courtney knew those people were few and far between, the kind of people that lived out in the middle of nowhere, off the grid. Even then, their name was likely recorded as a person who owned the property.

No, privacy was gone. No one was anonymous anymore.

A quick search of the Internet didn't reveal anything recent about Emily Tizzano, the woman who was visiting Lou's house, but there were news reports from more than a decade before. Courtney raised her eyebrows as she read, her face illuminated just slightly by the glow from her cell phone. Emily was a former cop? A dirty one at that? Courtney looked in the direction of Lou's house. Were they friends? Was she a new girlfriend? Courtney hadn't heard anything of the sort at the office. She expected she would have by now if Lou was dating someone. Cops were notorious gossips. An officer could barely go buy a coffee without it stirring up the rumor mill.

And the rumor mill had never been quicker to note when Lou started acting temperamental at work, the news filtering out quickly that his wife had left him. Courtney hadn't been with the homicide division at that time, but when she had been brought in and paired up with him, Captain Braylon Ingram met with her privately before making them partners. "Lou is one of our best detectives. You'll learn a lot from him, but I have to warn you, he's been kind of temperamental over the last couple months. Wife left him a while ago. His divorce was just finalized."

It wasn't news to her. Courtney hadn't really noticed, but then again, she'd only been with homicide for a couple months. She didn't know what Lou was like before, so it was hard to compare with how he was after. He might be a good detective, but all she knew was that his style was plodding, slow. It was irritating.

Courtney stared at her phone for a second, skimming through the articles about Emily Tizzano. Was this worth reporting? She shrugged. Those had been her orders.

Courtney thumbed through her contacts, found a single, unassigned number toward the bottom of the list that had no name attached to it and tapped it. The instructions were clear — no text messages, no voicemails. Only voice to voice any time of the day or night.

"Yes?" a voice answered.

"I'm at Gonzalez's house. Keeping an eye on him like you asked. There's a woman here."

"Who?"

Her contact wasn't known for wordy conversations. "A woman named Emily Tizzano. She brought her dog. I asked a friend at dispatch to run the plate."

"Anything else?"

"No."

20

Emily stood in the garage, her arms crossed in front of her chest. She stared at the information that Lou had compiled. "All right. Walk me through what you've got."

Lou shook his head. "It's what I *don't* have that's making me twitchy. My gut's telling me there's something going on with this case that I haven't found yet." He pointed to a set of pictures he'd assembled on the murder board. "You know, with everything connected electronically now, the only way I can work on this in isolation is if I print this stuff off and bring it home. The department's got eyes everywhere. Worse than it's ever been." He shook his head. "All this technology. I'm not sure it's actually helping anyone."

Emily was glad she wasn't wearing an earpiece. If Mike had heard what Lou was saying, he'd probably beg to differ. But Emily knew exactly what Lou meant. Technology wasn't her favorite. She maintained no social media profiles and only had a single e-mail address — the same one she'd had for the last twenty years, which she barely checked. She only had it in case she needed to order something online and they required it. "I know what you mean. Not a huge fan myself."

Lou continued. "I've got the body, but the coroner hasn't ruled yet. I guess they're backed up with autopsies. She called me when I was on my way home from work today. Said she'll have something for me in the morning. Nice gal."

"New?" Emily asked.

Lou nodded. "Yeah, Elena McMillan. Probably about our age. Very by the book. Doesn't want anyone even touching the bodies until she gets there. Very concerned about cross contamination and her ability to testify in court honestly."

Emily raised her eyebrows. "Honesty as a priority? That's refreshing."

"I know. Kind of funny to have somebody so old school in the middle of the mix. But anyways, I'm getting off track." Lou pointed at the series of pictures. "I'm not sure how much you've been able to dig up with your fancy tech guy, but the victim, as you know, is Ander Sabate, star forward of the Chicago Fire. He's the face of the organization. He was found yesterday morning by a woman with her dog walking along the beach. Washed up out of the lake."

Emily shook her head. Her mind started to clatter with the information that Lou was giving her. It was a very different process than she normally went through with Mike, who dug around online. She felt herself start to get excited at the familiarity of the run-down but tamped the feelings back deep inside of her. *Stay focused on the facts. Don't forget about Lou's motivation for pulling you into this. He has a badge. You don't.*

Putting together the pieces of a case was something she loved to do. Emily had single-handedly closed more Chicago Police Department cold cases during her tenure than any other detective. But her talent was what got her fired.

She pushed the thoughts aside. *Focus on the details, Tizzano.* "Any water in his lungs? Any possibility it was a drowning?"

Emily knew that in the case of drowning, water would actually be inhaled into a person's lungs. It was one of the tests that the coroner would do to determine cause of death.

Lou shook his head. "I don't know. Like I said, Elena hasn't done the autopsy yet. Was tied up with a couple of other cases."

Emily walked closer to the pictures, staring at them. Lou had printed off a series of them, eight in total, from different angles of the body. "Tell me more. What's got your Spidey sense all worked up?"

Lou stopped and sighed. "You know, it's not so much all of this, it's what we didn't find at the scene and what I've been able to dig up on his background check."

"Which is?"

"Sabate had no markers of someone who was suicidal. He was involved in the community. Did a bunch of charity work for Chicago Children's Hospital and not just because of his soccer fans. Was just there last week. Spent the entire day on an orthopedic floor, kicking soccer balls with kids and eating pizza. He's got a wife at home and a new baby."

Emily shrugged. "So what? Maybe the pressure is too much? Lots of men lose it when they find themselves responsible for a wife and a kid." Emily couldn't help but think of her own situation with Luca. He'd been different after they married. It had been like his interest in her had abated once there was a gold band on her finger.

Lou shook his head. "I did some more digging. Sabate didn't have any money issues. He just signed a big endorsement deal with Nike, was about to sign another one with some sort of an energy drink. He was set up for his future. He'd make more money than he needed to have in order to raise a family." Lou pointed to a sheet of paper he'd taped to the board. "I tracked his doctor's appointments, his prescriptions, and his family contacts. None of it adds up to somebody who was suicidal. No one reported that he was down. He wasn't on any anti-depression or anti-anxiety medication. He hadn't seen a psychologist or a psychiatrist that I could find, and he even called his mom and dad in Portugal every single day on his way to practice. He'd recently bought them a house paid for in cash."

Emily frowned. To her, it sounded like somebody who may be a closet depressive. "You know, there are lots of people that appear to be fine on the outside but they're really struggling." As the words came out of her mouth, she wondered if she was one of those people. "I'm still not seeing a huge discrepancy. You gotta give me something concrete."

Lou didn't seem deterred. "Then there's this." He pointed to a single picture on the board. It was of Ander's feet. "Here's the thing that really tipped me off. Not only did Ander come out of the water without his shoes, but I spotted puncture marks between his toes."

Emily walked over to the picture and cocked her head to the side. This was not one of the images that had come over when she and Mike had looked at the case earlier. She tapped on it with her fingernail. "Are you saying he was tossed in the water with his shoes off? What do you think this means?"

"I don't know. Could he have been doing drugs? Sure. But if he was doing something he was taking a big risk with his career. These pro athletes, they're tested left and right now, especially the international ones. Some guy named Paul Pogba was just benched for four years for using performance-enhancing drugs. Sure, there are ways to game the system, but shots between your toes? That's kinda obvious. I mean, the marks are right there."

"It's definitely not as obvious as in the arm, but the placement seems strange." Emily frowned. She stared at the picture and then looked at Lou. "You know what's even stranger?"

"What's that?"

Emily's eyes widened. "There's only one puncture mark."

21

Ana Sabate had just got done doing a few dishes that had been left behind in the sink. "Oh, Mrs. Sabate, I am *so* sorry. I got caught up with the baby. I was coming right away to do those." Christina, the Sabate's housekeeper, turned nanny, said apologetically, handing Ana a kitchen towel.

"It's no problem, Christina. I needed something to do."

Christina blinked but said nothing. Ana had been up early, pacing around the house. It was a fact that everyone who worked for her knew. She hadn't slept. Ander, her husband and the father of their baby, hadn't come home the night before. It wasn't like him. He'd left her with a kiss and a promise to come back at a reasonable hour after meeting a friend.

He hadn't.

Where he was, Ana had no idea. She'd tried to access his location, but for some reason her phone couldn't find his. She'd called and left messages, as well. Nothing. All she knew was that Ander had said he was going out with a friend for a boat ride, then to dinner, but he hadn't returned home as expected.

Ana leaned her hands on the edge of the counter as

Christina bustled around the kitchen. Ana glanced at her. Christina was just one of the people that helped around the house. They also had another nanny and a full-time security/driver available to them. Most of the time Ander just drove himself to practice and back, so Ana was the one that took advantage of whoever the agency sent to watch over them. There were times she was glad for the help and other times she just wanted to be left alone.

At that moment, the only person she wanted was Ander.

Ana clicked on the electric kettle to make herself a cup of herbal tea. Christina tried to intervene and make it for her, but Ana waved her off. Ana was capable of making a cup of tea for herself. As she waited, she caught a look at her face in the glass cabinet door. Her black hair was tied back in a ponytail, and she was wearing her trademark black leggings and a body-hugging T-shirt. Despite her recent pregnancy, her body had rebounded like a champ. Ander had told her that she looked even better than before she got pregnant. She wasn't sure she believed him, but it was a nice sentiment anyways. What she did notice was the dark circles under her eyes. Lack of sleep from the baby was one thing. Lack of sleep because Ander hadn't come home was something else.

A knock at the door of their penthouse got her attention. Max, the guard on duty that day, opened the door, the coil of a white earwig evident behind his ear, a gun prominently displayed on his hip. Ana glanced toward the door, seeing Max open it up.

From the hallway outside their condominium, three people stepped inside. Two of them, grim-faced men, had formal police uniforms on. The third person, a woman with a coil of blonde hair twisted behind her head, wore a skirt and blouse, and had black-rimmed glasses on her face. She carried a briefcase.

Ana walked to the door. She looked at the people who had

just arrived, then felt her entire body go numb. They looked at her with pity. Later, she'd remember that she thought they looked so official. One of the men stepped toward her, a serious expression on his face, pity in his eyes. "Mrs. Sabate?"

"Yes, I'm Ana Sabate." Ana could feel the tension building in her body. What was wrong? Why were they here?

"Ma'am, I'm sorry to bother you this morning. I'm Captain Ingram." He pointed behind him. "This is Lieutenant Hoffman and Mary Vargas." Ana recognized Mary Vargas. She was the team psychologist. He cleared his throat. "I'm sorry to inform you..."

22

Emily started to slowly nod. She was coming around to the idea that there was something up with Ander's death. "Did you happen to look at his other foot?"

Lou nodded. "Yeah. We only found a puncture mark in his left foot. Not the right. The right still had the sock on while we were at the scene."

"And only one?"

"So far, unless Elena finds something we missed."

That was a possibility. "So, either there are injection sites we didn't see, Ander Sabate has incredible powers of self-healing, or there was only one puncture."

Lou's eyes got wide. "So this wasn't somebody who was a regular drug user, then was it?"

"Not likely, not even for PED's."

"How do you know?"

Emily traced her finger across one of the pictures. "The gym where I work out has a lot of hard-core guys. A bunch of them are into performing enhancement drugs, or PED's. They cycle them. It's not just one shot. That wouldn't do the trick. If Ander was on them, he'd have more than one mark on him if he was running a tight cycle. That would be the best way to get the benefit without getting caught. Do a bunch of it in a week, then lay off while it clears his system."

Lou let out a low whistle. "This is getting more complicated by the minute."

Emily stared at the pictures again, walking by them. She'd let Miner off the leash once they started looking at the images on the murder board. He'd finished sniffing around all of Lou's belongings and had taken up a spot on the floor near her. She glanced at him. He seemed fine and happy. "Single overdose? An accident maybe?"

"Then why dump him in the lake?"

"I mean, it's possible that the fact the body was found in the lake and the puncture wound aren't even related. Ander could have experimented with some drug the day before, gotten high, then decided he was gonna end his life or maybe fell off a friend's boat or something like that." Emily stepped back from the pictures and glanced at Lou. "Did you talk to the wife yet?"

Lou's face grayed. "That's the thing. The brass won't let me interview her because of his notoriety. They are supposedly sending a liaison over to take care of it, but you know what that means."

Emily pressed her lips together. This kind of handholding only meant one thing — more politics were in play. It would be hard to get to the truth if Lou couldn't even interview Ander's wife. It was shoddy police work, that was a fact.

"They are playing nice with the powers that be, probably some rich team owner who doesn't want any bad press on his team."

Emily threw up her hand. "You're gonna have to talk to her if you wanna figure this out."

"I can't, not without disobeying a direct order. They've got me locked down on this one, but something doesn't smell right. I mean, honestly, this guy had too much to live for."

"I think the question we have to answer first is if there's water in his lungs. The medical examiner said she's gonna do it in the morning?"

Lou nodded. "Affirmative. She's probably getting the same kind of pressure I'm getting. I'll bet they'll try to do the funeral this weekend, but they're going to have to get the exam done before they can release the body."

Emily adjusted the brim of her baseball hat. "From where I stand, you could be looking at something or you could be looking at nothing at all."

Lou shook his head slowly from side to side. "There's something here, Emily. I'm telling you. I can feel it in my gut."

"Then someone is gonna have to talk to the widow."

23

Emily grabbed Miner's leash and walked out of the garage, Miner's collar jangling behind her. She made her way to her truck, opening the door, waiting for him to jump inside. As she closed the door, Lou waved. She did nothing but lift her chin as he disappeared into the house.

Driving home, she tapped her fingers on the steering wheel, thinking about what she'd seen. It was no wonder that Lou was being so cagey about the details. Ander Sabate's death was a much bigger deal than she thought. While soccer might not be on her radar, Lou was right, it was a global enterprise, one with billions of dollars behind it.

And those billions of dollars made it likely that something had gone awry from an investigative standpoint. There was branding and reputation to protect, a global enterprise to defend. She shifted in her seat as she drove, headed for the freeway. An old quote rattled through her mind — "Absolute power corrupts absolutely."

In her mind, there was an even more potent corollary. "Money corrupts absolutely." Not that there was anything wrong with money itself. The love of it was problematic for sure. She'd seen too many times — the worst of which was Vasso Stamatea's scheme to rob people of their money — how money could drive people to do things they normally would never do.

She could only hope that in this case, money wouldn't get in the way of the truth.

Biting the inside of her lip, Emily realized the first thing she needed to do was to somehow talk to Ander's widow. Nobody knew people better than the ones that they lived with. She would be the best judge of Ander's mental state and whether he was capable of suicide or had left any notes or information behind. But how? Public figures like Ander were usually heavily protected.

Emily picked up her phone and dialed Mike. He answered after one ring, as if he'd been waiting for the call. "How did it go?"

"Honestly? I don't know. I'm going to help him take a look at this, but I can't figure out if there's something there or not."

"What do you need from me?"

"I need a way to see Ander's widow."

"Lou hasn't interviewed her? Seems like a pretty basic first step to me."

"Nope. The brass has her locked down."

With the concerns about overly aggressive police particularly in urban areas, a lot of departments had attempted to save face by bringing in people like social workers to handle certain types of cases. Emily was of the opinion that social workers held a critical place, but not in law enforcement. But knowing the direction of CPD, she imagined that the liaison that Lou had talked about was probably somebody more along that ilk than somebody who was a sworn officer of the law.

"Let me see what I can figure out. I'm at the house right now."

"Great. I'll see you when I get back."

By the time Emily navigated her way through Chicago traffic, almost forty minutes had passed, a good portion of them spent in slow-moving bumper to bumper traffic. That was the thing about Chicago, there was no actual rush hour. There was always traffic on the freeways. It just varied how slow it actually moved. But no matter the hassles and her personal history, it was home.

Jumping out of her truck, she waited for a second as Miner made his way to the driver's side and then jumped down. He ran to the gate that protected her backyard and sat attentively, waiting for Emily to open it. As soon as she did, he found a spot, relieved himself, then ran to the water dish she kept outside and gulped down half of it. His thirst quenched, he trotted around the backyard, likely sniffing for a chipmunk, a bug or some other critter he could spend time investigating and most likely harassing.

Emily locked the gate behind her and went to the back door. As she opened it, she saw Mike perched at the kitchen table. His computer was open. He glanced up at her. "Where's Miner?"

Emily shook her head. She wasn't sure if Mike liked her better or Miner. *Probably Miner.* "He's outside hunting critters."

"Okay. I brought him a bone. Not that rawhide stuff. I know you don't like that. It's a soft one."

Emily raised her eyebrows. He was like an uncle, always plying the child, in this case a dog, with treats. "You find anything?"

"Oh yeah. A whole bunch of stuff." He nodded slowly.

Emily sat down at the kitchen table, resting her elbows. She was tired. Why, she wasn't exactly sure. The driving maybe? Seeing Lou? It felt like a heavy weight was sitting on her. "What did you find?"

Mike spun his computer around toward Emily. On the

screen was a picture of an attractive woman in her late twenties to early thirties. "Meet Ana Sabate."

Emily frowned. "This is Ander's wife?"

Mike nodded. "Yeah. She's a looker, isn't she?"

Emily rolled her eyes. "You're in a relationship, Mike. Don't say stuff like that."

Mike shrugged. "A guy can still look, can't he?"

Emily closed her eyes for a second. She had never thought of Mike that way. She thought of him more as a little brother than a guy on the hunt.

"Give me the rundown."

Mike gave a nod. "Ana and Ander have been together for years. She's a Portuguese national just like him. Was given a spousal visa when Ander got his job with the Chicago Fire. They grew up together."

"From childhood?"

"Yup."

"Are they related?" It seemed like a crazy question, but there were still places around the world where arranged marriages were a thing. Her own grandparents had an arranged marriage.

Mike shook his head. "Not as far as I can tell. They actually have known each other since they were kids. Families are from the same town. Went to school together. That's where they met." Mike tapped the screen and scrolled through pictures of Ander and Ana, clearly much younger than they were currently. She was standing awkwardly near him, her legs skinny and not filled out.

Emily could see why Mike had made the comment about her being a looker. Ana was beautiful. She had long dark hair, tanned skin, and in the picture that Mike had found of her, she was wearing athletic gear. Emily looked at a few more of the pictures that Mike had pulled up. Ander's wife could have been a model. She had wide-set dark eyes, a small nose, and a square jaw. One of the most recent pictures was of her when she was pregnant, professional photos from out on a beach somewhere, her hair long dark hair blowing in the wind, her hands resting protectively under her baby bump. The final picture in the stack was of Ander, Ana, and their baby together. They were an adorable family by any count. They looked so perfect that they could have been featured in a magazine shoot.

"What else do we know?"

"Ana is one of three daughters. She's the middle child. Parents were both teachers in Portugal."

"So she's got her education?"

Mike nodded. "Yes. "Graduated with a degree in art history from the University of Lisbon. She's been the one who has quarterbacked the Sabate's community service. She also runs their foundation and is on the board of the children's hospital downtown."

That spoke of someone who was smart, had refined taste, and was a lover of travel as well as history. She narrowed her eyes. Something told her that Ana Sabate was not someone she was going to be able to take lightly.

"What else?"

"Well," Mike cleared his throat dramatically, "because of my genius, I was able to piece together her daily schedule. The Sabates have a live-in nanny — two of them actually — though it appears by the amount of time that Ana spends at home, she's very involved in her son's life."

"What's his name?"

"Christopher." Mike spun the computer back toward him and then turned it back towards Emily again, showing her a close-up of Ana, sitting and holding the baby, another woman in their kitchen standing behind where Ana was doing dishes. From the expression on Ana's face, it was clear she didn't know she was being photographed. Emily frowned. The picture felt almost intrusive. "Where did this picture come from?"

Mike cocked his head to the side. "The dark web. You know, photographers get paid tons of money to get shots like this. And now there's the option to hack into security cameras inside the house. That's what this one looks like."

Emily's head snapped towards Mike. "What? What are you talking about?"

Mike nodded slowly. "Yeah, it's the newest thing. Instead of using a telephoto lens and hiding in a tree for a shot, hackers are being hired by some of these news organizations to make their way into security feeds that are in people's homes. They grab the video, slice the images out of it and then they doctor it up using some of the newest AI tools to improve the resolution and the colors. It's pretty cool, honestly."

Emily's eyes got wide. "Are you kidding me? That's not cool. That's a complete invasion of privacy."

"It's still cool," Mike mumbled under his breath.

Emily made a mental note to never allow Mike to install security cameras on the interior of her home. She wanted her privacy. As much of it as she could get.

Though frustrated by the turn in the discussion, Emily refocused, taking a deep breath. "So, what do we know about her daily schedule? Any security?"

"From what I can tell, she does have security. A group called Red Hawk. They are a private company."

Emily nodded. She knew them. It was a mid-range firm. Not someone you'd use for a serious threat, but good enough.

"You're looking for an intercept point, correct?"

"Yes." Emily knew she needed to get access to Ana Sabate to figure out if there was any chance Ander had committed suicide or if Lou was on to something. Walking up to her front door wasn't going to be a possibility.

"Lucky for you, as much as you hate the idea of somebody hacking your accounts, I was able to hack hers. Even better, she keeps her entire schedule online."

That wasn't exactly a surprise to Emily. Professional athletes, no matter what sport they played, had responsibilities outside of just practice and games. There were personal appearances, visits to fundraisers, trips to the local hospital to visit children who were ill. The list went on and on. With as beautiful as Ana was, and the storybook tale they could tell about growing up together, getting married, and having a baby, Emily didn't need anyone to connect the dots. The Sabates were a hot commodity, likely not just in Chicago, but around the world.

"Ana likes to work out. She posts about it on her social media a lot. It's all carefully curated, though." Mike handed Emily his phone. She thumbed through some of the images, most of them featuring Ana with her personal trainer. "Who is this person?"

Mike smirked. "One of Ana's two personal trainers. One puts her through cardio and weights, the other one does yoga and Pilates. She seems to alternate them, working out Monday, Wednesday, and Friday with weights and cardio, Tuesdays and Thursdays are yoga and Pilates."

A fixed schedule was one of the easiest ways for criminals to plan an attack. Emily wasn't a criminal, but she loved the tactic. *Gotcha.*

Emily nodded slowly, staring at the picture of Ana in front of her. "That means tomorrow is a Pilates day unless you think she's not gonna go. After all, her husband just died."

Mike typed something on his computer and nodded, as if having a conversation with himself. "I think she'll be there. The time is confirmed on her calendar. They just did that about an hour ago. Maybe she just needs to get out of the house for a bit?"

Emily sighed. Ana had lost her husband. People did strange things when they were grieving. There were those that stopped their entire life and others that gripped hard onto what they knew, fighting through it. From the little Emily knew of Ana, she seemed like Emily, a fighter. "Then tomorrow is my only opportunity."

"Correct. It's one of the few times that she leaves the house. The other trainer comes to her. Unlike her other excursions, from what I can tell, she goes to Pilates solo. I checked her financials, too. She generally works out, hits up the coffee bar next to the studio for an herbal tea, and then heads home."

"Then that's how I'm going to meet Ana Sabate."

24

The next morning, Emily got up early, showered and dressed in a tank top and long workout leggings, adding a zip-up hooded jacket to cover her gun plus a baseball hat. By the time she got downstairs, Mike was already at his computer, wearing the same clothes he had the day before. He'd spent the night on the couch as he typically did when they were working on a case. There was an extra guest bedroom upstairs, but for some reason Mike preferred the couch in Emily's living room. That was fine with her.

He glanced up when she walked into the kitchen. "I'll take Miner for a walk while you're gone. I'll be on comms if you need me." He pushed a set of white earbuds toward her. "They look like typical earbuds, but you only need to wear one. People will just assume that you're listening to music or a podcast or something."

Emily raised her eyebrows. "I'm assuming you did something to them?" Customizing technology was part of what made Mike so effective at what he did.

"You'd be right about that." He pointed to the earbuds. "You can use those like any other earbuds if you want to listen to something while you're waiting for Ana to show up. They'll function just fine. But, just like our other earbuds, if you tap them, it'll open a channel between the two of us. I kept the configuration the same. Figured it was something that would be familiar to you."

Emily narrowed her eyes. Did he just give her a slam about her ability to deal with technology? "I can deal with changes to technology just fine."

Mike held his hands up. "No, I didn't mean it like that. I just know that sometimes you get yourself into a situation where you need to move quickly. Didn't want you to have to think about how exactly to get a hold of me. Wanted it to be more intuitive, if you know what I mean."

Was he just handling her? "Are you doing a little CYA right now?"

"No," he protested. He shoved the earbuds closer to her. "It was a tactical decision. Nothing more." He looked up at the clock on the wall of her kitchen. "Listen, if you don't get going..."

Emily held her hands up. They would have time to spar later. "I know. I'll be late."

Moving toward the drawer where her gun was, Emily slipped a belly band holster on, secured the Velcro and inserted her gun. For the most part, she preferred a Kevlar holster, but with leggings on, she didn't have much choice since she wasn't wearing a belt.

As she tugged her jacket down over her gun, she heard Mike's voice. "The location for the coffee shop is already programmed into the truck's GPS. As soon as you turn it on, it'll pop up." Mike's computer beeped. "All right. She's on the move heading toward Pilates."

How do you know that? Her expression must have said everything that she was thinking.

Mike grinned. "I tapped into the traffic cams. Her SUV just left the building where the Sabates have their condo."

Emily licked her bottom lip. She knew from the information Mike had gathered the night before that Ander and his wife occupied the penthouse in the Wilshire building, one of the most luxurious condo high rises in Chicago with views that took in the skyline and the lake at the same time. "Alright. I gotta go."

Emily headed outside, tugging on her jacket again. To anyone else, she would look like another one of the women that frequented the high-priced boutiques and workout facilities in downtown Chicago. She jumped in her truck and pulled out of the driveway, sticking one of the earbuds in her ears. She tapped on the side of it. "All right. I'm on the move."

Mike's voice echoed in her head. "Yep. I see you. The GPS in your truck should be online by now."

Emily glanced at the screen. According to the read out, it would take her twenty-eight minutes to get to the coffee shop. She would need a couple of minutes to find parking, although it was possible Mike could help with that. With any luck, plus the cost of a high-priced cup of coffee, she would be in position well ahead of when Ana showed up after her Pilates class, ready to intercept her.

Emily drummed her thumbs on the steering wheel as she drove. She wove the truck through the side streets of her development, past Sammy's Butcher Shop, where she saw Carl's square figure behind the counter. Eight minutes later, she jumped on I-90 and made her way downtown.

By all accounts, it was a beautiful late summer morning. The sky was almost completely clear, save for a few wispy clouds that were out over the lake. The leaves on the trees had taken on the dark green of the end of summer, their final stage before the colors changed in the fall and winter arrived yet again.

But for now, it was pretty out.

Emily positioned her pickup truck behind a box truck in one of the center lanes of I-90 as she made her way downtown, reviewing the plan she and Mike had put together in her mind. Ten minutes later, Emily angled for the off-ramp, watching the traffic surge around her. Though it was a pain, at least it was cover for her, not like she was the only vehicle on the road, which had happened so many times in the past. She heard Mike's voice in her ear. He sounded like he was out of breath. "I see you just got off the freeway."

"Why are you out of breath?" Emily had chided him a million times about the fact that he spent more time flexing his fingers than any of his other muscles.

"It's not my fault. Miner's in a mood. He already barked at a trash truck and launched himself at a dachshund."

Emily shook her head and tried not to laugh. She wasn't sure exactly who she was laughing at, whether it was Mike's inability to control Miner or Miner's ability to fluster him so quickly. Miner was a typical cattle dog, always herding. It didn't matter if it was an enormous truck or if it was a tiny dog. If Miner decided that something was in his territory, he'd figure out how to get rid of it.

"This dog needs leash manners training. Man, he's just dragging me."

Emily shrugged as she drove around a corner, waiting for a cluster of people to cross the crowded downtown sidewalks. "He doesn't drag me. Maybe it's a you and him thing."

Mike didn't answer.

Emily made two more turns and then looked around. The street was littered with vehicles everywhere. That was the problem with downtown — trying to find parking anywhere was a nightmare. "You got any suggestions for parking?"

"I'm assuming you'd prefer a parking spot around the corner where you can slip in and flip out?"

Emily nodded. "Yeah. That would be ideal. I have no idea what I'm getting myself into." If Ana Sabate had security nearby, which she might, it wouldn't take them long to figure out that Emily wasn't just someone else in a coffee shop. Emily's skin prickled. She was suddenly glad she had taken a moment to grab her gun. Not that she would have left the house without it, though. Security for high profile people were typically ex-cops or ex-military, the kind of people that had a happy trigger finger. They'd be quick to react. Emily would have to be subtle. She frowned, then chuckled under her breath.

"What are you laughing about?"

"Was busy thinking about Miner dragging you all over the street."

"Very funny." There was a pause. "All right. If you go a hundred feet up on the left-hand side, you'll see a parking lot. I'll open the gate. I can handle that from my phone."

Emily didn't bother asking Mike how he had access to a private parking lot gate, or how he could take care of it while he was out walking Miner. Correction, while Miner was walking him. All she knew was that when she pulled up, the gate mysteriously opened. She chose a spot near the exit and slipped out of her truck, locking it behind her. Starting to walk, she tugged her shirt down over her leggings, dipping her baseball hat a little lower on her forehead.

Emily looked around, choosing a place on the sidewalk that was nearest the stores. That made it easy to slip inside if she needed to avoid someone's eyes. The sidewalks were occupied by a mix of people who looked like they were headed off to their jobs, and others that looked like they lived in the area, one's that had decided being downtown was better than being in the suburbs. It was a decision she couldn't quite understand. But then again, there were also people that made decisions to live in places like New York City and Rome, like her sister. "Different strokes for different folks," she muttered under her breath.

"What?" Mike asked.

"Nothing. I'm talking to myself."

Emily made her way around the corner and found the coffee shop exactly where Mike had described it. During their discussions the night before he'd even provided her with pictures of the inside of the coffee shop, the blueprints that had been submitted to the city's building department as well as the menu. "To make ordering easier," he'd quipped at the time.

Now staring up at the menu, which consisted of chalkboard writing that took up an entire wall, Emily was glad that they'd had that discussion. She quickly ordered herself an Americano black, extra hot and took a seat at the back of the cafe, pretending to play with her phone. Every few seconds she looked up, using her peripheral vision to fill the gaps.

There was a nearly constant stream of people making their way in and out of the cafe. To her right there was a man with a shaved head and glasses hunched over his computer as if he was busy writing what he hoped would be the next great American novel. To her left was a woman wearing a headset, having a hushed conversation with someone on a video conference call. From what Emily could hear, she was in medical device sales, hawking some sort of a product for the repair of shattered ankles. Closer to the door there was a table of four women, all of which we're wearing expensive workout clothes that Emily guessed ran easily into the multiple three figures, probably just for their shoes alone.

She sighed. Yes, there was a reason she didn't live downtown. Emily dipped her head, pulling her baseball hat a little farther down.

Now, all she could do was wait.

25

Emily didn't have to wait for too long for Ana Sabate to arrive. About eleven minutes into her vigil, three minutes earlier than she expected, Ander Sabate's now widow, Ana, walked into the coffee shop. Emily was only partially surprised that she showed up. If Ana was like anybody else, she'd hold on to what she could that seemed familiar. Maybe it was a comfort to her to be with her trainers, who had known her for a while. In Emily's mind, they were just paid friendships.

But then again, sometimes paid friendships were better than none at all.

Emily sized up Ander's wife as she walked to the counter. The question that she and Mike had not been able to resolve the night before was how to make the approach. They were in a public location, which worked to Emily's benefit. What didn't work to her advantage was that Ana didn't know Emily at all. Typically people in the public eye were suspicious of strangers, more suspicious than your average person. That, plus security, could spell trouble. Emily looked around the room slowly. None of the customers had moved, save for a couple of the women at the table who were wearing the expensive workout gear. One of them had looked over her shoulder at Ana and then back at her friends, picking up their laughter exactly where it had been, as if seeing someone who was married to a star was no big deal.

Emily watched as Ana ordered something from the barista. It was too far away for Emily to hear her, but based on Mike's research it was likely an herbal tea. Ana stood still for a moment, which gave Emily a chance to size Ana up. She was dressed all in black, her hair pulled into a ponytail at the nape of her neck, a matching black baseball cap on her head. It had to be her nod to widowhood.

A few seconds later, a man wearing jeans, a T-shirt and an oversized jacket walked into the cafe. He stood by the door, leaning against it. *There you are. I've been waiting for you.* "I've got a problem."

"What is it?"

"Security. He's waiting for her at the door. If she leaves, there's no way I can get to her."

"I can try to distract him?"

"How?" Emily whispered.

By the sound of the tapping in the background, Emily figured Mike and Miner had made it home. "There's a cop right around the corner writing parking tickets. Ana's SUV is parked in a no-parking zone." Mike paused for a moment and then added, "I can make a call and report it. Maybe get a little distraction going."

Emily's heart skipped a beat. It wasn't much, but it was something. "Do it." Mike would have to be fast, otherwise Ana would be gone by the time the cop arrived.

As Ana waited for her drink, Emily watched, glancing out from under the brim of her baseball cap every few seconds, but not letting her eyes rest on Ana. People had a sixth sense about being watched. The last thing she wanted to do was to alert Ana that she was being watched.

Out of the corner of her eye, she saw a tiny black and white car that looked more like a golf cart than anything else pull up in front of the cafe. The security guy eyed up the officer as she got out of her vehicle and made her way to his SUV, pointing to Ana who nodded. He disappeared outside.

Emily's throat tightened. This was her chance, what could be her only one. She got up from the table, shoving her phone into her pocket and strode to the counter, tossing her cup in the trash as Ana turned to walk toward the exit. Emily grabbed Ana by the elbow and leaned toward her, whispering into her ear. "Ana, I need to talk to you about your husband."

Emily saw the flash of fear in her eyes. It was followed by anger. She pulled away from Emily. "Who are you?"

Emily set her jaw. She needed Ana to cooperate, but she had to be careful not to overplay her hand. "I don't think he committed suicide. Come with me." Emily pointed to the bathroom.

The comment must have startled Ana. She blinked then nodded almost imperceptibly.

Emily walked stiffly behind Ana, following her into the ladies' room, feeling tension build in her body. She'd at least gotten Ana to cooperate a little bit. She'd have to see how far she could take it. Emily looked over her shoulder, getting a glimpse of Ana's security before the door closed. The guy was still outside with the parking monitor, waving his hands in the air, clearly irritated and pleading his case. It wouldn't take long for him to figure out that he didn't have Ana in his sights and likely start a search for her. Emily didn't have any time to waste. She felt the breath catch in her throat. She strode towards the stalls. Luckily, there was no one in there with them. By the time she looked back at Ana, the woman was pale as a sheet. "Who are you?" Her English was nearly perfect, with only the most subtle tinge of an accent.

"Let's just say I'm a friend of somebody on CPD." It was true enough.

"What do you want?"

"Just some information." Emily held her hands up. She didn't want Ana to think that she was being threatened in any way. That wasn't the way to get information. At least not at that minute.

Ana looked confused. "Information? I told the person they sent over from CPD everything I knew."

"They think it's a suicide. My friend isn't so sure." Emily narrowed her eyes. "What do you think?"

Ana turned away for a second, the blood flushing her cheeks. She muttered something under her breath that Emily couldn't make out. It sounded like it was in another language. "Mother of God, he would *not* commit suicide. I keep saying that, but no one is listening to me! We are good Catholics. We just had a baby. Is that what they think?"

"That's what the department is saying."

"He told me he was going out on a boat with some friends. I don't know who. He never came home. I don't know what to think, but there's no way he killed himself." Ana narrowed her eyes. "The police department thinks that or was it the *club*?" She stressed the word club as if it was a bad word. "You know, the Chicago Fire is worth billions of dollars. They get what they want. It's horrible." Ana crossed her arms in front of her chest.

"So why would they try to cover it up? Who would want to do that?" Emily thought she knew the answer but wanted to hear what Ana said.

"Because they want to protect their reputation." She frowned, then leaned toward Emily. "Wait, who did you say you are? Why didn't they send a regular detective to talk to me?"

Emily shook her head. She ignored the first part of the

question. "That's what I'm trying to get to the bottom of. So you don't think Ander committed suicide?"

"There's no way. Why?"

"He wasn't depressed or anything? You guys weren't having issues at home?"

"No. Geez, no. Me and Ander, we've known..." She looked down and away. When she looked up her eyes were filled with tears. "We've known each other for years. He was the love of my life." She covered her mouth with her hand, grief rushing over her.

Emily looked away for a moment.

A second later, there was a knock on the door. "Mrs. Sabate? Are you in there?"

Time's up. Emily didn't say anything. Ana held her hand up as if she was well aware of what needed to happen. "It's okay! I'll be out in a minute."

By the time Ana looked back at Emily, Emily noticed the wave of emotion had left her. "Did your husband owe anyone anything? Did he have enemies? Anything that would help me figure out exactly what happened?" Emily took a half a step closer to her, continuing. "Whoever came after your husband, if that's the case, and I think it is, could potentially come after you. It's better if you tell me anything you can think of right now."

Ana looked at Emily, her face frozen for a moment as if she was considering Emily's question. "I'll be honest with you. Ander was a good man. But like every person, there were people that didn't like him. Enough to kill him? I have no idea. He was just about to get another big endorsement deal. Some of the other players weren't too happy about that. But were they unhappy enough to kill him? I can't imagine that that's the case." Ana looked over her shoulder. "I gotta go. Security is gonna break in here in a second."

Emily nodded. By the calm way that Ana had handled their

interaction, she wondered if this had happened to her before. "I understand. Watch your back."

As Ana started for the door, she looked over her shoulder. "I hope you are who you say you are, not just for my sake, but for our son's. I need all the friends I can get right now. Will I hear from you again?"

Emily shook her head. There was no point in trying to reassure Ana about her motives. Nothing she said was as good as what she could do.

"Probably not, but keep watch. You'll know when I figure things out."

26

Emily waited as Ana disappeared out of the bathroom at the coffee shop. She counted to ten in her head then cracked the door open, just in time to see Ana walking with her bodyguard out to the SUV. Apparently, the issue with the parking person had been resolved. Whether the man had ended up getting a parking ticket or not, Emily had no idea.

She didn't care.

Instead of following Ana out of the main entrance of the coffee shop, Emily slid out the side entrance, choosing the door closest to the bathroom. She walked in the opposite direction from the curb where she was sure Ana was being ushered into her vehicle. Heading down the block, Emily made a loop to the parking lot where she'd left her truck. She stopped a few times, looking in the windows of the storefronts that she was passing, trying to determine if she was being followed. As best she could tell, she wasn't. For a moment, she wondered if she was just being paranoid, but then again, this was Chicago. There were lots of people who had lots of reasons to come for her, some of them she was sure were still lurking at CPD.

She picked up her pace as she got closer to the truck, quickly sliding inside and locking the doors. As she started the truck, she tapped the earbud. "I'm back in the truck."

"I see that. Interesting conversation," Mike replied.

"Maybe," Emily responded. *Was it?* She stared straight ahead, letting her mind drift, thinking about the interaction she'd just had with Ana.

"Anything you want me to follow up on?"

"No. Not yet. We'll talk when I get home."

As Emily drove, she realized she was surprised by the conversation. Ana Sabate didn't seem like the typical widow. She was sad to be sure, but another part of her almost seemed defiant and angry. Most interesting, it seemed like she was surprised by the news that CPD was considering Ander's death a suicide. What had CPD told her? Emily shook her head and sucked in a sharp breath. It sounded like whoever had notified Ana had been vague. *Typical.* Police departments had become vulnerable. The minute a victim was offended, they got their own lawyer and went after everyone. It was crazy in Emily's mind. Life was rough and brutal. Why couldn't people see that? People were barely human at times. If you didn't develop a thick skin, you'd end up getting run over by the stampede.

But that brought her back to Ana. Despite the fact that her husband had just died, Ana stood her ground. She hadn't become overly flustered when Emily had approached her, and she seemed surprised about the idea that Ander would have committed suicide.

Emily drummed her fingers on the steering wheel as she drove, continuing to process the conversation she'd had with Ana. The thing that puzzled her the most was the fact that Ana's attitude wasn't what she expected. She didn't crumble when Emily basically pushed her into the bathroom, a complete stranger asking questions about her husband. Emily knew that grief came in a lot of forms — everything from hysterical sobbing to fits of rage. She'd seen it all during her time as a cold case detective. Even with crimes that had happened years before, the people left behind were still prone to dealing with grief even years later.

No, Ana wasn't typical. Yes, she was clearly grieving, but it came from a position of power, not weakness.

But why?

That was the question that hung with Emily as she pulled into the driveway back at her house, locking her truck and making her way through the gate into her yard. Miner was outside digging a hole in the backyard. Emily just shook her head. He'd been a digger since the minute she'd gotten him as a puppy. The only way for her to keep her yard halfway decent was to keep bags of soil and grass seed constantly available. She looked down at him as she walked to the back door, dirty pawprints collecting on her back step. "Let's go inside, buddy."

Emily opened the door, letting Miner trot inside first. She followed, closing and locking the door behind her. Mike was sitting at his computer station at the kitchen table, a bag of chips open. He glanced up, blowing the long hair out of his face. "How did it go?"

"You need a haircut," Emily said, taking off her gun and putting it back in the drawer.

"Alice said the same thing. Said it's like living with Sasquatch."

Emily arched an eyebrow. She liked Alice. "Alice is a smart woman."

"She is, but you didn't answer my question."

Emily shot him a look. "I was getting to it. There's something definitely off."

Mike leaned back, crossing his arms in front of his chest. He frowned. "What do you mean?"

Emily reached into the cabinet and got out the coffee, starting a pot to brew. She liked the fact that she and Mike could spar like brother and sister and then get right back to work. "I don't know. She's clearly grieving, but she seems mad too."

"Probably about the money," Mike mumbled under his breath.

It was a fair point. Ander had given Ana and her baby an amazing life, one that a lot of people would have killed for. "Maybe. But there's something else. It was in her attitude. It's almost like she doesn't want to be handled."

"But that's the life she signed up for."

Emily pulled a mug out of the cabinet. "Normally I would agree. But there is something more going on here. I feel like the history she had with Ander really bonded them. She's mad. She seemed to get even more agitated when I told her that we suspect that he didn't commit suicide."

Mike cocked his head to the side. "Yeah, tell me again what she said. It was a little muffled in the bathroom. Not good reception."

Emily went on to describe the conversation in detail to Mike, how she managed to guide Ana away from the security guard, how she seemed irritated that the police department was dealing with the case with kid gloves.

"What do we do now?"

Emily poured herself a cup of coffee. "Well, based on her reaction, I say we get to work and try to figure out what really happened. If Ander didn't commit suicide, then somebody needs to pay."

27

Emily stared out the window. She couldn't get Ana's expression out of her mind. "I need to go to the crime scene."

Mike shook his head. "I'm not so sure that's a good idea. The place has been crawling with media and cops. I guess somebody set up a memorial for Ander at the park. Must have been leaked on the Internet." He blinked. "I mean, I already saw it on the news *I* watch."

Emily was surprised and not surprised at the same time. "I'll be fine. I'll take Miner with me. I can disappear into a crowd better than if I'm alone anyway."

"I'm telling you, I don't think it's a good idea. If they get wind of who you are, there's no telling what could happen."

Emily took another sip of her coffee and walked to the drawer where she kept her gun, retrieving it. What would they do? It wasn't like there were warrants out for her arrest or anything. As far as CPD was concerned, she'd been a thorn in their side, but that was well past. What Emily did now was under the radar, and generally not within the Chicago PD's jurisdiction. Something else was going on. Emily put her gun on her waistband. "What is this about, Mike?"

Mike looked away and then back at her. "It's about you, Emily. It's about Lou."

"You don't trust him."

"Do you? Have you forgotten what he did to you?"

Emily set her coffee cup down slowly. "Last I remember, this happened to me and not to you. I can handle myself."

"I know, but —"

"But nothing. I'm going." She clucked to Miner, who hopped off his dog bed. From a hook near the back door she attached a leash to his collar. "Send me the exact coordinates for the crime scene, will you?"

Mike nodded but didn't say anything. He clearly wasn't happy, but that wasn't her problem. That was his.

The drive to the park where Ander's body had been found didn't take long. Luckily, Emily was able to take the back roads. Pulling into the lot at Scenic View Park, she saw exactly what Mike had told her — the lot was about three-quarters filled with cars. There were two Chicago PD cruisers sitting nearby. A makeshift memorial had been set up at the trailhead with a picture of Ander. A pile of flowers and teddy bears had been left at the park just since his body had been found, a group of people milling around the memorial, some of them kneeling reverently in front of the display.

Emily sized up the situation. She looked at the patrol cars. They were from the 15th District, not the same precinct where she used to work. At least that was something.

She got out of the car, grabbing Miner's leash and locking her truck behind her. She shoved the keys in her pocket and set off toward the trailhead, glancing at the memorial as she walked by. She could hear the quiet hum of low conversations as she passed. Emily kept moving, walking toward the beach where Lake Michigan intersected with the shoreline. In her ear, she heard Mike. "The spot where they found the body is just east of your location."

Emily stopped for a moment, taking stock of where she was. Despite the fact that someone had died, the park was breathtaking. There was a gentle breeze coming off of the lake, a few seagulls calling in the distance. Emily could hear the lap of the water as it hit the shore. From where she was standing, she realized she had a panoramic view of the rounded shoreline where Illinois intersected with Michigan. She could see a peppering of small beach homes off in the distance. Her imagination drifted for a minute. She wondered what the people in the homes were doing, what kind of jobs they had, what kind of challenges they faced, if they had regrets about their life.

Don't go there.

Emily focused on the ground where she walked, focusing on the case, not the state of her life. She could hear Mike in the background. "All right. Let's try this new software I found. It's already installed on your phone. It'll get you within a few feet of where you need to go. I just enabled it. Check your phone now."

Emily stopped, looking over her shoulders and then pulled out her phone. People had become so dependent on the miniature computers in their hands that they had lost what was tactically called situational awareness. People were thinking about the recipe they were looking at, the bar their friends had visited the night before or researching the next sale at their favorite store. In the process, they lost any idea of where they were or who was around them. Their lack of attention gave criminals an open permit to hunt. It wasn't as though Emily was completely opposed to technology. She just knew that awareness came first.

Her cell phone flashed for a second and then a bright green circle emerged on the screen with an arrow pointing out in front of her. She heard Mike's voice in her ear. "All right. You should see an arrow."

"Yeah. I do."

"Just start walking in the direction it's pointing you. You'll see a countdown at the bottom of the screen. That will tell you how far you have to go."

Emily frowned and then glanced around her. Based on the information on the screen, it looked like she was about seventy-five feet from where Ander's body had been found. There could be evidence anywhere in this vicinity. She knew from her experience with CPD that water could drive debris in all different directions. "What is this app?"

"I'm so glad you asked!" Mike responded excitedly. "Some tech geniuses decided to break up the entire globe into ten-foot squares. Instead of assigning them those complicated GPS numbers that no one can understand, they decided to assign them all a combination of words. All I did was convert the GPS coordinates that Lou gave us into the system. It's easier to use than the pinning system that was already on your phone. More exact too."

"Clever," Emily muttered.

"Me or the system?"

Emily lifted an eyebrow. Mike was trying to be funny again. "The system."

"Yeah. It is, but they need to work on their back end. I already broke through their firewall three times just to clip some of their code."

The beginning of a smile tugged at Emily's cheek. Mike. He was always on the lookout for tools he could use. He was a collector of sorts, except not antiques. He liked to collect technology, snippets of programs here and there. From time to time, he'd cobble them together to make something new or tweak a system to make it work better. Though a lot of it was black hat work that he could be arrested for, Emily didn't care as long as it helped with her cases.

Emily looked down at her phone, noticing she was approaching the spot where the GPS said that Ander's body had been found. She stood for a second, bent over to pet Miner and used her finger to put a line in the sand, marking the spot so she could put her phone away. She did it quickly, hoping that no one would notice. Standing up again, she stared out at the lake, pretending to take a moment for herself. People did that when they walked their dogs by the lake, didn't they?

Emily sensed movement behind her and turned. A man had made his way down to the beach. He didn't even look in Emily's direction. That was good. He did a couple of cursory stretches and then headed off at a slow jog, moving away from her. He had earbuds in and did nothing more than give her a nod as she passed by. Miner spun to face him, eyeing him up as he did. "Easy, boy."

The man went off for his run, Emily found herself nearly alone on the beach, the crowd of people sad over Ander's death sticking to the parking lot area. Emily walked a few steps forward, heading eastbound. She moved slowly, looking at the ground, hoping to see something, anything that would give her something more of a clue about what had happened to Ander. There was a collection of rocks, some glass that had been weathered by the lake in blues and greens and whites, an occasional shell from a zebra mussel. There was a collection of deadwood scattered nearby, branches and trunks stripped of their bark and leaves thrown up onto the beach during the last storm.

After walking slowly about another hundred feet, Emily turned, feeling a knot in her gut. She hadn't found anything. *What were you expecting?* This was the tricky thing about bodies that were found in water. The very clue she could be looking for might be buried in the sand a few inches below where she was walking or offshore in just a few inches of water. They could also be miles away at the bottom of the lake, tangled on sunken wreckage left from years past. But Emily needed something. She needed something that she could use to leverage the case in a forward direction, either proving that Lou was right or that Lou was wrong. Right now, everything she and Lou had was based on their mutual gut instincts. She licked her lip as she walked, considering that fact. The reality was that her gut had never deceived her, unlike so many people in her life, including Lou. Her gut was reliable, a north star, something she could ground herself in no matter the situation.

And her gut was telling her that Lou was right. Something was going on.

Emily turned Miner around and started walking back in the other direction, pulling out her phone and briefly checking to see how far she was from the spot she'd left, then putting it away. She'd drawn a line in the sand but having the technology as a backup certainly was helpful.

As she approached the spot where Ander's body had washed up, she looked to the west. Along the shore she could see a trickle of people walking, some of them by themselves, some of them with someone else. She couldn't blame them. It was a beautiful day, the noise of the water lapping on the shoreline somehow comforting and stimulating at the same time. Overhead, she heard the cry of another seagull, which made her think about the ocean. It always surprised her that seagulls found their way this far inland. But then again, the Great Lakes were almost like an inland ocean if you combined them all together.

Emily kept walking, heading westbound, looking for anything that might have been missed during the initial investigation. She had no idea how wide or far Lou and his partner had scoured the beach. Based on what Lou had said, they hadn't bothered to call out the DCI techs. The scene was so fluid, with it being right on the edge of the lake, that it wasn't as if there were fibers or fingerprints to pick up that the experts from the Division of Criminal Investigation could gather. The medical examiner would just have to do her best with what information she could get from Ander's body. Emily could only hope that the new coroner would get to work on Ander soon. They needed something, something that would push the case forward.

Mike's voice cut through her thoughts. "You're getting a little far off target, aren't you?"

"What do you know about evidence paths in water?" she asked, her tone not just a little sarcastic.

"I know a thing or two," he chided.

"I'm sure you do." Emily was serious that time.

She had started to answer Mike when she saw something on the ground. She stopped and stared at it. The glint of gold among the rocks caught her attention. It wasn't any bigger than the size of a dime. Emily blinked, then frowned, a knot in her gut forming. Was she seeing things? For a second, she thought that that's maybe what it was — someone had dropped a coin, and it had just caught her eye and only appeared gold in the light. Emily gave a tug on the leash, Miner walking with her, getting closer.

Emily squatted down, using a single finger to brush some of the sand away from what she saw. She thought for a second it was nothing, just an old piece of metal. But as she pushed the sand off of the surface, she noticed that it actually was gold. Her eyes weren't deceiving her.

Using her phone, she took a couple of pictures and then finished cleaning it off. It looked like a man's heavy gold chain. As she uncovered it, her heart skipped a beat. She looked over her shoulder, a knot forming in her throat. Two Chicago PD officers were not more than about a hundred feet behind her. They were talking to each other, their radios squawking, probably sent to manage the crowd up in the parking lot. She couldn't blame them for taking advantage of the beautiful day, but the last thing she wanted them to see was her picking up what potentially could be a piece of evidence in what very well might be a murder. The breath caught in her chest. She had to move quickly. Tugging on the chain, Emily quickly pocketed it and stood up, turning and walking toward the officers instead of away from them. She knew the psychology. People who were guilty walked away. People who walked toward the police were innocent.

Emily was neither.

As she got close, one of them lifted his chin. "Hey, you find something good there?"

Emily could tell it was nothing more than a friendly question. She stuck her hand in her pocket and then opened up her fingers to show the officer. "Just a shell."

The officer nodded. "Nice one. Have a good day." They kept walking, going in the other direction.

So did Emily.

28

Back in her truck, Emily started the engine and looked around her. The cluster of people at the memorial had grown since she'd arrived. It was a good time for her to leave, but not before she took a look at what she'd found. Emily felt her stomach start to settle after her interaction with the officers. She'd been quick enough to grab the shell when she saw them coming. That was a good thing. The last thing she wanted to do was to have to explain why she was out digging for evidence at their relatively fresh crime scene. They would have grabbed her and the necklace and taken her back to the precinct for questioning in a heartbeat.

The good news was they had no idea. Given the number of people they saw at the beach, she figured by now they had already forgotten about her.

Emily glanced back at Miner. After his excursion to the beach, he was lying down happily on the back seat, his lips open, showing off a set of perfectly white teeth and a pink tongue. "We might have found something," she whispered to him.

Digging in her pocket, Emily pulled out the chain that she'd found on the beach, keeping it low in her lap so no one could see what she had. Her heart skipped a beat. It was close enough to the actual crime scene that she had a feeling that if it wasn't Ander's then it would be a huge coincidence. Lots of sports stars wore thick gold chains on a regular basis. They looked tacky to her, but then again, Emily wasn't much for dressing up, only forcing herself to do so if it was an absolute necessity.

Emily held the chain in her hand and stared at it, brushing a few grains of sand off of it onto her floor mats. She'd moved so quickly that she'd basically grabbed the handful of sand it was sitting in. There would be time to clean that up later.

What she hadn't noticed as she jammed it in her pocket was that there were two gold lockets attached to the links, plus a ring floating loose on the chain. Both the ring and the chain were wide and thick. By the size and design, Emily knew it was a man's ring. She pinched it between her fingers and looked at the inside of it, then quickly glanced up to make sure that no one was approaching her vehicle. A tingle ran down her spine. She couldn't sit there for long. The two police officers that were down at the beach were likely going to make their way back up to the parking lot soon. The last thing she wanted was more questions from them. But her curiosity was getting the best of her, her stomach tightening.

As she examined the ring, she saw that on the inside there were initials — AS + AN. Was this Ander's wedding band? It made sense. He probably didn't want to practice or play soccer with his wedding band on. Emily, not knowing anything at all about soccer, had no idea whether that was a regulation of the Major League Soccer organization, some international rule to prevent injuries, or simply Ander's preference. She frowned and let the ring slide down a few links of the chain as she examined the two lockets. Emily opened the first one. Inside, there was a damp but still discernible picture of a man, a woman, and a baby. She immediately recognized Ander and Ana Sabate.

She blinked. This was definitely Ander's chain. She realized it must have slipped off of his neck and the waves pushed it away. How it ended up there, Emily had no idea. At the moment, it wasn't important. What was important was that this was a man who was wearing pictures of his wife and baby around his neck. He hadn't left it behind in the apartment before he'd supposedly committed suicide.

It was another point in favor of Lou's theory.

Emily glanced up, checking the area around her truck. She saw the police officers making their way up the trail, getting closer and closer to where she was. Her mouth went dry. She didn't want to be sitting in her truck when they got to the parking lot. People sitting in their cars not moving were something that officers looked for, wondering if they were hiding something.

Emily quickly cracked open the second locket and looked inside. It was a picture of Ander Sabate and another, younger man. There was no way for her to know who it was, but they definitely looked related — the same dark hair, same thick eyebrows, same square-shaped jaw. Emily blinked, chewed her lip and pocketed the chain, then put the truck into gear, pulling slowly out of her parking spot as the police officers walked over the rise and into the parking lot.

As Emily pulled out of the parking lot she heard Mike's voice. "I see you're back in your truck. Find anything interesting?"

"You bet I did. Get Lou over to the house."

29

By the time Emily arrived back at the house, a four-door navy blue sedan was parked out front. Emily knew for a fact that none of her neighbors owned a vehicle that looked like that. In fact, she had chronicled exactly the makes and models of most, if not all, of the vehicles on her street, plus their license plate numbers.

With her history, it was important to know who was around.

The navy-blue sedan was definitely not one that she'd seen before.

Lou.

As she walked in the door, unclipping Miner's leash, her dog gave a single bark of hello and warning, the hello for Mike, the warning because Lou was standing in Emily's kitchen. Emily closed the door behind her. "You got here fast."

"I was in the neighborhood." Lou shrugged." He was dressed in a pair of dark blue pants, a gray shirt, a blue tie that matched his pants, and a charcoal sports coat over the top. He looked every bit like a CPD detective, almost the same guy she'd met years before except for a little gray at the edges of his hair. As Lou turned toward her, Emily saw the flash of gold on his belt from his badge. This was Lou at his professional best. She knew that under the right side of his coat he had his service weapon, and likely a backup on his left ankle as well. Habits died hard, especially for police officers.

"Mike called. Said you needed me over here. You find something?"

"I think so." Emily knew it was false modesty, but she didn't really care.

She tugged the gold chain out of her pocket and laid it on the table. Lou picked it up, frowning. "Where did you find this?"

"According to Mike's fancy tech, thirty-three and a half feet west of where you found the body. Was buried in the sand."

Emily watched as Lou rolled the chain ever in his hands. "This is definitely a men's chain."

Emily nodded. She pointed at it. "Yeah, and the ring has initials engraved on the inside. You'll never guess which ones?"

Lou raised his eyebrows. "AS and something?"

Emily nodded. "Exactly. But there's more. Check out the lockets."

Lou cracked open the first of the two lockets, holding it up for Mike to see. "Cute baby." He closed it with a click. He frowned as he opened the second one. "Who do we think this is?"

Emily shrugged. "Not sure. If I had to guess, somebody that Ander was pretty fond of."

Mike interrupted, holding out his hand. "Here. Let me have a look."

Lou handed over the chain. Mike laid it out on the table and grabbed his cell phone, taking a picture of the image that was on the inside of the locket. He tapped his phone a couple of times and then stared back at his computer. He'd blown up the picture already. How he'd managed to do that in so few keystrokes, Emily had no idea.

"Give me a second to run facial recognition," he said, sitting back down at his computer. A second later his computer beeped. "Oh. That was fast."

Lou frowned. "Who is it?"

"That is George Sabate." Mike leaned closer to his screen. "Looks like Ander's younger brother."

"I had absolutely no idea he had a younger brother," Lou said.

Emily shot him a look. What was CPD doing? "You didn't start your profile yet?"

Lou shrugged. "I only have the stuff I have in the garage at home. Courtney was supposed to be on that part of the case. I've been busy working a couple other files, trying to get stuff closed."

Emily looked away. Her stomach sank. This was one of the prime examples of why police work had become so hit or miss. The officers were saddled with too many cases at one time. That gave her a distinct advantage. She could focus on one case at a time and work on it until she got a solution. She set her jaw. "All right. What do we know about this younger brother? Is he here in Chicago?"

Mike nodded, never taking his eyes off the screen. "Yes. As a matter of fact he is," Mike said slowly. "Hold on, let me see what else I can find." Mike sat straight up. "Not only is George in Chicago, but as a matter of fact, George lived with Ander and Ana for a while. But now," he drew the words out, staring at his computer screen, "it looks like George has his own place, a condo that Ander bought for him on the edge of downtown. It's in a nice neighborhood, but not as nice as Ander's."

Emily shrugged. "It makes sense. If George came over from Portugal and needed a place to stay for a while, it'd be only natural he would stay with his brother. But then when Ana got pregnant, it would also make sense for Ander to get him out of there. He probably wanted time just with his wife."

"And then with the baby coming along he'd still want his privacy..." Lou finished Emily's thought.

Mike blinked. "Yeah, but if this guy was suicidal, wouldn't he have had his brother living with them to help Ana and the baby out?"

"Maybe the suicidal thing is recent?" Lou offered. "Not saying I buy it though, but if we are arguing that point..."

"Hold on, there's more."

Emily walked toward Mike, putting her hand on the back of his chair. "What you got?"

Mike winced. "There might be another reason that Ander moved George out of his condo."

"What's that?"

Mike spun his computer to where Emily and Lou could see it. From where she was standing, it looked like a mug shot of George. Mike raised his eyebrows. "Looks like George has gotten himself into a bit of trouble since he arrived here in the United States."

Emily sighed. Things were getting more complicated. "What kind of trouble?"

Mike hunched over his computer. Emily could hear the tapping of his fingers on the keyboard. It always amazed her how quickly he was able to get information. "Drugs."

Lou took half a step forward. "Wait. Are you in the CPD database?"

Mike nodded, his expression blank, the same as if Lou had asked him if he was breathing air. "Yeah. That and the criminal records database." He grinned. "I've also got access to a bunch of other databases you probably don't want to know about."

Lou held a hand up and closed his eyes. "No, I do not. All I know is you are a heck of a lot more efficient on those databases than I have ever been."

Emily tried not to laugh. She was glad Mike's talents were on her side, even if he was showing off. That said, they didn't have time to get distracted. She shot a look at Lou. "Is this gonna be a problem?" What she actually meant was, "Are you going to make it a problem?"

"No. If this gets me the information I need, then so be it."

Emily looked at him, cocking her head to the side. *Shouldn't Courtney be doing some of this work?* "Where's your trusty new sidekick?"

"I think she's back at the office doing paperwork. I don't know." Lou rubbed his forehead. "Talking about her gives me a headache."

The entire time they had been talking, Mike hadn't stopped looking for things on his computer. He drummed his fingers on the table. "You know, it occurred to me that I've heard of Scenic View Park in the news before. I mean, it's not the kind of news you guys listen to, but it sounds familiar."

Lou took a half a step forward. "What does that mean?"

Mike didn't bother to look up. "I tend to get the unadulterated version of what's going on in the area from the dark web." He blinked. "Anyway. I feel like I've heard about this park before. I was doing a search a while back on the places with the most crime in Chicago," he looked up, "you know, because of Alice. I wanted to make sure she wasn't going into dangerous neighborhoods."

Lou did a double take. "You *do* realize you live in Chicago, don't you?"

Emily closed her eyes for a second and reached for Lou's arm. "Don't start. We'll never get him back to work."

"Yeah, yeah. I hear the two of you." Mike looked back at his computer. "Anyway, I feel like I've heard about Scenic View Park before." There was a pause. "Where was it? Oh yeah. Actually, I have." He turned his computer around again for Lou and Emily to look at. "This blogger calls it 'Suicide Park' instead of Scenic View. Seems like there have been more suicides there in the last couple years than any other place in Chicago."

Emily frowned. "How many suicides are we talking?"

Mike stared at his computer. "Well, if you count Ander —"

Emily interrupted him. "I'm not sure we are." Emily shot a look at Lou. He nodded, the expression on his face telling her that he thought the pieces were starting to fall together. It was the same look he used to give her when they worked in the Cold Case Division together.

"Almost a dozen in the last two years."

"That's a lot," Lou responded. "Is there a breakdown on method?"

"There were three hangings, six people overdosed, three gunshots."

Emily rubbed the back of her neck. "Any way you look at that, that's a lot of suicides. "Are there more, Mike? If you go back a little further?"

Mike was silent for a minute, then nodded. "Yeah. Even if you adjust the time for ten years, the park has more than earned its reputation. It has more suicides and drownings, now that I look at it, than any other place in the metropolitan Chicago area over the last decade. Like a lot more."

Emily folded her arms across her chest. "How many more are we talking?"

Mike leaned toward his computer, then looked up at her. "At least fifty percent more."

Emily shot a look at Lou. Was that a coincidence? Something in her gut told her they had just stumbled on something.

"What about drownings?" Lou asked. "Is it because they have that big beach there? Maybe people were playing in the surf when they shouldn't?"

Emily turned to look at Lou. "What are you thinking?"

"Maybe some of those suicides got categorized wrong. Maybe they were accidental deaths?"

There was no part of Emily that thought Lou was right, but it was worth a look. "I don't know. Mike?"

"It's hard to tell right off the bat. I mean, for the most part, they just characterize a drowning, a drowning."

Lou shook his head. "That's on the past medical examiner. Honestly, the city is so busy, we could probably use two of them, one for the east side and one for the west. He had a bad habit of using the most general cause of death and then only going back to revise if we found other evidence. He was kind of lazy that way."

To some degree, Emily could understand why the coroner would do that. The medical examiner and the investigators had to work together on the cases. A narrow cause of death by the coroner could hamstring the investigators. On the other hand, being too general could also stall a proper inquiry. "So you're saying that unless there is a suicide note or something, there's no way to tell whether the drowning was an accident or not?" Emily had a hard time believing that was true.

Lou scratched the side of his face. "That's not what I mean. There are some that are definitely uncategorized for good reason."

"What does that mean?"

Lou pulled out one of the kitchen chairs and sat down as if it was going to be a long explanation. "Well, sometimes a suicide is obvious — like if someone writes a note, or their methodology is in your face."

Lou was dancing around the obvious. Emily cut to the chase. "Like if somebody shoots themselves in the face and there's a note next to them."

Lou looked down and then back at Emily. "Yeah. I didn't want to say it that way, but yes." He paused. "Other times it's not quite so obvious. Someone will take a bunch of pills. If they have a history of drug use and depression and they don't leave a note, it's hard for us to always tell which way the wind was blowing that day. Were they just having fun and got ahead of themselves, or did they get so depressed that they decided to end their own life? You know as well as I do, Emily, that not every case is cut and dried as much as we'd like it to be."

Emily walked over to the sink, poured herself a cup of cold coffee that she'd brewed earlier and popped it in the microwave while she thought. In her mind, things were not always that gray. What she'd seen over the years since she'd worked cases on her own was that people fell into one of two camps — good and bad. No one was perfect, but there were times when people needed to pay for what they had done. That was the job she'd taken on, happy to make that judgment when the justice system failed, but she could understand Lou's point. "How does that help us with Ander's death?"

Lou looked up at the ceiling for a second then back at Emily and Mike. "I think just to the degree that we don't have any obvious signs that it was a suicide. No note. No empty pill bottle. No gun. It might be a suicide, but then again..."

Emily pulled her coffee out of the microwave as soon as it beeped. "And yet your partner seems to think so."

Lou nodded slowly. "That's more troubling to me than anything else. I don't know if it's just a rookie thing —"

Mike finished the sentence, his expression tense. "Or something else."

30

Judge James Conklin had an hour left on the bench when he waved his paralegal over, adjusting the sleeve on his robe. He'd been distracted all day, thoughts running through his head about the governorship and the fact that Eric Atkins wasn't supporting his bid for the office.

"Your Honor? Is everything okay?"

James winced. It was a fake. "I'm not feeling well. I'm going to adjourn the court here in a second. I need you to push the rest of the hearings for this afternoon onto another day."

His assistant, a young woman named Heidi, nodded, knowing better than to argue. James was, after all, a sitting judge and her boss. "Of course, Your Honor."

A second later, Judge Conklin rapped his gavel on the bench calling the court to order over the chattering attorneys and the line of people filing in and out of the courtroom. He scanned the people in front of him with the gaze of a high school principal. "The remainder of the cases for this afternoon are going to be rescheduled. Please see my assistant for a new date and time. Court is adjourned."

As Judge Conklin got up and walked away from the bench,

he saw a few startled faces, people's mouths hanging open, a few hands raised in disbelief. It wasn't the normal course of business for a judge to simply walk away from cases that were pending and scheduled. But then again, he didn't feel the need to give any explanation at all. It was his courtroom, his schedule, and for all they knew he'd had a bad pastrami sandwich at lunch and was feeling ill.

Then again, he couldn't remember the last time he'd had pastrami.

James went down the hallway that led to the back entrance of his chambers. As he did, he unzipped the long black robe as it swished around his ankles.

The thoughts that had interrupted his job seemed to amplify as he walked, as if someone had driven by him in a car blasting music he had no choice but to listen to. He wanted the governorship. No, that wasn't exactly correct. He needed it. It was time for the next move in his career, one that carried more power and more prestige. He was tired of dealing with whiny attorneys who refused to do their jobs, and defendants who were obviously guilty who walked out of his courtroom without a care in the world. What had happened to justice? Even as a judge, there were limits to what he was allowed to do.

That would change dramatically as governor. He would finally have his voice heard.

He opened the door to his chambers and closed it firmly behind him, shrugging out of the long black robe that he'd worn for a good part of the day — or as long as he could stand — and hung it on a hanger resting on the hook of a coat rack in the back of corner of his office. He would have preferred to hang his robe in a closet, like the one he had at home, but his office didn't have one.

Yet another issue that would be eliminated when he was governor.

James's mind drifted to the Governor's Mansion in Springfield. Yes, he'd have to uproot his kids from Chicago, but they would adapt. Or, even better, he'd already come to the realization that perhaps he should leave Janice and the kids here — make an excuse about not taking them out of their schools — and spend the majority of the time in Springfield alone, where he could concentrate on his work. He paused for a moment. It wasn't that he didn't love Janice anymore. He did, but it was a partnership type of love, not the passion of a new flame. James didn't have eyes for anyone else. That had never been his style. The only thing he had eyes for was becoming the next governor of the great state of Illinois.

And, like everything else in his life, James knew he would get what he wanted.

From a drawer in his desk he pulled out a set of keys and dropped them near the keyboard for his computer. He retrieved the suit coat he'd worn to the office that morning from the back of his desk chair, tugging it on over his shoulders. He grabbed his cell phone and keys and checked to make sure his wallet was in his pocket. As he did, he scooped up a set of files filled with pretrial motions he had yet to read and slid them into his briefcase. He had planned on getting to them sometime that afternoon but hadn't had the chance. If he had the time later, he'd look them over. It was as good of an excuse as any to lock himself in his home office.

James heard some rustling on the other side of the door, the opposite one from where he had walked in, the one that led to his paralegal's desk. Heidi was probably back at her desk, quickly working to get people reassigned if they'd had their cases canceled that afternoon. James looked at the door for a second, his eyes settling on the dark wood. His normal route out of the building would involve going through that door, but he knew it would be a gauntlet of irritated attorneys not only trying to get his attention but trying to get to Heidi's desk first to get their cases rescheduled. They'd be sizing him up, wondering whether he was sick or bored or something else.

Instead of charging out through the throng of people he was sure would be in his way, he strode to the door he had just come through, pulling it open and closing it behind him just as he heard a knock. He was leaving in the nick of time. Inevitably, it would be Heidi attempting to ask him a question. She had the same habit as Janice, asking him things that she was capable of handling on her own. It was annoying. He scowled as he heard another set of knocks and stepped out into the hallway. *You're a smart girl, Heidi. Figure it out.*

Feeling frustrated, James strode down the hallway and decided to take the stairs instead of the elevator. With all the running he did, his legs moved efficiently. He made it out to the parking lot and to his car in record time. As he got to his car and slid inside, the first thing he did was lock the doors. The second? Shut off his phone. He imagined that there were going to be calls, not only from Heidi, but from his family and God only knew who else. The last thing he wanted to do right now was talk. He needed to think.

Judge Conklin pulled out of the parking lot that was reserved for the judges and administrators of the Cook County Courthouse and turned down West Washington Street, then headed toward the freeway. He knew where he wanted to go. That was part of the reason he shut off his phone. The new phones, with their ability to track their owners, were, in his mind, a positive and a negative, not just for legal purposes but for social ones as well. He was in no mood for Janice to be calling him and making demands. Luckily, unlike so many other people in the younger generation, he didn't need a GPS to get where he was going. James had lived in Chicago his whole life, long before there was GPS.

Where he was going, he didn't want to be found.

James realized that if someone was very clever, they could

log into the onboard navigation of his car to see where he was headed, but no one in his family would do that.

That was what mattered at that moment.

Twenty-seven minutes later, James turned the car onto the exit ramp that led to Naperville. Naperville was one of the more upscale neighborhoods of suburban Chicago, a place where successful Chicago businesspeople chose to live. The kind of people that had families and wanted a large yard and a dog and a housekeeper and a nanny, the kind of people who took pride in the azaleas in the spring and had an annual clambake every fall near their pool. James had little or no interest in mowing the lawn or working outdoors. That was why he and Janice had settled downtown, not far from work.

By any standard, the homes in Naperville were large and expansive. It seemed one neighborhood had homes bigger than the next.

Especially in the neighborhood where Eric Atkins had come from.

After doing some cursory research on the state senator, James had learned little that he didn't already know. That was true of most things. James was always ahead of the curve. He had been in law school, and he still was. It was something he prided himself on. Eric Atkins was born and raised in a small farming town in southern Illinois called Three Oaks, had gone to the University of Chicago for both his undergraduate education and law school, and then had married his college sweetheart. After working as a contract attorney for the better part of ten years, Eric had decided to throw his hat in the ring and become a politician. He'd first been the Mayor of Naperville — nothing more than an honorary position in James's mind — then had moved on to become a congressman. Five years ago, he had stepped over the line from the Congress to the Senate, taking on the responsibility of running the Appropriations Committee. Eric held the purse strings for the entire state in his hands. It was a prestigious position, to be sure, one that could have easily taken him to the governorship.

But from what James could tell, Eric wasn't that way. He had no idea if Eric was ambitious or not, but if he had to guess, he was.

After all, who wouldn't be?

A chill ran down James's spine. That was probably why he was blocking his run for governor. He probably didn't want James in office. Eric would want one of his allies from Springfield, not a hardened judge from Chicago who would set things right. Though he didn't like the truth of the situation, Layla had been correct in her analysis, and he respected her for telling him. Then again, she hadn't told him the full story. Whether she knew and was just trying to cushion the blow, he didn't know. He rubbed a damp palm on his pant leg. It was even worse than he thought. He didn't need any evidence. He knew he was right. Not only was Eric backing someone else, but he would also do everything in his power to block James's run for governor.

That couldn't happen. The position *belonged* to James. He could feel it in his gut.

James had seen on a news report that morning that Eric Atkins was traveling from Springfield, Illinois, where the state capital was, back up to Naperville for a fundraiser that evening. Not only was Eric backing someone else for governor, but he was also running for reelection, his eyes on the Senate President position. James knew that the people of Naperville would turn out in force for their hometown hero, the one that was bringing such pride to the sleepy little city. If they hadn't had a large opinion of themselves before, James reasoned, when Eric became the Senate President, it would do nothing more than increase their delusions of grandiosity.

On the news report that morning, it had been mentioned that Senator Atkins would be attending two separate fundraising events that day — the first one was the opening of a new playground at three o'clock that afternoon. Many of the children from the local school district were being bussed over to join the Senator for a photo op, followed by a walking tour of the renovations in the center of his adopted hometown.

Afterward, Eric would be joined by his wife, Nancy, for a private fundraising dinner at a new restaurant that was making a splash in Naperville called Red Bistro. As James parked his car, he tried not to roll his eyes. Red Bistro? Could they have come up with a name that was more creative?

From the reports, the fundraiser, priced at five grand a head, would give some of Naperville's finest a bit of face time with their soon-to-be leader of the Senate. James parked his car in the back lot of a specialty tea shop, stepping out into the afternoon sunshine. He sniffed the air, realizing he could practically hear the blow dryers at the local hair salons revving up, getting the ladies of Naperville ready for their debut that evening.

James walked to the trunk of his car, popping it open by pressing a button on the key fob. Inside, there was a dark green duffel bag, one that Janice had gotten him a few years before for Christmas. Which Christmas it was, he couldn't quite remember. They were all beginning to run together — the same strange egg and bread bake laced with bacon, the same running gear, tennis shoes, and new briefcase every single year as his gifts.

When did his home life get to be so boring?

Pushing the thought away, Judge Conklin unzipped the duffel bag and rummaged through it. He kept his golfing gear with him just in case anyone called him to go play nine holes on the fly.

They rarely did.

From inside, James pulled out a baseball cap, putting it on over his head and pulling out a pair of sunglasses. Although the day was relatively warm, he dug out a charcoal-colored windbreaker, tugging off his suit coat and pulling it on over his shirt, stripping the tie away from his neck and tossing it into the bag. He wanted to be invisible for the next few hours.

As James strode away from the car, he walked down the street towards the center of town. The playground was on a side street, near one of Naperville's three elementary schools. As Judge Conklin made his way closer to the site of the afternoon rally, he noticed a throng of people had already gathered at the playground. Security, wearing their dark sunglasses and their white coiled earwigs had formed a loose perimeter around a hastily constructed podium complete with patriotic red, white, and blue banners. Many of the people in attendance had already been given red, white, and blue balloons emblazoned with "Atkins for Senate" on them. As he approached the crowd, two children ran in front of him, laughing and screaming and pointing. The woman Judge Conklin expected to be their mom looked up, apologies written all over her face, and chased after them.

At least she was sorry.

A moment later, the music from the makeshift stage started, blaring through a set of large speakers positioned on either side, the group of people growing like flies attracted to honey. James couldn't identify the song. It was something relatively new and catchy. It was instrumental, or at least the first song was. After that, whoever was in charge of the music moved on to more traditional favorites like "Don't Stop Believing," "The Best is Yet to Come," and "I Won't Back Down."

James wrinkled his nose. *How cliché.*

He kept his head down as he moved around the edge of the crowd, watching them. Some of them were clapping along, some were smiling and talking to their friends. Others were focused completely on the stage, their eyes wide, their mouths open. James pressed his lips together. He wanted that kind of attention, the kind where people paused their lives to hear what he had to say. He stopped and stood behind two women with their children, waiting, not wanting to move around too much. People that moved to try to get a better angle were often the ones that security teams watched the most. He wanted to be just like every other rally goer who stood and waited to hear Eric Atkins politely.

James took a couple of steps forward and then stopped, looking at the security detail. The same question kept running through his mind over and over again — What did Liv Gardner have that he didn't? Why had Eric chosen to back her and not him? Did James not seem to be a legitimate enough candidate? Was there something about James that Eric didn't like? James thought back to Eric's weak response to the idea of getting together. He felt a ripple of disgust run through his stomach. No one from Eric's office had taken the time to call. No one. That was about as big of a rejection as anyone could get, almost worse than the way his father had treated him.

It was frustrating, to say the least. James couldn't have anyone who was blocking his road to the governorship. No one. Least of all Eric Atkins.

As the thought passed through him, a glossy black SUV pulled up at the curb near the podium followed by a matching trail car. Four suited men with sunglasses and earwigs poured out of the vehicles almost before they came to a full stop. The men fanned out before someone gave a nearly imperceptible signal that had Eric emerging from the SUV a moment later.

James had forgotten how tall Eric Atkins was. He had a shock of thick brown hair, combed neatly over to the side and wore a blue suit with a bright red tie. He looked more like a newscaster or a pilot than a politician. As Eric waved to the crowd, a cheer went up, people hugging each other and cheering and clapping for him like their savior had arrived home.

Eric Atkins strode to the podium, taking the steps two at a time as if demonstrating to the audience how young and spry he was. He immediately headed to the microphone, shaking the hand of the Mayor of Naperville, an older man who James didn't know. Eric stood behind the podium, his hands wrapped around the edges. "Hello, Naperville!" Cheers erupted across the crowd. "In case we haven't met before, I am Eric Atkins, your state senator."

There was another round of cheering.

"And in just a few short weeks, I'm hoping to become your next President of the Senate, bringing the concerns of Naperville to Bloomington!"

The crowd roared even more.

James clapped politely, trying to look the part. The last thing he needed was some overzealous security person coming over, ripping off his hat and sunglasses and accosting him right where Eric could see him. No, it was better to play the long game, just to watch and wait and see...

And make Eric pay for not picking him.

31

"What are you talking about?"

Emily had picked up the phone, taking a call from Lou. He'd left a few hours earlier after she'd found the chain with the ring and the two lockets on it. While it didn't prove that Ander wasn't suicidal, it also didn't prove he was. And in Emily's mind, if he had been, a heavy gold chain like that — which had to be worth at least twenty grand — would have been left at the condo for his wife and son. But no, she'd found it on the beach. That meant he was wearing it. That was the only explanation for its location.

"He was high as a kite," Lou said matter-of-factly.

Emily looked away, glancing at Mike. He'd looked up from his computer with a confused expression on his face. She held a single finger up. He'd have to wait for a minute. "Is that conclusive?"

"Yes. Had a bunch of fentanyl in his system."

"That must have been from the puncture wound between his toes that you spotted." Emily started pacing back and forth. Something wasn't adding up. "I still don't think he was an addict."

"Neither do I. But I have no idea how to move forward."

That was another issue. There was a question that was more pressing in Emily's mind. "What about water in his lungs?"

"Oh yeah, I meant to tell you. Nothing. Not a drop."

A chill ran down Emily's spine. "Are you sure?"

"Yup. I asked Elena twice. He died from the fentanyl, not the water."

"How is she going to rule it?"

"Right now? Accidental death." Lou didn't say anything for a moment. "I think she's getting pressure too. She said that's the best she can do with the evidence she's got, but I don't believe her."

That was a problem. They had a bigger one, though.

"So how did he end up on the beach?" Emily asked, her voice low.

A silence grew between the two of them. There came a point in every investigation when the detectives knew that the answer to a single question would be the difference in figuring out what had happened to a victim and leaving a case unsolved.

Emily and Lou had hit that point at the same moment.

"That's the question of the day, isn't it? No idea, but he didn't drown." Lou cleared his throat. "I don't know if it's enough though. If I don't get something concrete soon, I'm going to get called into the captain's office and they're gonna make me shut it down."

Emily felt the heat rise to her cheeks. Bureaucracy was once again getting in the way of justice. With the fentanyl, the necklace, and the lack of water in Ander's lungs, it didn't feel like a suicide. It couldn't be. Something — or more accurately, someone — else was responsible for Ander's death. Couldn't the CPD brass see that or were they so worried about slipping out of the good graces of the Chicago Fire soccer team that they wouldn't tell the truth?

Emily gripped her hands into fists. "You can't let them do that. Hold them off, Lou. Let me look at a few more things."

"I'll do my best." The call ended. Emily tossed her phone down on the kitchen table, wondering if she could trust his "best." It landed with a clatter. She was frustrated. It seemed like every direction they moved in this case they hit a roadblock.

"Ander was high?"

Emily relayed to Mike what Lou had said, including the part about how he was under pressure to close the case and that there was no water in Ander's lungs. Emily glanced toward the door. "I need to go take a walk and clear my head. There's something we're missing and I'm not sure what it is."

Emily quickly clipped a leash to Miner's collar. There was no point in even trying to go outside without him. He would offer high, chirpy barks and protest until he was included.

Closing the back gate behind her, Emily took off walking down her driveway and then headed in the direction of the meat market. Not one bit of her was hungry or interested in talking to Carl, but she needed a destination, one that was familiar. She could feel her brain churning away at the information they had found so far. She ran through it in her mind — Ander's dead body, Ana's report that he had no suicidal tendencies, the fact that he was a high-profile athlete, the puncture wound between his toes, the lack of water in his lungs. The most perplexing part of the entire thing was that Ander had been found on the beach. If he hadn't drowned, how had he gotten in the water? Emily's gut tightened. She wheeled around and strode back to the house, pushing the door open. Mike was still sitting there in his customary position hunched over the computer. He looked up at her. "You got back fast. What is it?"

"I can't figure out how he got in the water. He didn't jump in. He was already dead."

Mike shrugged. "Well, there's a pier out there. He probably got high and then got in the water. Or maybe he waded out on the beach and then his body washed back up."

It was too pat of an answer for Emily. It sounded like something that someone at CPD would say in order to get the case closed. She chewed her lip. "No. That's too easy. I need facts, not a guess. Aren't there tide charts or something that would help us figure this out?"

"Tide charts," Mike muttered under his breath. "Yeah, I know what you're talking about. I thought those were just for the ocean."

"No. They work for the lakes too." As the words came out of Emily's mouth, she wasn't exactly sure that that was accurate, but she needed to know for sure how his body had ended up in the water. While Mike worked on the problem on his end, Emily walked into her office, booted up her own computer and started looking at pictures on recent news stories of Ander Sabate. He looked happy, seemed to be loved by his teammates and coach, and did a lot of charity work. On the face of it, the guy didn't seem suicidal, but then again people could hide their pain well.

Even if that was the case, it still didn't explain how his body got in the water and washed up on the beach. A quick search revealed that there were sixty-three miles of shore in Illinois, twenty-two of which were near Chicago. On top of that, there were a million places that Ander could have been found — his condo, his car, the training facility for the Chicago Fire, or a bathroom at a restaurant or a club.

Why the water?

Emily was looking at some maps of Lake Michigan when she heard Mike call to her. "I think I've got something!"

Emily shut the lid on her laptop and walked back into the

kitchen, her feet padding along on the wooden floors. "What is it?"

"You were right."

"About?"

"Where Ander was found."

"Show me."

Mike cleared his throat. It gave her the impression he was about to launch into one of his lectures. "The National Oceanic and Atmospheric Administration, called NOAA, tracks daily water current charts for every major body of water. That includes all of the Great Lakes. I'm not an expert in this, but they have a net of buoys throughout the lakes that track water temperature, direction, wave height, and a bunch of other things." He stopped for a moment. "If it works like it's supposed to, that's pretty cool."

"And that would tell us what direction the tide was moving?"

Mike nodded. "Correct. Yeah, it's simple geometry. They also have this nifty little tool," he grinned as he clicked on the screen and pointed, "that will tell you if you drop something in the water where it will end up. I think it's mostly meant for hypothetical analysis, but it'll do the trick for us." Mike zoomed in on a map. "The problem is we have to run it in reverse. You know, because we know where Ander ended up, not where he started and that's what we are trying to figure out."

"Can we do that?"

Mike looked offended for a minute, as if she was questioning his ability. "It's not designed to run in reverse, but I fixed it for us."

Emily frowned. She knew that based on what Lou had said, Ander had been in the water somewhere between twenty-four and forty-eight hours. "And did you account for variations in timing depending on when his body entered the water? The currents could have been moving in different directions."

Mike nodded. "While you were in the other room, I ran this eight times. Only takes a few seconds. The program uses some pretty sophisticated three-dimensional modeling to help. I estimated his body weight, but then I grabbed the actual total from the coroner's report."

Another hack. Not surprising.

Mike continued. "There's only one way his body could have ended up over here where they found it."

Emily's stomach clenched. "And that is?"

"If he started out here."

Emily cocked her head to the side. The spot where the map had landed was out in the lake. She squinted at the screen. "How far offshore is that?"

"Two miles."

"Well, he certainly didn't swim out there, did he? Ana said he told her he was going out on a boat, but she didn't know with who."

Mike pointed to the map. "Based on what this is telling me, there's no way he got out there any other way than a boat."

"Agreed." Ander was a soccer player, not a distance swimmer. Emily rubbed her forehead. "I need you to check something for me."

"Sure."

"Can you see if there were any boats registered to Ander or if there were any boats the Coast Guard reported as being adrift in the lake in the last couple of days?"

Mike's eyes widened. "I see where you are going. Good thought. Give me a minute."

Emily paced while Mike searched. A second later Mike looked up. "No boats registered to Ander or his wife and no boats adrift in the last fourteen days."

Someone owned a boat that got Ander out onto the lake. The question was who.

Emily looked up from the computer, her eyebrows knitted

together. Miner was acting strange. He had trotted to the front window, his toenails tapping on the wood floors. He'd climbed up onto the couch and was looking outside, using his nose to push the curtains aside, his breath leaving a fog on the glass. Every few seconds he'd growl and then bark. Frowning, Emily walked into the room. She knew better than to ignore her dog's instincts. She walked into the living room. "What is it, boy?"

Miner jumped off the couch, paced back and forth, and then jumped back on the couch again pushing his nose through the curtain. He uttered a low growl and then a bark. Emily pushed the curtain aside looking for herself. She didn't see anything. Even Lou's cruiser was gone. The hair on the back of her neck stood up.

Emily knew better than to ignore Miner's warning.

32

Courtney Green made her way back to her car. She'd parked it around the corner after following Lou Gonzalez to a house in the suburbs of Chicago. He was supposed to be on duty. He was supposed to be helping her with the reports on the suicide of Ander Sabate.

He wasn't.

She had sat in her car for a few minutes, parked down the road, but then she realized that if Lou came out, he'd likely spot it. Not that her car was that notable. It was just another white Ford sedan that crisscrossed the streets of Chicago on a daily basis. But Lou was no fool. And she didn't want to take any chances.

Concerned that she'd be spotted, Courtney drove around the corner and slid her car into a spot in the back of a strip mall that was just up the road from where Lou had parked. She pulled on a denim jacket, leaving her blazer in the car. Digging around in the back seat, she found a green bucket hat she'd gotten at a White Sox baseball game a few years before. How it was still in her car she had no idea, but it was as good of a distraction as any. She pulled it on over her blonde hair and started walking back in the direction where Lou had parked his car.

Making her way down the street, she saw that the houses were not new, but they were neat, most of them brick bungalows, each of them well taken care of, their shrubs manicured, and their lawns recently cut. Most of them look to be closed up, their owners at work or out running errands. Courtney took a few pictures of Lou's car parked in front of the house. She thought she could hear barking from a dog inside, but she wasn't sure. If she did and someone was home other than Lou, they'd be alerted to her presence. She froze. She didn't want to get caught by Lou or by anyone else. Courtney turned on her heel and walked away.

As she got back to her car, she dialed the number she'd been told to use.

"Do you have an update?" The words were spoken with no emotion.

"Maybe." Courtney wasn't sure, but she'd been told to report everything. It wasn't up to her to decide what was significant and what wasn't. "It might be nothing."

"Go on."

"Detective Gonzalez is parked at a house near the Bayview strip center. Not sure what he's doing inside."

"He's not at work?"

"No."

"Do you know who owns the house?"

"Not at this minute." She had a guess but didn't want to offer up information that wasn't confirmed.

"Find out."

The call ended. A shiver ran down Courtney's spine. Lou was on the wrong side of what was going on. He needed to get out of the way, or the brass at CPD would do it for him. As much as she wanted to be a top tier detective, there was also part of her that felt sorry for people that got caught up by the system. Lou was about to be one of them. There were powerful forces at play, ones that she didn't want to mess with, ones that had promised reward for obedience. Part of her wanted to warn him, but then again, that wasn't her job. *She* was the rookie after all. He should have been looking out for her, but he wasn't.

The only thing she could do was look after herself.

33

By the time Emily and Mike finished with the 3D modeling of the scene, proving that Ander Sabate didn't just wander into the water, nor did he fall off the pier, and she had called Lou, the sun was starting to set. Emily still hadn't been able to explain why Miner had gotten worked up, but the situation had put her on high alert, enough that she kept looking out the window as she stood at the stove. There was nothing there. At least not yet.

Mike's phone beeped.

"What's that?" Emily asked, shooting a look over her shoulder as she stirred a pot of pasta on the stove. She quickly cooked up some ground beef and made a simple Bolognese sauce, a recipe she'd learned from her mother. There was already a salad sitting on the table. When Mike wasn't around, she didn't cook much. But Mike had an appetite like a hungry bear coming out of hibernation. If she expected him to be able to concentrate, she'd need to feed him.

"Hey, this is interesting," Mike said.

Emily knew that when Mike said something was interesting it could be anything from a random fact about a piece of technology to something that was pertinent to their case. "What is it?"

"Do you remember how we figured out that there have been more suicides at Scenic View Park than any other place in Chicago in the last few years?"

Emily nodded. "Yep."

He arched an eyebrow. "There are a couple of them that remind me of the Sabate case."

That got Emily's attention. "Really? What do you mean?"

"This gal, Elizabeth Gordon, she was a campaign manager for some local politician. She OD'd a few years back. She was found at the park. Her family told the same story. It's in the case notes. Said she was happy with her life, happy with her job. Had recently been working with a high-profile attorney and was excited about her future. Had just bought a house as well. Her life was on track and then all of a sudden, she was dead."

Emily frowned and walked over to where Mike was working. She quickly read the information he'd found. Elizabeth Gordon was beautiful from the photographs Mike had found — tall and blonde with a quirky half smile. "How long ago did this happen?"

"Three years ago."

"And there's another one you should have a look at."

Mike flipped the computer around closer for Emily to see it. He tapped on the mouse pad. "This guy. His name is Tony Rossi. He was a businessman. Specialized in imports and exports of Italian wines. Had just expanded his business and gotten a big contract to service some of the most exclusive restaurants downtown. Hung himself at Scenic on one of the trees. Had a baby at the time. From the date it looks like the kid's probably around ten or eleven at this point."

Emily glanced over her shoulder, watching to make sure her pasta didn't boil over. "That *is* strange."

Mike was right. The cases were very reminiscent of the

Ander Sabate case. The part that was troubling was that Ander, and now Elizabeth and Tony, had everything going for them, and yet they had committed suicide.

Unless they hadn't.

Emily's skin prickled. "What are you saying, Mike?"

"I don't know. But I smell a rat." His expression tightened.

Emily set her jaw. "So do I." Dinner was going to have to wait. Emily had some visits to make.

Ten minutes later, leaving Mike with instructions on how to finish dinner and a reminder to put it in the fridge when he was done, Emily was on the road. She left Mike and Miner back at the house. She'd lost her appetite. From the truck, she'd tried to call Lou to tell him she was going to do some more digging, but when he hadn't answered she just kept moving.

On her way out the door, Mike had furnished her with the address of Elizabeth Gordon's parents who lived about twenty minutes from where Emily did. After weaving her way through a few darkened neighborhoods and shopping districts, Emily ended up in the North Center neighborhood. The houses there were all small and boxlike but neatly cared for like hers was. Emily sat outside of the house for a second, taking it in. Elizabeth's parents lived in a home that was covered in white siding. But even in the darkness, although the homes appeared to be well taken care of, Emily could see the signs of wear. The paint was a little dingy, peeling in a few places. There were two pots by the front doors that weren't filled with flowers from what she could see. An older Toyota Camry was parked in the driveway, one that was probably at least fifteen years old, the paint dull and dusky.

Emily got out of her truck and adjusted her jacket to cover her gun. She crossed the street, striding up to the front door. She knew when she knocked on the door that she might bring back bad memories to Elizabeth's parents, but if she had any hope of figuring out what happened to Ander, she needed answers. Her gut told her they might be some of the only people that could help.

A second later, the door opened. "Can I help you?"

The woman standing in front of Emily was a little shorter than Emily herself, probably about five foot three. She had deep lines gouged in her pale face, dark circles that looked as though she was tired. Emily sized her up. "Are you related to Elizabeth Gordon?"

The woman pressed her lips together. "Yes, I'm Carol, her mother."

"I'm Detective Tizzano. I wanted to see if I could talk to you about your daughter?"

Emily knew it was a stretch to call herself a detective, but she did it out of convenience. It was far faster to just say that she was still a detective than try to explain that she was a former detective and now a private investigator without a license. In fact, it was worse than being complicated.

The woman looked surprised, then her face drooped, as if she was already disappointed. "Elizabeth? Is there news about her case?"

"I just have a few questions." Emily knew it was a deflection, but it was as close to the truth as she could get.

"All right. Come on in."

Carol hadn't asked for ID, a badge or even a business card. It always surprised Emily how few people asked her for any type of identification. Despite the high level of crime in Chicago, people were still too trusting. Carol shut the door behind them. She folded her arms across her chest as if she was preparing for battle. "You're investigating Elizabeth's death again?"

"Yes." That part was true at least. "I just have a few questions about the circumstances and her mental state if that's okay."

It always surprised Emily how quickly she was able to

morph back into the cold case detective that she had been almost a decade before. Old habits died hard. "We were going through some old files. I found your statements in the paperwork that Elizabeth had seemed happy with her life."

Carol nodded. "She was. Elizabeth was very excited about her life and what it looked like." Carol looked down. When she raised her eyes, they were filled with tears. "She had so much to live for. I still have a hard time believing she's gone."

Emily narrowed her eyes. "You don't believe she committed suicide?"

"Everyone said she did, but I can't understand why. She seemed happy. A mother would know." The words came out measured.

After that, it was difficult to get any more information out of Carol. She said she had to go. Whether or not that was actually true, Emily didn't know. There was something about the way that Carol rushed Emily out the door that didn't seem right. Was she just unhappy about talking to Emily? Having her evening interrupted? The dredging up of bad memories?

There is something definitely off, Emily realized as she walked back to her truck. Emily tapped the comm in her ear as she pulled away from the curb. "Mike?"

"Yeah. I heard the whole thing."

"Seem weird to you?"

"A little. Especially how she shut you down."

It wasn't as if Emily needed verification that the experience had been strange. It had been. There was no doubt about that. But then again, when people lost their loved ones, things could definitely seem strange. Hopefully, she wasn't reading into things.

Emily looked in their rearview mirror in time to see a car coming around the corner following her. "I'm gonna head over to Tony Rossi's house. See if I get the same reaction."

"Sounds good. Updating your GPS now."

A moment later, Emily's truck navigation updated all on its own. What magic Mike had done to be able to remotely interface with her truck, she wasn't sure. But then again, he'd probably installed all sorts of technology around her house and on her vehicle that she didn't know about.

She shrugged. Maybe ignorance *was* bliss.

Tony Rossi's family lived on the other side of town in Naperville. Emily made her way through the evening crosstown traffic and got off, winding her way through strip centers filled with upscale boutiques, restaurants with more BMW's parked in the lot than a dealership. There were a slew of spas and beauty salons, all of them closed at the late hour. Emily drove into a neighborhood with large homes. She'd been in one that looked similar a few years before when she had been working on a case that involved gambling. That house had belonged to Frank Battaglia, a notorious crime boss. These homes were smaller versions of the palatial ones she'd seen before. That said, they were still probably at least three times the size of her little bungalow.

The house where Tony Rossi's widow and son lived was no exception. There was a shiny white Suburban parked outside, one of the newer models that Emily knew cost close to eighty grand, the windows of the house lit up with a gentle yellow glow.

Emily got out of her truck, leaving it on the street and walked up the driveway. Unlike the house where Elizabeth Gordon's parents lived, this one was completely manicured, every detail taken care of. By the looks of it, Tony Rossi's wife used a landscaper, an expensive one.

As Emily got to the front door and pressed the doorbell, she saw a light kick on from a small box next to the door frame. A video camera. They were everywhere these days. The doorbell itself rang with a deep bonging noise, sounding more like she was requesting entrance to a castle than a house out in Naperville.

From inside, she heard the scrambling of nails against tile. It sounded like there was a small dog living in the house. A second later she realized her assumption was correct as a cascade of barking began. There were a few clicks in the door as the locks were opened and then a woman with a mane of dark, wavy hair opened it. She didn't say anything.

Emily started first. "Are you Isabella Rossi?"

"I *was*. Who are you?"

Unlike Carol Gordon, Isabella Rossi was noticeably suspicious. Her posture was stiff, one hand still on the door, her chin lowered. Emily didn't blame her. It was dark, late for someone to just drop by unannounced. "I'm Detective Tizzano. We're looking into the death of your husband Tony?"

As Emily waited for her reaction, she saw a young boy with dark hair run down the stairs inside the house, glance her way, and then run right past heading for what Emily imagined would be a snack in the kitchen. He was wearing a blue and white striped shirt and had dark hair like the pictures of his father. Isabella looked at her, her expression stony. "You're investigating my husband's death again?"

"Yes. We just had some questions after doing a routine case audit."

"A routine case audit? Who are you with exactly?"

"Like I said, I'm a detective."

"With what department? Let me see your ID."

Emily narrowed her eyes. It wasn't an unreasonable request, but it wasn't one she could comply with either. She stepped forward into the house. "I'm not with the department," she said blocking Isabella's ability to slam the door closed. "I'm a private investigator."

Isabella pushed on the door, but Emily's boot was wedged at the bottom. Isabella's dog, a Pomeranian mix, kept charging at Emily's boot and biting it, but the small teeth weren't going through the leather. Isabella swatted at the dog and tried to close the door, but it wouldn't budge with Emily blocking it.

"What do you want?" Isabella asked, her voice thin, panic on her face.

"Like I said, I'm not here to cause trouble. I just have a few questions."

Isabella narrowed her eyes, her voice a hiss. "I don't know who you are, but my son is home. I'll talk to you for a second, but then you have to leave."

The woman pointed outside. Emily nodded and stepped back. The woman swung the door closed and locked it before Emily could put her boot back in the door again. She heard a voice from inside. "I don't know who you are or what you want but get off my property. I'm gonna call the police."

Emily moved close to the door. "I don't think you wanna do that, Isabella," Emily hissed.

"Why is that?"

"Because I don't think that your husband committed suicide."

There was silence from the other side of the door. Emily waited for a beat, then another.

All of a sudden, she heard the lock click in the door frame, Isabella pulled it open, her face pale. "I don't know who you are, but I've been waiting for ten years to hear someone say that." Isabella called over her shoulder, "Enzo, I'll be outside on the front porch. I'll be back in in a minute."

"Okay, Mom!"

Isabella closed the door behind her and pointed to a set of chairs on their front porch. From how new they looked, Emily guessed that no one ever sat on them. Although Emily didn't much feel like sitting, if it would make Isabella more comfortable to act like a hostess, then that was fine. She settled herself into one of the chairs, adjusting the cushion around her back. Isabella looked at her, pushing her long, dark hair back over her shoulder. "You said you don't think Tony committed suicide?"

Emily raised her eyebrows. Isabella was getting right to the point. "I'm not sure. What do you think?"

Isabella looked away for a second, then back at Emily. "Start again. Who are you exactly?"

"I'm Detective Tizzano. And no, I'm not with CPD. I used to be. Now I work as a consultant." Emily was ready to trade a little truth with Isabella to get answers.

The explanation seemed to satisfy Isabella. Her shoulders dropped. "That's why you don't have a badge."

"Correct."

"And why are you looking into this case again?"

It was a fair question. "It's come to my attention that there have been a series of issues at Scenic View Park, including recent events." Emily knew she was being vague, but she needed to get Isabella to talk about Tony.

"You mean Ander Sabate."

Emily cocked her head to the side, surprised. How the information had gotten out she wasn't sure. "You heard about it already?"

Isabella nodded. "Haven't seen anything about it in the news, but my son, Enzo, he's a big soccer fan. Somehow, one of his friends found out."

Emily made a mental note. Whether the soccer team or the city liked it or not, information was going to get out about Ander's death. A trickle had already gotten out. Pretty soon the news would be overflowing, rife with speculation.

Isabella's voice interrupted Emily's thoughts. "And you think that somehow the two are tied together?"

Emily needed to be careful. "I don't know that. What I *do*

know is that your husband seemed to have an awful lot to live for. Am I wrong?" *C'mon, Isabella. Time to talk about your husband.*

Isabella shot up out of her seat. "No, you aren't! That's what I don't understand. Tony was an amazing husband. He was excited about being a father. He had just expanded his business when all of this happened." The words came out rapid fire as if Isabella had been waiting to say them for years.

Emily shifted in her seat. "Would anyone have stood to benefit from his death? Like say a competitor who might want to take him out?" It was worth asking. If Tony's death wasn't a suicide, there had to be another answer. Emily needed to establish some sort of motive or connection between the cases.

"No. The business didn't change. When he died, I needed to figure out a way to support me and our baby. I took it over. Rossi Spirits is now the third largest distributor of premium wines and liquors in the city."

Emily raised her eyebrows. That was not a small accomplishment given the amount of competition in Chicago. "What do you think happened then?"

Isabella continued to pace. Emily noticed that every so often she would look in the front window, checking on Enzo. She threw her hands in the air, clearly frustrated. "Do you have any idea how many nights I have laid awake asking the same questions? I don't know. It's a mystery to me. Everything seemed to be going fine. We had just had Enzo. Tony had just made the deal to expand the company. We were on a high. We hardly slept, we hardly spent any time together, but everything was amazing. And then he was gone." Isabella snapped her fingers. "Just like that."

Emily frowned. It was so similar to the story that Ana Sabate had told that it was striking. "Can you think of anything that Tony was doing in the weeks leading up to his death that was unusual? New people that were in his life? New activities? Anything out of the ordinary? Trips?" Emily rattled off a long list.

"Well, yeah, there were a lot of new people hanging around with the business expansion — everyone from new attorneys to architects and builders while we were trying to get the warehousing put together. Not to mention the bankers. Always the bankers. I had joined a new mom's group to get some support. Having a newborn wasn't fun either."

Emily didn't know anything about that. She'd never had kids and given where her life was now, she didn't want them. She and Luca didn't have a chance to even try for a family before she'd been arrested, and he'd ended up leaving her. It was probably for the best. Warm and fuzzy wasn't exactly Emily's forte. "Any of those people get involved with Tony?"

Isabella shook her head. "No. The only other thing that was different was that court case. He was on the jury."

Emily frowned. In their research they hadn't found anything about a court case. "Can you tell me more about that?"

Isabella shrugged. "I don't remember a lot of the details. All I know is that it had something to do with a murder. It seemed like Tony was downtown for weeks. He was trying to run the business, trying to be a new dad, and then of course, this jury duty pops up. He tried everything to get out of it, but the judge was a real stickler."

Emily had been in court enough to know that there's no convenient time to go to court. It was likely nothing. Jury duty was run of the mill, but given that Isabella remembered it, it was worth asking a few more questions. "Was there anything significant about the trial? Or was it just that he was gone, and it put a lot of stress on him?" Emily started second-guessing herself. Maybe just the amount of pressure between the new baby, the new business, and a trial sucking up his time had pushed Tony over the edge?

Isabella tapped a set of manicured fingers on the edge of her chair, looked away, and then back at Emily. "There was one thing that was significant. It ended in a hung jury."

34

"A hung jury?"

Isabella nodded. "Yeah. They deliberated for two weeks. No matter which way they looked at it, nobody could agree on a verdict."

Emily leaned forward. "Who was the defendant?"

"It was a guy who was a gang member, but I don't remember his name. Big African American guy from what Tony talked about. Said the guy was frightening just to look at, had to be about six foot five and three hundred pounds. All muscle. Tony somehow ended up being the jury foreman. The prosecutor was coming at him for trafficking drugs and three murders somehow connected to that. They rolled it all into one trial. But the guy's attorneys were top of the line. Tony said he'd never seen anything like it."

Isabella shifted in her seat. "The prosecution would present a fact and within three minutes the defense had it taken apart either the way it had been collected, who had relayed the information, or what it meant. Tony said by the end of the trial the entire jury was upside down. He said it was like being Alice in Wonderland. There were certain people that thought that the defendant had committed the murders, other people that thought he hadn't, other people believed that he was out of town. The worst part was they couldn't agree on whether the guy was guilty or not guilty. The jury froze."

Emily cocked her head to the side. "There was no verdict at all?"

"That's exactly what happened." Isabella sighed. "If I remember right, the judge didn't have a choice. Tony said he could tell how furious the judge was, but he had to declare a hung jury. The guy walked away, scot-free."

"Why do you think the judge was mad?"

"No idea. Tony said something about the guy having a reputation for being tough on crime. We went back to our life and then two days later Tony was gone." Isabella looked over her shoulder into the house. "Listen, I'm sorry. It's late. I gotta get back inside to Enzo. Feel free to stop over again if you have more questions. Let me know what happens, okay? It would help both of us to move on."

Emily nodded and watched Isabella disappear back into the house. Standing up, she made her way down the front walk of the house where Isabella Rossi now lived alone with her son and her dog after putting her life back together again. Emily couldn't help but wonder if the attorneys that had turned the case upside down had somehow also turned Tony Rossi's life upside down too.

35

"Something's not right," Emily said to Mike as she got back into the truck.

"As far as I'm concerned, there are a lot of things that are not right. Exactly which one are you referring to? Would that be the fact that insane people have access to nuclear weapons, there are literally thousands of terrorists living within our borders, our water is being spiked with nanobots or something a little closer to home?"

Emily tried not to roll her eyes. "Let's go with the third option." Emily spent the next couple of minutes describing her interaction with Isabella Rossi. "She seemed so convinced that there was no reason for Tony to kill himself."

"Sounds like we have a theme."

It was the same conclusion Emily had come to. "I was thinking the same thing. We have at least two families that are convinced that their loved ones didn't commit suicide in the same park. I don't really like the odds on that. Do you?"

Mike snorted. "A conspiracy? Heck, you are living in my backyard. I love a good conspiracy. What are you thinking?"

"I'm thinking that there's something else going on here.

Sure, some of the people that have died at Scenic View Park probably *did* commit suicide. But Tony and Ander in particular? My gut tells me there's something else going on that's been covered up." Emily felt like she was on the verge of coming up with a plausible hypothesis that would link the cases together. She drove for a second, drumming her fingers on the steering wheel without saying anything. "Isabella Rossi said that Tony had been involved in a court case. He was the jury foreman or something. Can you get me some information about that?"

"Sure. I'll have it ready by the time you get back."

During the rest of the drive home Emily let the details of what they'd found out so far roll around in her head, trying to make sense of them. There was something tying these cases together. She could feel it. But what it was exactly, she wasn't sure yet.

When Emily arrived home, she walked in the back door of the house, closing and locking it behind her. It was getting late, but she knew she needed answers before she tried to get any rest. "Did you find out anything?" she asked Mike.

"A little something." His hand darted into an open bag of potato chips that was next to him. He glanced up at her, looking suspicious. "Sorry. I got hungry again. I DoorDashed myself a box of snacks. He glanced down at the floor. Emily's eyes followed. He wasn't kidding. There was a literal cardboard box overflowing with snacks — three different kinds of chips, three bags of cookies as far as she could tell, two jars of what looked like queso, and a bag of taffy. Emily shook her head. "You have a hollow leg. How does Alice keep you fed?"

"She doesn't. She gave up months ago."

Mike sighed then used the back of his hand to wipe the salt from his face. "I did a little digging on that case you mentioned. It was exactly as Tony's wife described it. Guy named Reginald Jackson, street name Striker, was being tried for multiple drug and murder charges. The jury got hung up on a technicality, something having to do with the way the evidence was handled and then also the way that Striker's paperwork was submitted during his booking. I'm sorry to say, but it looks like the detectives on the case bungled the front end of the investigation. It led to a hung jury. Prosecutor wouldn't retry it because there was no way to get around the paperwork issue. Striker's attorneys would have done the same thing again."

Emily shrugged. "It's no skin off my nose." Maybe she should be more sensitive about the reputation of the Chicago Police Department. After all, she had been one of them. But she wasn't. They'd betrayed her. If they got caught doing something wrong, it just was more evidence to prove her case. She knew that as much as there were good officers out there, there were also people that were not only inept, but completely corrupt. It happened in every industry — doctors, lawyers, businesspeople.

"So what happened?" Emily slumped down into one of the kitchen chairs, kicking off her boots, noting the scratched leather from where Isabella's dog had tried to take a chunk out of them.

Mike cleared his throat. "Well, it looks like the trial went on as usual, but then the jury ended up arguing among themselves once Striker's attorneys made a big deal about the paperwork issues. There were people that simply didn't agree on a verdict. From what I could find it was kind of a mess. The judge kept sending them back to deliberate more, but it was no use. Striker walked out of the courtroom a couple of weeks later completely free and clear. Prosecutors couldn't retry the case since everything was so messed up."

Emily frowned. "The judge in the case — Isabella said that he kind of went nuts after everything happened. Wanted a verdict."

"I didn't find anything about that. The reports just have to do with the fact that it was a hung jury. Why?"

Emily stood up and started pacing. She stared at the floor as she did, furrowing her eyebrows. "I don't know." She stopped in her tracks. "Wait. Wasn't Ander's brother in legal trouble too?"

Mike nodded slowly. "Yes, he was." Mike's hands ran across the keyboard of his computer. "It was here in Cook County, same as the Striker case. And it was the same judge. Some guy named James Conklin."

Emily raised her eyebrows. "Well, isn't that an odd coincidence?"

36

"I need to go back to the scene," Emily said to Mike, putting her gun back on her belt.

"For what? It's the middle of the night."

"I don't know exactly." Emily wasn't lying. She really didn't know why. She had a gut feeling that there was something at the scene she'd missed, a detail that would tie everything together. So many people had died at Scenic View Park. She could feel the weight of them on her shoulders, just like she felt the weight of the victims with unsolved cases when she used to work for CPD.

Unfortunately, Emily took things like murder personally.

The look on Ander's wife's face and now Isabella Rossi's face rose in her mind. All she could think about was two little boys that were going to grow up without their fathers. What had happened to them? Lou was right. There was more to Ander's case than a suicide.

Without another word, Emily double-checked her gun, grabbed a flashlight from her equipment drawer as well as her cell phone, wallet and keys, and headed outside.

The summer evening was cool but humid. The wind had

picked up. She could hear the leaves rustling in the trees as she climbed into her truck. Starting it up, she headed back toward Scenic View Park. Luckily, the roads had emptied significantly from earlier that day.

By the time Emily made it to Scenic View Park it was after midnight. The darkness was complete, save for the glow of the moon overhead. It was partially blocked by a few latent clouds that drifted across the sky.

As Emily opened the truck door, she could hear the chirp of some night birds in the trees near the parking lot. She sat, listening, for a moment. Just beyond them, she could hear the waves from Lake Michigan hitting the shore. The wind had kicked up. So, apparently, had the lake. Emily bit her lip as she looked around. There were a few other cars in the parking lot. It was dark enough that it was hard to tell whether there was anyone inside — a desolate parking lot was an ideal place for meetups, affairs, and one-night hookups.

She didn't care about all that. What people did was their own business.

Emily slid out of the truck grabbing the flashlight and stuffing her cell phone in her back pocket. She slammed the door to the truck closed, hearing the alarm system chirp as she walked away. The case was nagging at her. In the back of her mind, she wondered how much she should actually tell Lou. He was part of the problem, wasn't he? And even if she gave him all the information, based on the lack of action she'd seen from Chicago PD recently, she wondered if they would actually get the case solved and prosecuted the way that it should be.

Maybe she needed to handle business herself.

But then it hit her. She didn't even have enough to contact Lou, at least not yet. At the moment she had two suspicious deaths that only had two things in common — the location where they happened and the fact that the people were in legal trouble. There was something else. She was missing it. Maybe she could find it at the crime scene.

Emily walked down to the beach, accessing the program Mike had sent her to find the location where Ander's body had been found once again. A second makeshift memorial had been set up on the beach in a spot away from where the water was coming up, a cluster of more teddy bears and signs, a picture of Ander in his uniform, dimly lit by a few flickering candles. Someone had heard the news and found the exact location. Who it was, she wasn't sure. She blinked. The Chicago Fire better be ready. The news of Ander's death was coming out whether they liked it or not.

Emily looked toward the lake. It hadn't been her imagination. The waves had definitely kicked up. In the distance, Emily could see the white caps cresting with the help of the moon. On the horizon, an ore ship moved silently. Emily used her flashlight to scan the beach again. She only felt comfortable leaving it on for a second, then clicked it off, the muscles in her back tensing. The beam of light told everybody around her she was looking for something. Not that there were lots of people at the beach at midnight, but then again there was no reason to draw attention to herself.

As Emily started to walk eastbound on the beach, the hair on the back of her neck stood up. She turned around expecting to see somebody following her, but no one was there. A wash of confusion ran over her. What was going on? Why was she feeling that way?

Emily shook off the thought and kept walking, staring at the beach, hoping that the moonlight would show her something that she had missed before. The case needed to be tied together. There had to be a reason why Scenic View Park had been renamed Suicide Park. She just wasn't sure what it was.

After a few minutes of futile searching, the only thing that Emily had spotted was the half-rotted corpse of a catfish that was bobbing its way to shore along with two new pieces of deadwood that the lake had thrown up from the depths. She turned and walked back in the direction she started. What had she hoped to find? Whatever it was, Lake Michigan had either hidden it underwater or buried it under the sand.

Frustrated, Emily started to walk up the path back toward the beach when she spotted someone coming toward her, a woman with long blonde hair that glimmered in the thin moonlight. As she passed, the woman deliberately averted her gaze. Emily thought it was strange. An obvious move to not be seen even though they were the only two on the beach. Emily walked three or four more steps, the breath catching in her throat. She whirled around, her stomach clenching into a knot.

"Elizabeth?"

The woman froze but didn't turn around. Emily saw the tilt of her head upward. She spun slowly. "You must be Detective Tizzano."

Emily walked toward her and then led her back down to the beach, her heart skipping a beat. "You're Elizabeth Gordon, aren't you?" Emily whispered as they walked. "You are supposed to be dead."

"That's true on both counts." Elizabeth frowned. "How did you recognize me?"

Emily's mind was racing. She'd seen a lot of things in her career, but a person back from the dead? That was a new one. "I saw your pictures. We were doing some research on the park. I'm helping one of the detectives with Ander Sabate's death."

"I know. My mom called me."

Emily thought back to the frumpy woman, Carol, she'd met earlier that night, who had cried and fussed about her daughter's death. But there was one problem with that.

Elizabeth wasn't dead.

Man, Carol was a good actress.

As they approached the water line, Emily convinced they

were out of earshot of anyone who might be lurking in the darkness, she turned to face Elizabeth. "How did you find me?"

"I didn't come here looking for you. I came to see where Ander Sabate died. I was actually hoping to slip in and out of here without being seen."

"But Elizabeth —"

Elizabeth interrupted. "I go by Veronica now."

Emily was becoming frustrated. She folded her arms in front of her chest. "Exactly what is going on here? Why are you here? How are you still alive?"

Veronica sighed. "My mom called me after you left. Said someone was sniffing around about the case again. We talked for a while and then I put two and two together about Ander Sabate."

"Ander Sabate? What does he have to do with you? And why are you here? How is it you're alive?" Emily felt like she was repeating the same question over and over again. Elizabeth, or Veronica, still hadn't answered it. The questions were coming hard and fast into Emily's mind. She felt her shoulders tense. Finding Elizabeth Gordon alive and wandering around at Scenic View Park wasn't exactly what she had expected. She'd thought — no, hoped — that going out to the beach would provide clarity. It was, but just not exactly the way she expected.

Elizabeth looked out toward the water. "Ander Sabate is just the tip of the iceberg."

"What?"

Elizabeth started to walk down the beach. Emily followed. "You asked how I'm still alive?"

"Yeah, that seems like a good place to start."

"Well, I OD'd. That part is true. Not by choice, though. I was really out of it. Really, really sick. I woke up here at the park, in that stand of trees over there." She pointed, her face looking drawn in the moonlight as she relived what she'd been through. "I could barely walk. A few years back, the park had become a place where everyone from a homeless junkie to a millionaire from Green Street would come to get high. The police were doing regular sweeps of the area to try to clean it up, but they were dealing with a lot of gang violence, so this place was still a good place to hide. When I realized what happened, I grabbed my ID out of my pocket and stuffed it in this woman's pocket. She was already dead. She looked like me — blonde hair and everything. I had to get away. I called my mom as soon as I could to tell her what happened. I didn't want her to worry. I figured the police would come around to do the notification. I told her she had to act like she'd never acted before."

That only explained part of the story, the part where Carol was so easily choked up at the mention of her daughter's name, Emily realized. Carol had been practicing for years.

Emily stopped walking and faced Elizabeth for a second. "Hold on. I feel like you've jumped ahead in the story. What are you saying here? You overdosed but you didn't mean to?"

Elizabeth shook her head. "No. What I'm saying is someone tried to kill me."

The words hit Emily like a punch to the gut. She held her breath for a moment. "All right. Tell me more."

They started walking again. "I'd been working as a campaign manager. My client wasn't happy. I was just starting out. It was supposed to be an easy gig, just doing local stuff. Didn't have a ton of experience but was really into the idea of helping good people get positions where they could help others. My client got more and more angry. He took me out to dinner one night after we had a big donor that bailed. I thought it was to console me. I had been working really hard. We had dinner and then he brought me here. Said something about how a walk at the park might give me new life."

"So you're saying that your client tried to kill you?"

"Yes."

"And you've hidden it all these years?"

Elizabeth nodded. "Yeah. I couldn't risk that he'd find out I'm alive. He'd probably try to do it again. So I disappeared. They had a funeral. I have no idea who that woman was that got buried in my casket. I hired some guy I found to get me a new driver's license, a social security card, and a birth certificate, and I became Veronica Anderson."

Emily frowned. "This person you're convinced tried to kill you."

Elizabeth set her jaw. "He did try to kill me. Almost succeeded. Just a little bit more cocaine and I would have been long gone."

"Who is he?"

Elizabeth blinked. "You haven't figured this out yet?"

Emily shook her head. "No, I've only been working on this for two days."

Elizabeth smiled. "Well, you're making faster progress than anyone who has ever gotten near this case. The person you're looking for is the same person that was my client. James Conklin."

Emily frowned. "The judge?"

Even in the moonlight, Emily could see Elizabeth's face pale. "Yeah. That's the same one. He was my client at the time. Was trying to get on the bench, the seat he holds now. He didn't feel like I was moving fast enough. Kept complaining that he'd paid me too much money and that I needed to *accelerate* his career. I'll never forget that. Who uses 'accelerate' that way?"

Emily kicked at a shell on the beach, thinking. *A homicidal judge? Are you serious? What was the motive?* "He was that upset that he tried to kill you? Why not just fire you?"

Emily knew that with every homicide case something usually set the perpetrator off. There were lots of reasons — jealousy, anger or even just cold hard cash. "I'm not exactly sure. I was at his house a bunch of times. Never seen anything like it. Everything is perfect. His wife — they were newlyweds at the time, so no kids — she was like a robot. Practically said 'yes, sir' to him. You ever seen that movie called *The Stepford Wives*?"

Emily hadn't.

"It's about this neighborhood where everybody looks like either Barbie or Ken. It's really scary. Janice was the closest thing to a Stepford wife I've ever seen."

"And you came out here tonight because?"

Elizabeth cocked her head to the side. "I come out here every time there's a suicide. I always wonder if the person really did kill themselves or if it was the judge." Elizabeth lifted a finger. "Did you know Ander Sabate was tied to Judge Conklin too?"

Emily didn't want to play her hand. She still didn't know much about Elizabeth. "How?"

"He was the judge in Ander's brother's case. George."

"How do you know all of this?"

Elizabeth shrugged, then sighed. She looked down and then back at Emily. "I feel like since the guy tried to kill me once already, I should probably keep an eye on him. So, that's what I do. I don't wanna leave the area because of my mom. She refuses to move. Her health isn't that good. I live about an hour and a half away. It's far enough out of the city where I don't have to worry about bumping into the judge, but close enough I can get to my mom if I need to."

Emily was starting to put the pieces together. "It sounds like you've been solving this case for years on your own. Did you take any of this to the police?"

Elizabeth shook her head. "No, I couldn't. For all intents and purposes, I was dead. And even if I did, who would believe me? All the paperwork points to the fact that I'm no longer Elizabeth Gordon. I'm Veronica Anderson. I'd have to admit to a whole bunch of crimes in order to get Judge Conklin prosecuted. Don't get me wrong, I feel bad," she said as they continued to walk. "He's killed other people. Seems like anybody that gets in his way, he kills. I'm sure of it. I just can't be the one to stop him. Not without risking my own freedom."

Part of Emily was frustrated. Elizabeth had known about the threat that Judge Conklin was for years. She'd done nothing about it. Then again, she understood the need to prioritize her own safety. If Conklin was half as dangerous as Elizabeth said, then Emily was sure Elizabeth was right. Killing someone once was probably not enough.

Emily held her hand up, a knot in her gut. "Help me out here. Judge Conklin went after you. He went after Ander Sabate. Why? What's the connection?"

Elizabeth looked down at the sand for a moment, then tucked a stray lock of hair behind her ear. "I don't have the full story. What I have pieced together so far is that Ander's brother George had a drug problem. He got dragged into Judge Conklin's court. Got pretty mouthy while he was there. Told everyone his brother was a hotshot and that he'd never get convicted. I guess somehow Ander, who was trying to protect his brother, offered to make a sizable donation to Judge Conklin's election fund, but when his brother was convicted anyway, Ander pulled back on his promise. No money for the fund. It's something that Conklin definitely needs."

"Election fund? For his role as a judge?" Emily frowned.

"Nope. He wants something bigger. Conklin's making a run for the Governor's Mansion."

Emily shook her head. She could not believe what she was hearing. "So Conklin kills Ander because he doesn't make the donation?"

"That's what I think. Conklin seems to go after the people that get in his way. It's his own brand of handing down justice, his own deadly verdicts, but there's no jury and no hope for the people he sets his eyes on." Her voice was thin, wary.

Emily's stomach clenched. Was any of this true? Was Elizabeth making all of this up? "How do you know this? You're supposed to be dead."

"I have friends, Detective Tizzano, friends who work on the edges of Judge Conklin's life. I pay a few of them to get me information. A couple do it for free because they know how much I lost when the judge decided to go after me." She looked away for a moment. "There aren't many. It's not safe for me to have a real life until he's out of the picture, but I have a few people help me watch my back."

"You're saying they watch Judge Conklin?"

Elizabeth nodded. Emily started to ask who they were and then stopped. It was none of her business. Worse yet, if Elizabeth revealed who they were it might put them in danger. Without speaking, the two women turned around and started walking back the way that they came. The conversation paused for a second. Emily tried to process what she was hearing. It was a lot, but the bottom line was that Lou's gut instinct had been right. "You said Conklin has attacked other people? Any ideas who they are?" Emily was trying to sort out which of the many suicides that Mike had tracked at Scenic View Park were the judge's handiwork.

Elizabeth nodded. "I don't know all of them and I only have suspicions. I don't even know if I was the first or not, but I think that another one of Judge Conklin's 'suicides' was from a case a few years ago. The jury foreman — a guy named Tony Rossi. I don't know anything for sure, but I heard the judge went nuts when Tony couldn't get the jury to a verdict. Went on a rant in his chambers they could hear all over the building."

"Yeah, I talked to his widow a few hours ago."

Elizabeth nodded. "How did you figure it out?"

Emily pressed her lips together. "I've got a guy that helps

me. We realized that there are significantly more deaths in this park than anywhere else in Cook County. Seemed a little odd, so we started doing some digging. Isabella Rossi, Tony's widow, doesn't believe that he committed suicide."

Elizabeth scowled. "I don't have any evidence, but I can promise you he didn't. The fact that a notorious criminal went loose because of someone else's ineptitude would be enough to trigger Conklin."

"But why go after Rossi? He was just the foreman. I heard the issue was with the booking paperwork. Why not go after the officers who were responsible?" As the words came out of Emily's mouth, she realized that the judge may have done just that. It was something worth checking into. Maybe there were more ghosts hiding at Scenic View Park than Emily could ever imagine.

Sighing, Elizabeth said, "I snuck into the courtroom for the verdict. It was my way of facing the judge. I figured he'd be so concerned about the mass of media in the room he'd never see me. I put together a good disguise — I bought a short, dark wig, used a bunch of tanner on my face so I looked like I had just been out in the sun and even got a set of tinted glasses and wore a hat. The courtroom had been packed with people. I grabbed a seat in the back. Figured there was no way Conklin was going to be looking for me. I was already dead, right?"

It was a ballsy move, one Emily could respect. "Right. What happened?"

"Conklin disappeared for a little bit with the attorneys, Striker, and the jury foreman."

"Tony Rossi."

"Yep. The same one." Elizabeth stopped to zip her jacket up a little higher at the neck. The wind had picked up. "When they came back into the courtroom the look on Conklin's face was one of absolute fury. I've never seen anyone with that expression before. He didn't even look like that when he tried to kill me. He was cool as all get out that night."

"Why was he so upset? It's a hung jury. Happens all the time."

Elizabeth cocked her head to the side. "Not in Judge Conklin's world. Judge Conklin gets the verdict that he wants. He wanted a guilty verdict. He wanted to put Striker behind bars so he could add it to his resume of being the crime-fighting judge."

"So this is all about political aspiration?"

Elizabeth nodded. "That and people that disappoint him. That was my crime. People that get in the way of Judge Conklin's political aspirations tend to end up like me."

"Dead? That's a little extreme, given what you are telling me."

"In a worst-case scenario, yes. He's gone through more campaign managers, fundraisers, and PR people than I can count. If you can't give him what he wants, he freaks out. It's subtle though. I had no idea he was coming for me until he did."

"What happened, exactly?"

"I met him for a working dinner at a restaurant downtown. I'd been on the hunt to get him some bigger sponsors. Even back then, he wasn't just thinking about being a judge. He's always wanted more. We got through dinner. He paid. I told him that the sponsors I had been looking at weren't interested. I told him he was basically too small of a fish for them to take a look. I wish you could have seen the look on his face. It was something I'll never forget." Elizabeth folded her arms in front of her chest. "Anyway, he walked me to my car. I told him we'd try again, that I wouldn't give up. The last thing I remember before I woke up at Scenic View Park was a stabbing pain in my neck, like I'd been stuck with something. The next thing I remember, I was waking up at the park. When I pulled all of the things out of my pockets, there was a suicide note he'd written for me." Elizabeth shook her head. "Looking at it now, I can almost laugh about it. Didn't even sound like me."

"So he planned it. Was ready for you to fail him."

"Pretty much." Elizabeth glanced toward the walkway up to the parking lot. "Seems like that's what happens. Someone blocks Conklin's path to success, and he just can't move on. He's gotta eliminate them permanently."

The words hung between the two women for a moment. Emily felt a chill run down her back. This judge was nothing other than a sick SOB who got violent when he didn't get his way. He was like a two-year-old who got mad and had a temper tantrum. The problem was that his tantrums included a death sentence.

Elizabeth sighed. "Luckily, there's only a few of us that ended up on the wrong side of the dirt, if you know what I mean."

Emily knew exactly what she meant, but it was an understatement. Only a few? From the sounds of it, Judge James Conklin was a serial killer.

The women made their way up toward the parking lot. They stopped near the entrance to the walkway where Emily had parked her truck. "Listen, I have a contact over at the FBI that might be able to help you. Or at least get you and your mom into witness protection. They could give you a new life and get you out of the city, so you don't have to hide anymore."

Emily was thinking of Cash Strickland. She'd done a couple of cases with him. At first, their relationship when she was in Louisiana looking for a serial killer had been contentious. But more recently, they had been more friendly, maybe even close to some sort of a relationship, though that seemed to have cooled. Emily hadn't heard from him in a while. In her mind, it was no surprise. Cash was all about the regulations. Emily was not. Cash was on the right side of the law. Emily was too, just not in the same way. She thought back. Cash had texted her six weeks before, telling her that he was going on a month-long training. She hadn't heard from him since.

Elizabeth shook her head. "No. I'm better off if I keep doing what I'm doing. My mom's health isn't good enough that we could relocate someplace else. We've talked about moving, but she doesn't want to leave the city. And I can't leave her." Elizabeth met Emily's eyes. "I'm glad you found me. It's good to finally tell my story to someone."

Emily nodded. This was the reason she did what she did — to help people like Elizabeth. "Stay out of sight for a while. Let me see what I can do." Emily knew what she wanted to do, but the fewer people that knew, the better.

Elizabeth nodded, then started to walk away. She called over her shoulder. "Detective?"

"Yeah?"

"Be careful. Judge James Conklin is dangerous. Very dangerous. He'll stop at nothing to get what he wants."

Emily set her jaw, feeling her stomach harden into a knot. "Thanks for the warning."

What Elizabeth didn't know about Emily Tizzano is that neither would she.

37

After attending Eric Atkins's fundraiser, James slipped out of the park and walked back to his BMW. He'd parked around the corner so as not to be seen by Eric or his security detail, which was seemingly getting heavier by the moment, evidence of his rising stardom. James looked over his shoulder. The bile rose in the back of his throat. Why wasn't that him with the crowds of happy people, the balloons, the band? What was Layla doing? Why was his own campaign manager not putting together events like this one? James's thoughts turned to Eric. It was Eric's fault, not Layla's. He needed someone to support his campaign for governor. Eric was the perfect person to introduce James to everyone outside of Chicago, but he wasn't doing that. He was doing exactly the opposite, in fact, blocking James's efforts. James glared at the ground in front of him. *How dare you not support me, Eric?* Who did Eric think he was? Was he the kind of man that just did exactly what he wanted, never taking into account the consequences of his actions?

James shoved his hands into his pockets. Eric had made a

mistake. A big one. James got to his car, slid inside, and pulled the hat and sunglasses off as he started the engine. As he drove, he gripped the steering wheel even tighter, so tight in fact, that his hands began to ache after a second under the tension. There was part of him that liked the ache. The pain reminded him of the same pain he'd felt when his father would grab the back of his arm when he was disappointed in something that James did, pinching it so hard his hand would turn blue, squeezing the life out of it before he let go.

James narrowed his eyes. He'd tried asking Eric nicely if he would support James. He'd asked to meet. He'd gone through the correct channels. Made the request exactly the way that it should have been made. There was no reason other than arrogance or stupidity that Eric wouldn't support him. Eric hadn't been overt about it, but if what Layla had heard was true, then Eric had already made the decision to support Liv Gardner and not him, not even giving him the courtesy of a meeting to talk details.

That was a mistake.

James looked out the window as he headed home. There was a high school football team out on the field practicing in the heat, the late summer Chicago sunshine beating down on their shoulders and backs. As he passed, he saw the players drop to the ground in unison and then jump back up, pumping their knees up and down as they did. James knew what they were doing — the infamous up-downs. He'd seen a program on the TV a few years back about the Detroit Lions and remembered pointing it out to his son. The thing that was remarkable to him was the head coach did the exercises with the team. James had been impressed. He remembered commenting to his son. "That's true discipline, son. They follow the rules. People need to follow the rules. That's what keeps order in our society." James Junior had only offered a weak smile in return.

But Eric Adams Atkins wasn't following the rules. And if he wouldn't, then neither would James.

At home, James put the hat and sunglasses back in his duffel bag in the trunk of his BMW before going into the house. As the back door clicked closed, he heard nothing but the quiet murmur of voices above him. Good. He thought. Janice was doing her job. The house was in order and peaceful.

Double-checking his assessment, he took a lap through the first floor of their spacious townhome and didn't see Janice or the kids. He walked up the steps to the second floor, feeling a sudden tightness between his shoulders, one that was threatening to give him a headache. This was not the time for Janice or the kids to be doing things that they shouldn't be. He was on edge.

He gripped the banister tightly as he marched up the steps. A minute later, he found Lisa, his daughter, sitting on the floor in her room playing with a puzzle, working on getting the pieces put together. Seeing him, she jumped up and ran toward him, wrapping her arms around his waist. "Hi, Daddy!" He half returned the hug by tapping her on the back. Looking down, he saw her face tip up to search his. "I missed you today." She pointed at the floor. "Mom said I should do a puzzle instead of watching television."

He couldn't bring himself to respond to her comment about missing him. He gave her a curt nod. "Your mother is right. Go work on your puzzle. I have work to do downstairs."

Without a word of protest, Lisa turned back to her puzzle, plopping down cross-legged and focusing on getting the next piece in place. James turned away without another thought.

In the next room over, James found Janice and James Junior sitting together. Janice had pulled up a chair next to James Junior's desk and was helping him with his multiplication tables. Seeing James appear at the doorway, Janice stood and gave him a peck on the cheek. Her lips were dry on his skin. "How was your day?"

"Fine," he lied. "What are you working on?"

James Junior looked up. "Multiplication," he groaned. "Mom said I need to practice."

Janice raised her eyebrows as if looking for support from James. James blinked. "Your mother is right. Finish them up."

He said nothing more.

Satisfied that Janice had things under control upstairs, James turned on his heel and went downstairs. He went into his office and closed the door, a signal to his family that he didn't want to be disturbed.

He stopped and stood, staring at his desk. His day hadn't been fine. Not at all. He had to figure out what to do about it.

James glanced at a space behind his desk. In the built-in cabinetry in his office was a refrigerator. He pulled out a bottle of water and set it on a coaster on his desk. From a cabinet next to it, one with a lock on it, he drew out an aged bottle of whiskey and a small crystal glass. He poured himself a finger of the whiskey, not more than an inch of the amber-colored liquid, locked it up in the cabinet again, and sat down at his desk. Janice thought he was being overly zealous by having a locked cabinet in his office, but the last thing he wanted was his children to have access to certain things that adults could indulge in, one of them being his liquor. They weren't quite old enough to be left at home on their own, but it was always good to be ready. Judge Conklin had seen too many times where people had gotten involved in drugs or alcohol and it ended up in his courtroom. He wouldn't allow his children to get involved in alcohol or drugs. Even James himself, with his family history, was excruciatingly careful around it.

Staying in control was the name of the game.

James allowed his body to relax in the thick leather desk chair. He lifted the glass to his lips, smelling the alcohol before it ever touched his tongue. Taking a tiny sip, the woodsy taste of the whiskey filled his mouth, covering his teeth and tongue. As he swallowed, the liquid burned its way down his throat.

James followed the single sip of whiskey with a guzzle of water to deaden the effect of the alcohol and then opened his computer. He typed in the password and then clicked on an Internet browser, tasting the whiskey still on his lips, even with the chaser of the water. He leaned toward the screen. This wasn't a standard browser. This was one that accessed the dark web. James quickly navigated his way through a few of the sites he knew to have information about people that were popular. He began looking at Eric Atkins, pulling out some bits and pieces, his fingers racing over the keyboard.

Within just a few minutes, James had collected basic background information on his newest rival. Unfortunately, it was things he knew already — where Eric had gone to school, how he'd ended up as a state senator, where he lived, and even his address. James wasn't surprised at the amount of information he could access, though none of it was helpful. If people thought that commonly used Internet browsers had information, they would be completely horrified at what was on the dark web.

A few minutes later, James found what he was looking for. A complete dossier on Eric Atkins, the kind of opposition research that politicians used all the time to get people out of their way, discrediting them, eliminating the competition. James read the description. It promised to have the kind of information he needed. Scrolling to the bottom of the page, James narrowed his eyes. The person who had the background on Atkins wanted ten grand for it. "Dream on, pal," James muttered under his breath. There was no way he was going to pay that much money for information he could find on his own.

If nothing else, James was an expert researcher. He'd had to become one as a judge. He needed to know the law better than any attorney that walked into his office and had taken that on as a personal challenge. If a cocky attorney came in with some random argument that he didn't understand, then he had to have the chops in order to go find the information he needed in order to either carry or deny their motion.

And now he needed information on something else, Eric Atkins.

An hour and a half later, James muttered under his breath. "Gotcha." He'd found exactly what he was looking for. James leaned back in his chair, studying the photographs that were displayed on the screen in front of him. Eric Atkins had been spotted with a woman. Better yet, it was a woman that wasn't his wife. Someone had taken photos and video of him at a restaurant, two of them holding hands. James smiled. That wasn't something you did with anyone other than your wife.

James studied the pictures. Could he go to Eric Atkins and show him the pictures and encourage Eric to change his mind and support him instead of Liv Gardner? He could, but something in James's gut told him that it wasn't enough. Eric had been in politics for long enough to know that those kinds of scandals, spun the right way, might make him look like every guy out there, like someone that understood his constituents' daily lives, building a "Hey, you were tempted and so was I," camaraderie.

No. It wasn't enough.

James took the last sip of his whiskey. He'd nursed it along, allowing himself one tiny sip every fifteen minutes and it was finally gone. He set the crystal glass back on the coaster and stood up, walking to the window, considering his options and the question of what to do with Eric Atkins.

Staring outside was one of his favorite things to do. Given the elevation of his office on the first floor of their townhouse over the sidewalk below, he felt like he was king of the castle, staring out at his domain. And if he had his way, someday his domain would include the entire state of Illinois. After that, the sky was the limit. Maybe even the presidency.

James turned and looked over his shoulder at his computer. But none of that would happen if Eric Atkins got in his way.

James bit the inside of his lip so hard he tasted blood. That couldn't happen.

38

Having finished his whiskey, James sat back down at his computer to do a cursory security check of his case files. Checking his data was normal for him, though he highly doubted any other jurist had even the slightest idea how to do it or why they would want to.

That was their problem.

He logged into the courthouse database, which with his position, gave him an opportunity to see who was requesting information about his cases, everything from who had filed the initial charges and the arresting officers to who had assigned them to him and when. More importantly, he could tell who had accessed the files.

Access depended on where the request came from. If it was from the media, they had to submit a formal Freedom of Information Act, or FOIA, request, which would generally be slow-walked by everyone from the County Clerk to the prosecutors, only to have the media person receive a heavily redacted, blacked out copy of whatever information they had requested.

Other law enforcement agencies had more ready access, their position as officers of the court giving them almost immediate access to everything. Well, almost everything. The exception was the most highly sensitive information on a case, information that could impact the prosecution or the fair trial of a defendant. James squinted at the screen. He saw that there were a series of searches on his cases, recent ones. And not just the current cases on his docket, either. James frowned. To him, it looked like somebody was sniffing around. This happened periodically. In the past, it had been a database administrator doing research on a new platform to manage their caseload digitally. This somehow looked different though. James blinked. It was different. The inquiries went back as far as a decade before, when he had just started on the bench.

Who are you? What are you looking for?

The whoosh of blood thundered in James's ears. He opened a program that tracked IP addresses. He'd managed to customize it to his needs a few months before when he was bored one afternoon, only a few adjustments to the JavaScript required to allow it to work with the databases he had access to.

He opened the DOS screen on his computer. To the uninitiated, it looked like nothing more than a black box with white lettering, type the command "run search bot" and waited, leaning back in his chair.

A second later a list of IP addresses came back, the majority of them collected within the last forty-eight hours. James copied the IP addresses, dumped the numbers into a document so he could keep track of them, and went back to the dark web, using a tool to identify the physical address of where the IP was located.

James had tried to explain to James Junior what an IP address was a few weeks before. It was a simple process actually. The IP address was similar to the street address of a house, only it simply identified the computer that was being used and where it was. The computer, once communicating with the Internet, would report its location. All James had to do was backtrack to see what location it was at, coordinating the computer's IP address with the physical street address.

James tapped his fingers on his desk, waiting. A second later, he had his answer. While a few of the requests had come from Chicago PD's offices, which he expected, the majority of them came from a location on the other side of the city. Frowning, James stared at the screen. He went into a property records database, one that was available to anyone, even those who never used the dark web. He typed in the address and waited for the records to populate. The title came back to Lou Gonzalez. James felt his chest tighten. Was that Detective Gonzalez? The one from Chicago PD?

He'd only met Detective Gonzalez once or twice when he'd appeared in his courtroom. James leaned toward his computer screen and went back to the dark web, searching for a combination of Lou's name and address to see what popped up.

"Are you kidding me?" he hissed.

James continued his research. After a few minutes, he realized that Detective Gonzalez wasn't the only one who was looking through his old cases. There was another IP address on the search records. James tried to backtrace it, but it bounced all over the place, everywhere from Toronto to Buenos Aires to Tokyo. James frowned. Someone with technical skills was after him, someone who knew how to hide their identity. James compared the search criteria. It was the same as the one that Detective Gonzalez had used.

What was going on?

His face began to redden just as there was a knock on the door. "Enter!" he barked. The timing couldn't have been worse. He had to track who was looking for him. He had to know. Shadows were collecting at his door. He could feel it.

Janice opened the door. "I'm sorry to bother you," she said meekly. "I know the door is closed, but I wanted to let you know that the children and I have just finished eating. I have a plate ready for you if you want it."

"Thank you, but I don't," James replied curtly, the heat running to his face. Could Janice have any worse timing? He looked up, sucking in a breath. "I appreciate the offer," he said calmly. "but I had a late lunch. Could you put it in the refrigerator for me?"

As the words came out of his mouth, a strange calm came over him, one that was tight-lipped and tense, but calm nonetheless.

"Of course." Janice backed her way out of the doorway as if she was afraid he was going to throw something at her. She clicked the door closed. James looked at his phone. He picked it up and dialed, his stomach in knots. As soon as he heard a voice on the other end of the line, he said one short phrase.

"We have a problem."

39

"Chief?" Lou said stiffly. He was walking through the lobby at the twelfth precinct, the building where the Homicide Division was housed. He nearly bumped into the desk sergeant as he answered his phone, a grizzled-looking man with a gold shield on his chest and a thick five o'clock shadow that desperately needed to be trimmed. Lou got nothing but a glare from him. Where the sergeant was rushing off to, he had no idea. Lou glanced around him. It was surprisingly busy in the lobby. There was a van out front. An early morning bust had brought in a bunch of suspects, all cuffed and cursing under their breath, calling everyone they ran into the worst names they could come up with, everything from a rat to comments that Lou didn't even want to think about. They were escorted by steely-faced officers who were trying desperately not to take the bait.

"Gonzalez, how are you?"

Lou ducked into an aged conference room that was near the lobby. It was vacant at the moment, filled with an old scratched wooden table with four chairs around it, a picture of the

Chicago skyline on the wall in a plastic frame. No glass for suspects to turn into a weapon. The room smelled like onions. Lou glanced down. The wastepaper basket was filled with sandwich wrappers. Apparently, the overnight shift had gotten hungry. Lou wrinkled his nose. Onions first thing in the morning weren't his idea of appetizing. "I'm fine, Chief. You?" Lou clicked the door closed behind him, the noise from the lobby instantly muffled, his stomach churning. Whether that was from the smell of the onions or the call from his bosses' bosses' bosses' boss, he had no idea. He didn't even know how many bosses there were between him and the chief of Chicago PD at that moment.

Lou looked down at the floor as he held the phone up to his ear. Why was the chief calling? The chief never called him. The chief never called anyone at his rank. It wasn't as if they had never met. They actually knew each other from the police academy, but Lou hadn't spoken to Chief Podarski since his swearing in ceremony five years before when the chief, a highly motivated, energetic guy with bright eyes and an eager attitude had gotten the notice of the mayor. He'd risen through the ranks quickly — much to the chagrin of other people who felt they were more qualified. Podarski had leapfrogged his way into the position after being on the job for only fifteen years.

"I'm good. Thanks for asking. Listen, are you on that Ander Sabate case?"

Lou felt his stomach clench. The chief wasn't calling for the answer to that question. Lou swallowed. He'd been waiting to get a call from someone about Ander's so-called suicide. He just hadn't anticipated it would be the chief. "Yes, sir." Lou was braced to give an update. Was the owner of the team putting pressure on the chief? The mayor?

"I just pulled up the report from the medical examiner. Good news. She's decided that it was a suicide. No need to waste any more resources on it. Just want to give you a heads up that I'm going to go ahead and close that. You can start working on your other cases. I'm sure Captain Ingram has other cases for you to work on."

Lou frowned. Since when did the chief get involved in the minutia of coroner's reports and case files? "I'm sorry, sir. Did you say you're going to close out the case?" It was unheard of. The job of the chief was administrative and political. His uniform elevated him above the daily grind of law enforcement.

"Yes, yes. I know it's unorthodox. But we're getting pressure from the mayor's office and from the Chicago Fire soccer team. Who knew soccer was such a big deal? I'm going to get it closed. Cut and dried according to the coroner. Just wanted to give you a heads up." The chief gave a nervous chuckle. "Good work on this, though, Lou. Thanks."

Lou started to answer, but the line was already dead. Apparently, the chief had moved on to more pressing matters.

Lou dropped the phone to his side and frowned. What had just happened? He bristled. He knew exactly what had happened. Someone had gotten to the chief. Who it was, he didn't know. It could have been the team, it could have been the mayor, or it could have been someone else. But that didn't change the reality. Lou firmly believed that Ander Sabate hadn't died by accident.

Unfortunately, with the chief closing the case out from under him, his hands were tied.

Lou opened the door to the conference room and instead of heading upstairs to his desk, he headed right back outside onto the street, passing another throng of cursing criminals being escorted inside. Lou walked down the block, his gait stiff, and turned a corner, out of eyeshot and earshot of the front of the precinct. Cops were notorious gossips. In Lou's mind, they were worse than a bunch of old women kibbitzing in a knitting circle. He thumbed through his phone and dialed. He heard a voice on the other end of the line.

"What's going on?"

"They closed the case right out from underneath me."

"What?" There was surprise in Emily's voice. Glancing over his shoulder, Lou moved farther down the block away from the police station. "Yeah. The chief just called me. The medical examiner just ruled it a suicide. Said the soccer team and the mayor want it closed, so he closed it."

"You're kidding me? What about the fentanyl in his system? And no one has answered the question of how he got out into the water in the first place. We know he didn't drown. And you told me you found some adhesive or something on his shoe. No explanation for that, either. What is going on?" Emily balled her hands into fists.

Lou closed his eyes for a second and then opened them. "I know. There are still a lot of questions, but you know what this means, don't you?"

Emily's words came out gruff. "That you can't work on the case anymore."

"Correct." Lou felt his stomach sink. He was in a bind. He could work on the case quietly in his off hours, but if he found something he'd be in a jam and that was if the tech division didn't rat him out to his superiors. The good news was that he still had the information in his garage. He could work the case old school, no tech, on the down low, but even if he got to the bottom of it, he could get himself jammed up. If he took the information to Captain Ingram or anyone else to get the case reopened, they could easily accuse him of insubordination. Lou knew he could lose his job, his retirement — everything. And given the fact that his wife had left him, and he was divorced and living on his own, he had too much to lose. Work was all he had left.

From the tone of Emily's voice, Lou could tell she had already come to the same conclusion. There was no one who understood the fragile nature of law enforcement better than his old partner.

"All right. Stand down. Let me see what I can do so you don't get your butt in a sling."

40

Lou couldn't just sit by and do nothing and let Emily take the heat, especially after everything she'd been through. Guilt nipped at his gut. Sure, Chief Podarski had told him the case was closed. Maybe it was in his mind, but Lou still had questions.

Lou pulled his set of keys from his pocket and stared at them for a second after hanging up with Emily. She was right. There were too many questions that had gone unanswered. Maybe the chief was happy with the outcome. Lou was not.

In his car, Lou made a beeline for the medical examiner's office. It was a trip he could make in his sleep. He'd literally been there hundreds of times during his career. He pondered what he was doing as he drove. If the chief found out he went to talk to Elena after the fact, he'd be miffed. Might even write up Lou. At that moment, Lou didn't care. Something was going on. He needed to find out what had happened.

Thirteen minutes later, Lou pulled into the Cook County's Medical Examiner's Office. He left his car outside in one of the spots marked for official vehicles and went inside. He sniffed. The air always smelled a little funny to him, like a combination of disinfectant and mold at the same time. Perhaps it was just stale air.

Lou pulled open the door that led through the waiting room into the lab and office area. He strode down the hallway and stuck his head in a few of the doors, looking for Elena. He found her a minute later in her office, leaning over her desk, talking to one of her interns, a young man wearing a white lab coat and blue scrubs, just like Elena was wearing. Her hair was tied up in a bun at the top of her head, a set of glasses on her face.

As soon as she spotted Lou in the doorway, she looked at the young man. "Dr. Diamonte, please excuse me for a few minutes. I'll come and find you." The young doctor eyed Lou as he brushed past. Lou closed Elena's office door as soon as he left.

Elena threw herself down on her desk chair. "Why am I not surprised to see you?"

"Maybe you're a good judge of character?"

"You're here about Ander Sabate." She said it like it was a fact, not a question.

"Correct. What happened?"

She raised her eyebrows. "You tell me. I did the autopsy and was basically told that my findings were consistent with a suicide. Actually had the head medical examiner from the state call my office this morning and close the case out from underneath me."

Interesting. Seems Chief Podarski wasn't the only one who was making sweeping decisions. "Same thing happened to me. What did you find on the autopsy?"

"Well, all of the stuff you already know from the report — no water in the lungs, a single puncture wound between the toes, enough fentanyl in his system to kill a small herd of livestock."

"Anything else?"

Elena frowned and then shuffled a set of papers on her desk. "Actually, I just got this back a few minutes ago. Printed it off to put in my set of records. It's about that sticky substance you found on his shoe." She handed Lou a sheet of paper.

Lou frowned as he read. The page was filled with a lot of four-syllable words that seemed to talk about compounds. "What does this mean exactly? I don't speak chemistry."

Elena smiled. "Yeah, I should have thought of that. I actually failed chemistry in high school. Turn to the next page. You'll see the summary."

Lou flipped to the next page, scanning it. "It's an adhesive. I was right."

"Yup, the kind used in duct tape."

Lou cocked his head to the side. "How would that get on Ander's shoes?"

Elena looked up at him, her expression even. "If his ankles were bound together. There was bruising that was consistent with that kind of restriction. Found it under the surface."

"Nothing on his wrists, though?"

"Nope, but I wouldn't expect that. The adhesive, and the tape for that matter, could have easily washed away with the prolonged exposure to the water. If I had to guess and I took another look, I'd bet I'd find residue somewhere on his wrists. The tape? It's probably at the bottom of the lake somewhere."

Lou narrowed his eyes. "So he was murdered."

Elena looked away, her voice hollow. "Not that I apparently have a vote, but yes."

Lou felt heat build in his chest. "You can't report this to anyone? Change your findings so we can investigate?"

"Not unless I want to lose my medical license."

That was serious. "Are you kidding?"

"Nope. That's what I was told this morning." Elena took off her glasses and rubbed the bridge of her nose. "All of my friends told me to stay out of Chicago. Too corrupt, they said. I told them they were wrong. They weren't. I'm already applying for new jobs. This might be the last time you see me, Detective Gonzalez."

Lou pressed his lips together. Elena might not be the only one looking for a new job.

41

It didn't take James too long to complete his little project. After doing some additional research, he realized that the pictures he'd found were of Eric Atkins with a woman who wasn't his mistress. Whatever idiot had posted them on the dark web hadn't bothered to identify the woman. But James had. He was smarter than that. The woman in the picture was Eric's sister. Based on the dates and the digging that James had done, he realized it had happened the same week that their mother had died. Clearly, Eric was consoling his sister.

James smiled. The public didn't know that.

Replacing Eric's sister's face with someone else didn't take any time at all. The AI, or artificial intelligence, tools available had become very easy to use. James had quickly found another video of a man and a woman, similar in height, walking together in a park holding hands. And then there was another one of them kissing. A few hours' worth of work and James had videos of a man and a woman in a park, kissing and holding hands at dinner. He smiled as he reviewed the videos one last time. Even though it was wholly untrue, it was the makings of a scandal, a scandal that would move Eric Atkins out of the way.

While the images processed, James thought about Ander Sabate. It was a shame, really. Ander was a great guy and would have made a great face to add to his campaign strategy. But he reneged on his promise and his brother was a druggy. Ander didn't have any control over what George did, but he should have come through with his donation. It would have made all the difference. Ander had embarrassed James. Who was he to do that? James was a judge. He was in charge. Not Ander.

So James had made him pay.

Getting Ander to the boat was easy enough. James had called and said that he wanted to make things right between him and Ander. Ander was more than willing. After all, who didn't want to have a great relationship with a powerful judge?

They'd gotten James's boat, a thirty-foot sailboat named *The Mistress*, off the dock with no problems. After motoring out of the marina, Ander handled the wheel while James got the sails set. The night was perfect, enough of a breeze to make the sailing fun, but not so much they couldn't relax. James had brought some food and drinks along. Ander showed him pictures of Ana and the baby and was all smiles, as if everything had been forgiven.

It hadn't.

James offered Ander a special bottle of water, one that had been spiked with a loading dose of fentanyl. A few sips later, Ander had passed out. James quickly dug through his toolbox where he'd stashed a syringe. He tugged one of Ander's shoes off, tossing it overboard, then stuck the needle between Ander's toes, giving him more than enough to stop his breathing. James waited for a moment, watching as the color drained from Ander's face, his lips taking on a bluish tinge. Unlike the other criminals in his court, James took no pleasure in ending a life. It was a means to an end, a way for him to get the justice he knew he deserved.

The rest had been child's play. James had bound up Ander's

ankles and wrists with tape and rolled him overboard, tossing his cell phone after him. Ten minutes later, James was turned back to shore, no sign of Ander on board.

James smiled as he sailed toward the marina, the sun at his back. There was a price to pay for not being a man of your word.

Ander had paid.

42

Emily had been outside on the phone talking to Lou when Mike poked his head out the door. In his hand he had an open bag of cheese curls. Emily frowned. It was early, just after eight in the morning. She'd told him all about Elizabeth Gordon and her rising from the dead when she got back from Scenic View Park the night before. Elizabeth had accused Judge James Conklin of being behind the murders when Lou had called, telling her that the case had been closed. Emily grimaced as she looked at Mike. "What are you eating?"

Mike looked startled like he hadn't even realized what he had in his hand. "I like these for breakfast."

"Can you check something for me?"

"Yeah," Mike mumbled through a full mouth. "What?"

"Any boats registered to Conklin?"

Emily continued her conversation with Lou. Mike returned a moment later. "Conklin owns a sailboat called *The Mistress*."

Emily blinked. That solved the problem of how Ander got two miles offshore. "Lou, I gotta go. I'll be in touch."

Mike looked at Emily. He shook his head. "That's not why I came to get you. You gotta come in here and see this."

Emily hung up with Lou, promising to get back with him as soon as she knew anything. As she walked into the house she could hear the television blaring, a newscaster talking in an overly controlled tone of voice. Mike pointed, holding an uneaten cheese curl between his fingers. "Watch. Ander's death finally made the local news."

The stories ran back-to-back. The first one featured the grieving wife of Ander Sabate standing behind a thick looking man who the banner at the bottom of the screen identified as Bill Driscoll, the PR person for the Chicago Fire soccer team. "With great regret, we are informing our fans that our star forward, Ander Sabate, tragically took his life a few days ago. We realized there has been a lot of speculation about where Ander has been. Please know that the team has been working in close concert with the family and the Chicago Police Department to give the family time to grieve and to come to grips with his tragic and untimely death, as well as make a plan to honor the contribution that Ander made not only to soccer but to the greater Chicago community." Driscoll stopped and scanned the media in front of him, his expression even and his tone professional, tinged with an appropriate level of sadness.

Driscoll continued. "A memorial space has been set up near the main entrance of the stadium. We know that there are those of you who already heard about this tragedy through various unauthorized channels in the media."

Emily blinked. *A shot across the bow?*

"Regardless, we ask that you give Mrs. Sabate and her family privacy as they grieve. Please know that the Chicago Fire soccer team family will care for Mrs. Sabate as if she was one of our own. Ander was an amazing part of our team, and we are devastated at his loss…" As Driscoll paused, Emily could hear the shutters on the digital cameras going off at high speed, capturing the scene in front of them, a stalwart Bill Driscoll, flanked by

Chicago Fire coaches and Ana Sabate. She was dressed in traditional widow's garb, a long black dress, black nylons, conservative black shoes, and a black headband holding her mane of dark hair off of her face. Her fingers gripped the handle of a small black handbag that she held in front of her at her waist, as if she was ready to swing it in the air to fend off the media. The outfit was so somber that the only thing Ana was missing was a black lace veil. Emily wondered if she would wear one for the funeral.

Emily was just about to say something when Mike pointed. "Hold on. There's more. Today is a juicy news day. Can't wait to do some research."

The news reader, a woman with dark hair and too much eyeliner, straightened. Emily noticed that she and her co-anchor had coordinated their outfits, the woman in a black dress with a purple scarf, the man in a black suit with a purple tie. Emily tried not to roll her eyes. *Who actually dressed like that?*

The woman continued. "And in other news, one of Illinois's most prominent political figures has run into some personal trouble. This video was leaked on the Internet this morning by a reputable source."

A second later, Emily saw a video of a man that Emily didn't recognize holding a woman's hand as they walked in a park. The next clip showed the same man kissing the woman as they entered a home, the door open for a split second, just long enough to capture their lips pressing together before the door completely closed. The newsreader continued. "State Senator Eric Atkins, who was poised to make a run for reelection and the prominent position of Senate President, found himself caught in a scandal this morning. This video was released to several major video media networks by an anonymous source. We have yet to identify the woman in the image. We've contacted Senator Atkins's office for comment, but they have not responded at this time. Stay tuned for more on both of these stories."

Mike raised his eyebrows as he crunched on another cheese curl. "Dude, that guy's career is over."

Emily was just about to tell Mike about the phone call she'd gotten from Lou when Mike stopped, frozen where he was standing. "Hold on."

"What is it?"

"I don't know." He frowned. "I thought I saw a flicker in the corner of the screen."

A flicker? Who cares? "So?"

"Something's wrong."

Mike dropped the bag of cheese curls on the coffee table in the family room and headed back to the kitchen. Miner, who had followed them in to watch the television, had his nose in the air, sniffing the snack Mike had abandoned. Emily scooped the bag up, not wanting Miner to finish them off. Cheese curl dog vomit wasn't exactly what she wanted to deal with that morning.

By the time she walked back into the kitchen, Mike was already at his computer. He'd pulled up the video that they had just seen on the television. Emily saw him open a few other programs on his computer, overlapping their windows like tiles so he could look at all of them at the same time. Emily wasn't exactly sure what to make of Mike's reaction. She knew he went off on rabbit trails. She was still thinking about the call from Lou. She looked at Mike while he was working. "Lou called me this morning."

"Really?" Mike answered without looking up. "What did *he* want?"

Emily ignored the tone of his voice. "He said that the chief closed the Sabate case. He can't work on it anymore."

Mike glanced up. "What? The chief did? That's not standard operating procedure, is it?"

Emily cocked her head to the side. The more she thought about it, the angrier she got. "No. It's not." In her tenure with the CPD, she'd never had a chief interfere in any of her cases, not even a sergeant or a lieutenant from another division. The CPD specialties were siloed — vice, theft, homicide, drugs, gang violence, domestic terrorism, and a few more she couldn't think of at the moment — and the officers kept to themselves. It was necessary, the best way to protect the investigative work they were doing. *What is going on here?* Emily felt like she had stumbled into a rat's nest of corruption. They had a judge that was killing off people and a chief close a case before all the work had been done.

Something wasn't right.

"Where are you?" Mike muttered under his breath, his eyes darting back and forth as he stared at his computer screen.

Emily stayed silent. She didn't want to interrupt Mike's focus. She watched him for the next couple of minutes, his head swiveling left and right as he was looking at things on his computer. The expression on his face was focused and intense, like a man on the hunt. It reminded her of when Miner was in the backyard chasing a chipmunk. Tunnel vision.

Emily stood up and walked to the window, staring out. Elizabeth Gordon had named James Conklin as her murderer the night before. And given what Emily now knew about Conklin's tie to Ander Sabate and Tony Rossi, Emily knew something would have to be done. There was a minimum of three bodies on Conklin. How many more there were, she had no idea, but her gut told her there were more. Probably a lot more.

What to do was the next problem. Lou had been paralyzed by the department. She was on her own.

"Typical," she muttered under her breath as Mike worked. If there was any reality in her life, it was that she could only really rely on herself.

"Oh, okay. I see you," Mike said, slapping his hands on the table as if he'd just discovered the location of the Holy Grail.

Emily walked toward him. "What is it?"

He looked up, his eyes bright, like a five-year-old who'd just been surprised with their first bicycle. His next words came out slowly. "This video is fake. The entire story is fake."

Emily walked toward him and looked over his shoulder, scowling. "What do you mean?"

"Okay, so the tech is a little hard to explain to somebody who's not in the business."

Emily fought off the urge to slap the back of his head. "Let's give it a try."

Mike sucked in a breath as if he was just about to go underwater. "Here's the deal. There's been this new surge of deep fake videos."

No kidding. "Yeah, I've heard about that."

"Well, then you know that photographs and videos can be altered."

Emily frowned. It didn't take a genius to see where Mike was going. "So this is one of them?"

"Yep. And you're going to ask me how I know." Mike's expression was smug.

Maybe he was a genius after all. "I am."

"There's image data loaded in the background of the video. Somebody who doesn't know where to look for it or how to find it would never be able to get to it. But then again, people have gotten to be very good at hiding the image data. Forensic technologists have gotten to be experts at digging through the background information on what we see. I'm not sure they would have found this," he said, giving himself a little pat on the back, "but see right here?"

Emily stared at the screen. All she saw was blank spaces. "See what? The dead space?"

"Yes. Exactly. There was code that was taken out."

"Okay...so?"

"Whoever made this video was trying to eliminate the ability for someone to go back and figure out where it originated."

"Are you talking about someone who took the pictures to start with, or the person who made the fake?" Emily felt confused.

"The person that did the altering. We usually call them an artist. It's a loose term, obviously. Whoever did this was not exactly a Picasso."

Emily was getting impatient. She had the urge to do something. "Can we get to the bottom line, please?"

"Yeah. Sorry. Hold on." Mike ran his fingers across the keyboard and then there was a beep. "Oh, gotcha," he mumbled under his breath as if the computer had said something to him. He looked up at Emily. "I have the location where this video originated."

"The original or the fake one?"

"The fake one. It just came in." Mike looked down at his computer. "Give me a sec."

Emily watched as Mike opened a series of screens, copying data over and then doing it again. "Here it is. It's coming from a townhouse downtown."

Emily felt her stomach tighten. "Who does the townhouse belong to?"

Mike paused for a minute, stared at the screen then started to nod. He leaned back in his chair. "Our good friend Judge James Conklin."

Emily knitted her eyebrows together. He was a judge, not a tech wizard. Had he paid someone to do it? "Conklin? He made the AI video that framed Eric Atkins?" Emily's pulse quickened. The pieces were starting to fall together. She started to pace near where Mike was working. It made sense. First, Conklin killed off his old campaign manager, not really though, since

Elizabeth was still alive. The next victims were a couple of people who embarrassed him in court. Now he was going after a political opponent. It was about one thing and one thing alone — ambition.

Emily stopped to stare at Mike. "How's that possible? Did he just send it, is that why? He's a judge, not a coder."

"That's where you'd be wrong, Emily. Conkin's not just a judge." The words came out low and slow. "The judge has been hiding a secret."

Emily threw her hands in the air. "What are you talking about?"

"I just pulled up his educational history. Most people that go to law school have an undergraduate degree in one of the social sciences — History, English, even Sports Management if they want to become an agent."

Emily rubbed her hands together. "But not Conklin?"

Mike shook his head. "No. Our new friend has a degree in computer science."

43

"Tell me where Eric Atkins is right now. He and I need to have a conversation." Before Mike could even answer, Emily ran upstairs, changed into a pair of jeans and a T-shirt, pulling her dark hair into a ponytail. She ran back downstairs, grabbed her gun from the drawer plus a set of earwigs, one for her and one for Mike. She tugged her T-shirt over her gun and added a light jacket, shoving her feet into a pair of running shoes. "Do you have a location?"

"Yep. Just sent it to your phone. He's hunkered down in Naperville. How are you gonna get to him?" The muscles on his jaw flickered.

"I don't know. But I gotta warn him."

"You think Judge Conklin's coming after him?"

"If he made the video, then it stands to reason he will, especially after what he did to Elizabeth, Tony Rossi, and Ander Sabate. Senator Atkins needs to be warned. I don't know what kind of beef Conklin has with him, but he's gonna have to be stopped."

Mike blinked, his eyes wide. "Senator Atkins is gonna have security all over the place, plus probably Naperville police."

"I'll handle them."

How exactly Emily would do that, she had no idea.

After striding out to her truck, Emily got it started and pulled out of the driveway. Mike had loaded up the location where Senator Eric Atkins was hunkered down, weathering the first few hours of the media storm that was circling around him.

The drive out to Naperville was easy, but dealing with the feeling in Emily's gut was not. James Conklin was guilty in her mind, guilty of two murders, plus an attempted murder and conspiracy against Eric Atkins. The sad thing, though it was the harsh reality, was that Chicago PD was somehow in on it. Whether that was a sin by omission or commission, she had no idea. The net result was the same. It was still sin. She knew there had to be a strong working relationship between the judicial and the law enforcement branches of government, but the unfortunate part was as soon as you got people involved, their own agendas tended to outweigh the actual good of the people that were around them. As Emily drove, she realized that it was likely no coincidence that the chief had shut Lou down. Was Judge Conklin being protected by the CPD? What was in it for them?

Could this get any worse?

Emily's mind was working so fast that the next piece to fall into place surprised her. It occurred to her that Lou had been uneasy around his new partner. Was she involved somehow too, or were Lou's concerns about her well-founded but unrelated to Ander's death?

Emily pushed the thought away. She had priorities other than dealing with corruption in the Chicago PD on her plate at the moment. Courtney was a problem for another day.

The scene in front of Eric Atkins's house was worse than Emily had imagined. There were no fewer than twenty media vans sitting in front of his house, kept largely at bay by four cruisers from Naperville PD, the officers looking bored as they stood at the end of the senator's driveway. Emily passed by, moving slowly enough that it looked like she was being cautious given the throng, but not stopping and drawing any attention to herself.

On the side of the road, she saw a young red-haired woman standing off to the side, a microphone held up close to her mouth, a camera pointed at her face. She was talking and pointing dramatically, clearly giving an update on the video that had been released about Senator Atkins that morning. As Emily passed by Eric's house, she realized it backed up to a golf course. She set her jaw realizing that might be her best way in.

Instead of parking near Eric's house, Emily drove down the street, following small wooden signs with a neat script that read "Clubhouse." A minute later, she spotted it. It was a newer two-story building with a circular driveway with a porte cochere over the front and two newer shiny sedans parked underneath the overhang. There were a series of golf carts parked off to the side, appropriately dressed golfers walking in and out of the clubhouse, getting ready to go out for their tee time. Emily didn't understand golf. The whole process of hitting a small ball as far away as you could manage, and then trying to hunt it down didn't seem entertaining to her at all.

She preferred hunting actual prey.

Emily chewed the inside of her lip, considering her next move. She knew she wasn't exactly dressed like a golfer. She parked her truck, pocketing the key fob. Glancing over her shoulder, noticing that no one was watching her, she walked to the back side of the clubhouse. There were four groups of people out on the patio, seemingly enjoying their breakfast before they headed out onto the greens, paying no attention to the drama unfolding in their neighborhood. Emily walked back toward the front of the building and then made her way over to the golf carts. A moment later, a cart filled with two men pulled up, they dragged their clubs off the cart and gave her only a brief nod. That gave Emily an idea. It might look strange if she walked along the greens to get to Senator Atkins's house. She walked by the golf carts slowly, glancing down at them. There were keys in the ignition. The last one in the line had tools attached to the back. Someone had left a jacket and a baseball hat on the seat. Whoever was doing work on the greens was probably taking a break. "Perfect," she muttered. Quickly stripping off her jacket, she replaced it with one that read Three Pines Golf Club and tucked the hat down over her dark hair. She put the golf cart into gear, backed it up and drove away.

Emily guided the golf cart down the well-worn paths and headed back toward Eric Atkins's house. Her suspicion was that security was so focused on keeping the media at bay that they assumed the back would not be a threat. Her theory depended entirely on how well-qualified Eric's security team was or if he even had a private one. After all, he was a state senator, not a national one.

Within a minute, Eric's house came back into view. Emily passed about ten houses on her way to his, each of them nearly identical in the back with groomed landscaping. Three of them had pools, including Eric's.

Trying to intercept a state senator under siege at his house in broad daylight was risky. Emily knew it. She felt her throat tighten, the breath shallow in her chest. As Emily approached his house, she looked casually to the right. The only thing to the left of her was some empty putting greens, their flags waving gently in the breeze. Emily kept her eyes focused straight forward. She didn't want anyone to get suspicious about who she was. The key to that was to look as relaxed as possible. If she pulled it off, to anyone looking out their back window, she would appear to be one of the greenskeepers headed off to maintain their pristine view. Even to someone who knew the greenskeepers, which many avid golfers did, she assumed, they might just figure she was a new hire.

Either way, she'd have to strike quickly.

As Emily approached Eric's backyard, she realized it was encircled with a fence. For all intents and purposes, it was primarily a decorative edifice, black wrought iron with pointed finials at the top of each spire. It was only a small deterrent, probably more to meet the city's requirements for cordoning off swimming pools from small children and drunk golfers than anything else. She spotted a gate that ran along the outside of the pool, the opening right next to what looked to be an outdoor building. What it housed exactly, she wasn't sure.

Getting close, Emily knew she had to make a decision. She decided to park the golf cart in full view. There was no point in hiding it. She was pretending to be a greenskeeper. A greenskeeper wouldn't try to camouflage their ride. She hopped out, grabbing a rake from the back of the cart and walked towards Eric's fence, raking at a few leaves that had collected near the base, pretending to deal with them.

She glanced up. From where she was positioned, she could see the back of Eric's house. It was expansive and wide, with large windows covering the back of it. Expensive cushioned patio furniture was artfully set around the pool, a long outdoor dining table near the back door where there looked to be a setup for an outdoor grill, a pizza oven, and even refrigerators. She heard voices from inside the house. They sounded heated. "I told you it's nothing!" A male voice boomed.

Eric.

A female voice responded, but Emily couldn't make out exactly what the person said. It was probably Mrs. Eric trying to exact her pound of flesh.

A minute later, Emily heard the sliding glass door open. She ducked behind the outbuilding, raking at the grass a little bit more. For some reason, there was no security around the back of the house. As she anticipated, they were all focused on the front, keeping the media from trampling the flowers.

Big mistake.

That was the only tactical error she needed them to make. A forty-ish man with dark hair walked stiffly out of the sliding glass doors and made his way toward the building, his shoulders slumped, his face downcast. She watched as he made his way to the pool building and went inside.

Emily's heart skipped a beat. This was her chance. She flipped open the latch to the gate and stepped inside, closing it quietly behind her. She made her way to the door just as it opened, the noise of a toilet flushing inside. She put a hand on Eric's chest and shoved him back inside with one hand, using the other to cover his mouth. "What the —?" he yelled as she released him.

"Shut up." Emily stood with her back blocking the door.

"Who are you?" He waved his hands near her face but didn't touch her. That was a smart move on his part. "I've got security out front. I'm gonna have you arrested for trespassing."

"Shut up."

Eric didn't listen. He lunged for her. Emily stepped out of the way and grabbed his hand as he bumped into the door. In a split second, she had twisted his arm behind his back and was pressing on the pressure points between the base of his thumb and his first finger. He groaned. "Okay, okay! Who are you? What do you want?"

Emily eased off the pressure just a bit. "I told you to shut up. I'm not here to hurt you. But you need to listen to me."

Eric decided that was the time to try to break free. Emily increased the pressure on his thumb and he groaned again, holding up his free hand. "Okay, okay."

Emily let go, just in time to see him try to swing up a left hook at her, she blocked it, grabbed his wrist as he came around and twisted his arm behind his back and pushed him up against the wall next to the door. "You are being really stupid right now," she hissed in his ear.

"I'm gonna have you arrested!" he bellowed.

Emily tried not to smile. At least he had a little fight in him. "I don't think that's gonna happen."

Eric didn't answer, apparently realizing that he was up against someone who had skills he'd never experienced before.

Standing pressed into his back, Emily whispered into his ear. "I need you to listen to me. That video. It's fake."

Emily felt that energy drain out of Eric's body. "What?"

She relaxed her hold on him and waited to see if he would swing again. He turned around slowly. "What are you talking about? How do you know that?" He looked down at the ground for a second. "I mean, I know it's fake. But nobody will believe me."

Emily rubbed her chin. It seemed to be a theme in this case. "It's not important how I know. But it *is* fake." Stepping back, she gave herself a little room in case Eric decided to attack again, but she kept her back to the door. She needed him to stay in the room with her for a moment. She hadn't bothered to look around when she followed him inside, but quickly realized by the humming in the background that he was in the mechanical room that also doubled as an outdoor bathroom. The pump for the pool and the heater were humming behind him. "What's your connection to Judge James Conklin?"

"Conklin?" His face twisted as if he was surprised by the question.

"Yes. Conklin. What's your connection?"

"Nothing, I mean not much." Eric stammered. He ran his hand through his hair. "I don't know. I mean he called me a few days ago."

Emily frowned. "About what?"

"I think he wants to take a run at becoming governor. He asked for my support but I'm already backing another senator, Liv Gardner. She and I have worked together a lot. If she's governor, it makes my job easy and we both benefit. Not that it's going to matter now that this scandal has come out."

Emily waved him off. "Don't worry about that right now. That will get fixed. What else do you know? Any other contact with Conklin? Anything you can tell me?" As Emily asked the question, she realized that Eric hadn't pressed her to explain who she was once he knew the video was fake. That was good. She'd prefer to stay anonymous.

Eric's shoulders sagged. "Well, he called me a couple of days ago, told me he knew I was going to run for Senate President once I got reelected, asked me if I'd back his run for governor, then mumbled something about us working well together. When I told him I wasn't available to meet right away, he got really silent. He probably heard I'm backing someone else."

So that was it. Atkins wouldn't play ball with Conklin. "Anything else?"

"Not that I can think of." Eric stared at her. "Who are you?"

"I'm an investigator."

"Do you work with Chicago PD?"

Emily shrugged. "Sort of. That's not important right now." The pieces fell into place. Eric Atkins was the last one in the way. If Conklin wanted to make a move for the governorship of Illinois, he'd need Eric Atkins to back him. And when Eric told him no, Conklin had started to do exactly what he had done to Elizabeth Gordon, Tony Rossi, and Ander Sabate. He was on a course to destroy the senator, and Emily was relatively sure the videos were only the first part of the plan.

"Conklin's gonna come after you."

Eric shrugged. "Let him. People come after me every day."

Emily shook her head slowly, her expression stony. "I don't mean like that, Senator. He's setting you up. He's gonna come at you, make it look like you committed suicide and get you out of the way."

Eric's face paled. "What? He's a judge. He wouldn't do that."

Emily stepped toward him. "Senator, you need to trust me. I need you to get yourself and your family out of town. Get out of here for a couple of days. Go back to Springfield. This whole thing will blow over. But if you don't get out of here, you're going to be risking your own life and maybe the lives of your family too." Conklin hadn't expanded his punishment to family members, but from her experience, Emily knew that would be the natural next step for a predator like him.

"Okay, I guess. We were gonna head back to Springfield this afternoon anyway."

"Not this afternoon. Now."

Eric frowned. "And what about the video?"

"I'll take care of the video. I'll make sure that evidence is released that it was a fake as soon as I take care of something."

Emily turned the knob on the door. It wasn't any of Eric's business what her intent was. As she slipped outside, she leveled her gaze at him. "Just get out of town. Right now."

44

Things were getting out of control, James realized. As he'd been afraid of, too many people were now involved in his business. The most troubling thing he had found was that people were snooping around his old cases. No good could come of that. There were secrets buried in his case files, secrets that, if they came out, would destroy him and any hope he had to further his career.

That couldn't happen. It wasn't just ambition driving him. It was survival. Sitting day after day in the same courtroom, listening to people whine, cajole, and downright lie their way through his day was taking its toll. Things had changed in the law. Not the statutes themselves, but the respect for his position. It used to be that no one would set foot in his courtroom without being properly dressed and on time, completely prepared for their case. Not anymore. The last few years had been a stream of people showing up for court in any manner of dress. Just the week before, he'd had a case of theft to preside over where the defendant had shown up in pajamas and slippers. James had called both attorneys up to his bench, read them the riot act and pushed the case to another day when the accused could arrive dressed more respectfully.

He had to get out.

James knew he would be a good governor, maybe even a great one, but he had to get there first. He'd administer law and justice from the sprawling mansion in Springfield, with plenty of space for a team of like-minded assistants and committee chairs to help him.

And now it wasn't just Eric Atkins that was in the way.

James had discovered that someone else had been skulking around in the shadows, looking at his cases. Not just his recent ones, but ones from a decade before. Some of the more recent inquiries had come from CPD, that was fine.

But there was someone else. And they needed to be deterred.

On his way to the office, James stopped at a hardware store. He picked up a jerry can and a canister of charcoal lighter fluid. The man at the checkout barely looked at him as he handed over the cash. "Nice day for some grilling."

"Uh huh."

After returning to his car, James made one more stop at a home about fifteen minutes from his own. It belonged to an anesthesiologist who James had done a few legal favors for. The man's wife liked to drink and had been behind the wheel after half a bottle of red wine and five shots of tequila. She'd plowed into the side of a building. The doctor had come to James's chambers, hat in hand, asking for leniency. James had considered the man's request. The woman had only hurt herself and some property. No one else had been injured. And the man might come in handy someday.

Today was that day.

James stopped at Dr. Walsh's mailbox and retrieved a paper bag with a canister in it, setting it on the front seat of his car.

James couldn't be sure, but he thought he saw the drapes flutter as he went by.

Another debt paid.

Now all he had to do was implement his plan.

45

Courtney was working on a stack of paperwork when she got a text.

"Meet me around the corner in ten minutes in front of the Silver Skillet."

Courtney gazed at the text for a moment, letting the word sink in. Why did he want to meet now? Hadn't she done everything he'd asked?

She stood up from her desk, pocketed her cell phone and wallet and grabbed her keys. Staring at her desk, she wondered if she had forgotten anything. She always had the sense that it might be her last time in the precinct, but she didn't know why. It was an eerie feeling, as if she was living on the edge of a cliff but didn't know when the dirt would collapse under her feet.

Going downstairs, Courtney took the back steps, avoiding the hustle and bustle of the precinct's lobby. She darted out the back door, nodding to a couple of uniformed officers who were headed inside, probably either to do paperwork, meet with their sergeant or head to a briefing.

Courtney didn't miss her uniformed days.

She winced at the thought. She loved being a police officer, but being out on the street was never her gig. It had been boring and nerve-wracking at the same time. There were shifts where she and her partner had literally done nothing but sit in their cruiser for hours. There were others where she'd been on the move for every minute of the shift, not even getting time to use the bathroom. But mostly, it was the moment they got the call that drove her nearly insane. To go from chatting with someone about what they'd had for dinner the night before to pulling her gun two minutes later was too much. She'd found she stopped sleeping and lost a lot of weight from the constant stress.

And then things had changed. Based on a suggestion from her sergeant, Courtney had applied to take the detective's test. She'd passed it with flying colors and had been offered a spot in the homicide division. Everything seemed fine until she'd gotten called downtown. It had happened suddenly, out of the blue, before she'd packed her locker from the second district and moved over to the twelfth.

When she'd arrived, she thought she'd be meeting with someone from Human Resources to discuss her new compensation package. Instead, a dark suited man met her at the front door and ushered her quickly back outside into the sunshine. His hand gripped the back of her arm tightly and he guided her down the street and around the corner. "What's going on? Who are you?"

The man didn't answer, simply pointing to a side door of the building. It was painted in a rust color and unmarked, but Courtney knew that it led into CPD headquarters. Where exactly it led to, she had no idea.

She ran out of time to consider the fact when the door creaked open. Emerging from inside the building was the police chief himself. Courtney stood at attention and waited. She glanced at the suited man who had brought her to the doorway and seemed to shake his head. Chief Podarski furrowed his eyebrows and held up a hand. "Relax, Green. This isn't that kind of a meeting. I have a job for you."

The meeting didn't take more than a few minutes. What Chief Podarski had asked her was to do a personal favor for him and a good friend of his, and this favor came with benefits she was very interested in — a fast track up the CPD ladder.

The meetings then came few and far between. In fact, she had only seen Chief Podarski one other time since that day and that was at a promotion event. He'd locked eyes with her from across the room, given her a nod and went on his way.

But somehow, today seemed to be different.

Outside in the bright morning light, Courtney walked around the block and found her way to the spot where Chief Podarski wanted to meet. She could smell bacon cooking from the restaurant's open door and her stomach rumbled. When had she eaten last? The thought registered and then left her just as quickly as a glossy black SUV came around the corner. The driver's side window opened up. The chief's security officer pointed to the back. "Get in."

The meeting didn't last long. Courtney slipped out of the SUV and walked away three minutes later. There had been a brief exchange. She'd left her gun and badge behind. As the SUV pulled away from the curb, an email pinged on her phone.

It was a one-way trip to San Diego.

46

Mike had been sitting and working on his computer when he heard a strange scratching noise at the back door. He looked around then noticed Miner was on his bed in the kitchen. Miner must have heard it too. His head popped up, his ears pricked. A low growl emerged from Miner. He stood up, taking two slow steps and then charged at the door. Mike watched in disbelief as the door flew open, a man wearing all black and a hood running into Emily's house. Miner charged, grabbing the man's lower leg, but it didn't stop him, at least not entirely. Before Mike could do anything, the man sprayed some sort of gas in his face. Mike felt suddenly woozy and felt his knees buckle.

Mike woke up in what seemed to be a few minutes, coughing and gagging. There was smoke all over the place. As he opened his eyes, he realized the entire kitchen was engulfed in flames. He stood up, dazed, his lungs burning, still not knowing what had happened. He had vague memories of a man and a funny smell. Now there was nothing but flames in front of him. What had happened? Mike coughed again, then gagged. He had to get out of the house. His head spun, his eyes burning and watering from the smoke. He covered his face with the back of his arm. "Miner! Miner! He could hear Miner whimpering by the back door. Mike grabbed his computer and ran, opening the door and letting Miner out.

Mike didn't waste any time. He ran to the garage, jumped in his car and pushed Miner inside. He had to get away. They were coming after Emily. Mike quickly made a spoofed call to Chicago's emergency services, bouncing the call off of towers all over the state, confusing the 911 system. He explained where the fire was and then hung up, his voice hoarse. He coughed a few times, smelling the smoke on both himself and Miner. He looked over his shoulder. Miner was laying down in the back of the car, panting, but he seemed to be okay. Mike called back to him. "It's okay, boy. I'm gonna take you somewhere safe."

47

Emily had been sitting in her truck for a half hour, waiting to see what Eric Atkins was going to do. Two minutes later, two sleek black SUVs rolled by the front of the clubhouse. "Okay, good," she mumbled under her breath. At least Eric Atkins was out of the way.

She had just put her truck into gear when her phone rang. "Why are you calling me and not using the comms?"

"There's no time. I think Conklin tried to burn your house down."

"What?" her heart thundered in her chest.

"Yeah. I was sitting there. He must have tracked our case file searches back to your house. He's better with tech than I thought. I masked those. I promise I did." Mike sounded breathless. "Anyway, somebody barged in through the back door and sprayed me with something. Knocked me out. By the time I woke up the house was on fire."

Emily was afraid to ask the next question. Luckily, she didn't have to.

"Don't worry. Miner's with me. We're going to my cabin. I gotta get off the grid."

Emily knew where Mike's cabin was. It was about an hour outside of Chicago, hidden on some vacant land out in the countryside. She and Mike had had a fight a few years before, Mike deciding to take Miner with him without asking her. She chased him down and retrieved her dog. He'd learned from that experience, apparently. This time he'd at least told her that he had Miner with him. "Good. Let me handle business here. Send me a message when you're at the cabin and you get Miner settled. Do either of you need medical attention?"

"No. I think we're okay."

Emily waved her hand in the air as she stepped on the gas. She needed to get back to her house. "I'm gonna send Angelica a message and have her call you just to be sure."

"Yeah. okay. And Emily?" Mike's words came out slow and measured.

"Yeah." Emily answered.

"Be careful."

48

Emily was furious. By the time she sped through Chicago traffic and made it back to her house from Naperville, there were two fire trucks parked, blocking her street, their red lights spinning and blinking, yellow hoses laying in thick tracks across her lawn. The front door had been thrown open, a trickle of smoke pouring out.

She parked her truck on the street and walked up the front steps ignoring the crowd of neighbors who had clustered on the sidewalk across the street. A firefighter met her at the door, a dour look on his face as if he'd sucked in too much smoke. "You can't be in here."

Emily pushed past him, ignoring his protest. "Yes, I can. This is my house." The smell of smoke was thick in the air, like someone had transported her into the center of a charcoal grill.

He paused. "You weren't home when all this happened?"

The guy was a genius. "No. I just got a call from a friend that there was a fire." No need to expose Mike.

The firefighter adjusted his helmet and followed her as she went into the kitchen. As she stood in the doorway, she blinked. The kitchen that she had spent so much time in was nearly unrecognizable. Emily took a few steps forward, tracing her finger across the soot covered counter. She could see the tracks where the accelerant was streamed, the marks dark and there were black lines on her floor and cabinets. Maybe the floors could be sanded and restored, but she wasn't sure. Emily walked over to the cabinet doors. Most of the stain and varnish had bubbled with the heat of the flames, forming bulging welts on the surface. She pressed her lips together. Emily had never really been a big fan of the cabinets Luca had chosen anyway. This was as good of an excuse as any to replace them.

The firefighter interrupted her thoughts. "Well, listen, lady, you're really lucky. It's mostly smoke damage and some surface stuff. You can probably have the floors refinished and get some new cabinet doors and you'll be back in business." The man walked over to the stove and turned on the knob. "Oh good, they've got your gas back on. See, your stove still works. Looks like somebody spilled something flammable, and it lit your kitchen on fire. Maybe it sparked from a burner or a cigarette?"

Not even close. "Maybe," she said slowly. The last thing she wanted to do was to have the Chicago arson investigators crawling all over her house. The police would become involved. They'd want to interview Mike. Things would get messy. No, it was better if she handled her own business.

The firefighter continued. "It's going to require some cleanup, but whoever called it in for you did you a solid. The fire would have moved rapidly if we hadn't gotten here when we did. We got it all put out before it spread. Not sure how livable it is, but you're good to go."

"Thanks." Emily watched as the firefighters moved their extinguishers, hoses, and fans out of her kitchen. She walked back toward the living room. Aside from some lingering smoke smell, it was untouched, everything exactly as it was when she'd left it a few hours before. She walked back to the kitchen, looking at the damage again. Yes, there were some char marks on the floors and the surface of a few of the cabinets had bubbled and cracked from the flames. The good news was that Mike and Miner were both okay and safe. She shrugged. It was probably time for a new kitchen anyway.

But first, she had a problem to solve.

49

James Conklin leaned down and massaged his leg, pulling the pant leg up as he got into his car which was parked a block away from the house he'd just torched.

There were two giant bite marks on his right calf. He had no idea that former detective Emily Tizzano had a dog, and a mean one to boot. The puncture marks were deep and were already starting to bruise. It was going to hurt later.

He grimaced. If it was any other circumstance, he'd insist that her dog be put down. But since he broke into her house, that might be a hard case to make.

Even James knew when he had no case.

It had taken some work, but James had finally figured out that it was Emily who had been helping Lou Gonzalez. She was the one who had accessed his records. How she had managed to do that and hide her identity so well, he had no idea. She was nothing. A disgraced cold case detective who'd been fired. What did she know? Maybe she'd ended up playing with tech in all her free time.

At least that's what he'd thought until he broke into her house. Seeing the young guy in front of a computer answered the question he had about who had accessed the files. It wasn't Emily. It was the guy he'd dosed with an aerosol version of Halothane, a powerful anesthetic that took just seconds to work. He'd crumpled as fast as a two-dollar suitcase, falling to the floor in the middle of a sentence.

Had the guy and the dog made it out? James didn't know. He didn't stick around to find out and he didn't much care. He thought keeping Detective Tizzano busy with a little fire at her house was probably a good idea. He hoped she got the message to stay out of his business.

He'd been wrong.

He was furious at the situation, but even more furious at himself. He should have known there was a dog and another person in the house so he could have prepared properly. He'd gotten no information on that. That was what he was paying his informant to do. She'd failed him. It was no surprise. Though she'd been highly recommended as someone that could be trusted, that apparently, hadn't been the case. It made him ineffective and sloppy. He could feel his father's disdain even after all of these years. Eric Atkins was his prey, not Emily Tizzano. He needed to get to him.

James reached down and massaged his leg a bit more at the next streetlight. He turned the car toward the courthouse and realized that if he didn't either get Eric Atkins on his side or out of the way, there was no way that James would be able to even step his foot close to the governor's race. There would be no point in even running. Even if he started having events, there would be no one there. He'd be the candidate that sunk to the bottom of the polls, newscasters giggling when they talked about him hanging at less than one percent support.

His face reddened, the embarrassment covering him already. He didn't want to be one of *those* people, the ones that failed. It couldn't happen. He was Judge James Conklin. He was a guardian of law and justice, the best man to be the next governor of the state of Illinois.

Couldn't Eric see that?

By the conversation they'd had, James knew Eric was willfully withholding his support. Layla was right. Eric had already made up his mind about supporting Liv Gardner. That couldn't happen. If something didn't change, and fast, James would be six years older by the time his next opportunity came. No, it was time to tidy things up. Time to get yet another obstacle out of his way.

50

After spending a couple hours cleaning up her kitchen, Emily decided that the damage wasn't too bad. She was keeping her hands busy, waiting to hear from Mike. He was as close to family as she had in the area. And Miner was her constant companion. She stared at the floor, scrubbing viciously at a black mark, thinking about what she would do to anyone who tried to hurt her dog.

She didn't get a chance to finish her thought. Her phone rang. It was Mike, reporting that he and Miner had made it safely to his cabin. Alice was on her way as well. They'd gotten the generator started, he'd given Miner plenty of water and the two of them were settling in. As soon as Emily hung up, Angelica called and said that she had already talked to Mike and that both he and Miner seemed fine. That was a load off her mind.

It was time to get back to business.

Judge Conklin was escalating in his violence. Something had to give. Judge Conklin was going to continue to come at Eric Atkins and her. That was unacceptable. After washing her hands, she called Mike back. "Where's Conklin now?"

"I just got my computer booted up. At his house. Looks like he just got home."

Emily set her jaw. "All right. Tell me if he leaves."

51

Judge Conklin had arrived home after work, the sun nearly setting over the horizon by the time he pulled in and parked his BMW in the back of his townhouse. There was no lingering smoke smell. He'd stopped at the gym after his trip to Emily Tizzano's house and showered, tossing his black clothes into the trash bin, then headed back to the office for an afternoon of hearings.

It had been a long day. With his side trip to deal with Emily Tizzano, he'd ended up having to stay late at the office, catching up on motions and paperwork. He would have preferred to do them at home, but then again, he didn't feel like dealing with his wife or his children. He was in a mood, the kind of mood that reminded him of his father. And he knew what his father had been capable of. Usually, going for a run tamed the beast inside of him, but he wasn't sure it would work this time. James called Janice on the way home, trying to sound pleasant. She answered after the first ring. "Did you have a good day?"

"It was challenging," he answered.

"Anything I can do?"

Deal with Eric Atkins and the annoyance of Emily Tizzano. Not be there when I get home? "Actually, I thought I would do something for you."

Janice sounded surprised. "Really? But that's not necessary, James. You're always so considerate." The words came out stiff and halting. If she was lying, and he knew she was, he didn't care at that moment.

"I know you and the kids have been dying to try the new rooftop restaurant at the Plaza Hotel. So I made the three of you a reservation and got you a room for the night."

"Oh, that was so considerate. The children will be so excited," Janice cooed.

"I'm glad you are happy, but the only thing is your reservation is in forty-five minutes. You'll have to get packed and get out of the house quickly if you want to make it." The accelerated timing had been by design.

"Oh dear. Yes. I can have the kids out of here in the next ten minutes. They will be so excited. Thank you, James!"

"Of course." James hung up the phone. He didn't say I love you. He never did.

52

As the sun set, Emily tapped the comm in her ear. She'd texted Mike a few hours before and told him to be ready. When she reached out, he was. "Where is he?"

"At his house."

"I'm headed there now. Where's his family?"

"They left. Heading downtown. Last I saw, they parked at the Plaza."

That was good. "Okay, keep an eye on them. I don't want them coming back any time soon."

"Will do. Stay safe. This guy's dangerous." Mike sounded concerned.

"I know. Don't worry about me. You take care of yourself, Alice, and Miner. I'll reach out when I'm done." Emily felt no pressure to explain to Mike what she was planning, probably because there was no plan. She felt in the mood to improvise.

On the drive over to Judge Conklin's house, Emily considered calling Lou. But his hands were tied. And unlike the way that he'd treated her, she decided to treat him better. She would handle his problems for him rather than getting involved in police politics. *Wasn't there some Bible verse about repaying good for evil?* She wasn't sure that would work in Judge Conklin's situation, but that remained to be seen.

Emily drove directly downtown, making her way into the expensive neighborhood where Judge Conklin and his family lived. The street was filled on either side by red brick townhomes and artfully placed streetlamps punctuated by tall planters filled with flowers. At this stage of the summer, the plants were nearly overflowing with foliage. Six months into the future, they would be overflowing with snow and ice.

As Emily passed by Judge Conklin's townhouse, she noticed the exterior of it was lit by two shiny brass fixtures on each side of the door. It was bright red brick, in a conservative Colonial style, with immaculate white trim and shutters around each window, a wrought iron railing at the edge of the steps. It was exactly as she would have expected. There were lights on inside. That was good.

Emily drove down the street, circled back, and then parked around the corner in the rear parking lot of a drugstore. She walked down the block and around to the back of Judge Conkin's home, sticking to the shadows. Judge Conklin had killed three people and was now attempting to go after two more — Senator Eric Atkins and herself. That couldn't be allowed.

Emily trotted up the steps to the back door and didn't bother to stop, ring the doorbell or knock. No such pleasantries were required at the home of a serial killer. She fished a lock picking set out of her pocket and after just a few seconds, managed to unlock the door. "You need better locks, Your Honor," she whispered under her breath. Pausing by the door, she waited for a second to see if the alarm system would go off. It didn't. She walked into the kitchen, which was just off the back entrance and opened a cabinet door, getting herself a glass of water. She took a sip of it as Judge Conklin flipped on the lights, his eyes wide, his hands clenched into fists as if he was ready to fight. "What the —?"

"Hello, Your Honor." Emily leaned on the counter, taking a sip of the water.

"How did you get in here?"

"I picked the lock."

"You have no right—"

Emily cocked her head to the side. "Kinda hypocritical after what you did to my kitchen. You could have killed my dog. That makes me very unhappy." The judge stiffened. Emily noticed that he was standing with his weight on his left leg. "Oh, I see you met him. He's kinda territorial, especially when a madman breaks into his house."

James sneered. "Nasty little animal. You should have him put down. Oh, actually I can do that. I'll write up the order in the morning. By the time you figure out how to fight it, he'll be dead."

That was all Emily needed to hear. It was one thing to threaten her, but an innocent animal? No. She pulled her gun and pointed it directly at James's chest. "I actually don't think that you are going to do that."

"Whoa, whoa!" James held his hands up. "What is this? Coming into a judge's house and holding me at gunpoint? Hmm. That carries a minimum of a twenty-five-year sentence. You've gotten away without going to jail before, Detective Tizzano. What makes you think that your luck is gonna hold?"

"I could ask you the same question, except that the sentences for murder are a bit longer. How does life sound? The names Elizabeth Gordon, Tony Rossi, and Ander Sabate mean anything to you?" As Emily said their names, she wondered how many more people James had killed.

Emily saw his eyes narrow. "I can't help it if people have problems with their mental health and overdosing."

"Really? Because Elizabeth Gordon told me differently."

Judge Conklin's face paled. "Elizabeth Gordon is dead."

Emily shook her head, then smiled. "No. She's actually very much alive. I talked to her the other day. It seems you didn't quite overdose her enough. She's been watching you for years. Told me all about you and your little vendettas."

Judge Conklin looked away for a second and then back at Emily. "You're lying."

"No. I'm not."

He straightened. "Her drug problem isn't any of my concern." He was sticking to his story. "She was a terrible campaign manager."

"You can tell yourself that all you want, but the reality is that's not the case." Emily glanced around the house. "Now, Your Honor, where are your guns?"

"I don't have any guns."

Emily chuckled, then waved her gun in his direction, moving her finger from the rail to the trigger. He must have noticed her slight movement. "Don't waste my time. Walk."

James walked her into his office and pointed. "In the safe behind the painting."

"Excellent. Open it."

Emily took a step back as he did, keeping the gun leveled at his chest, giving herself some room to maneuver in case James decided to be a bad boy and try to make a move on her. Head shots were more of a sure thing in terms of the outcome, but it was a much smaller, more agile target. With its much greater width, it took a fraction of a second longer for a torso to move out of the way, which might make a significant difference. Emily knew shooting a round into a bigger target was always a better idea.

As James turned his back to her, the safe clicking open, Emily holstered her gun and darted up behind him without warning. She wrapped her right arm tightly around his neck and braced her left behind his head, using a chokehold she'd learned. It was a risk, but it was one she was willing to take. He clawed at her arm as she squeezed tighter and tighter, pressing the carotid arteries against his neck closed, depriving his brain of oxygen. It was a simple submission chokehold, one designed to incapacitate an attacker and one she had practiced thousands of times with Clarence and the other trainers at the gym.

And incapacitate was exactly what she needed to do.

As James slumped to the floor, Emily let his body go. If she did nothing, he'd wake up in the next couple of minutes, still being combative, still a serial killer on the loose. He'd be the same old James, wanting to kill people who got in the way of his ambitions.

Leaving him alive presented a single, critical problem — his prosecution. Even if insurmountable evidence was presented against him, he was likely to never be properly prosecuted. Or if he was, she was sure he'd hire slippery, slick attorneys that would get him off, and then another murderer would go free. He'd be free to continue to go after people — including her.

Emily strode away from him. She knew she had at least two minutes of peace and quiet before he started to stir. She took the steps two at a time, walking through the upstairs bedrooms. The first one was done in a range of pinks and whites, clearly belonging to a little girl, the pieces of a half-finished puzzle strewn neatly in the corner of the bedroom, a white lace pillow on the pink bedspread next to a worn brown teddy bear. From the background information Mike had put together, she knew James had a son and a daughter. A shiver ran down her spine. She couldn't imagine being raised by a man like James, controlling and cruel. He was a father, not a dad.

The next bedroom was in blues and beiges, properly decorated for a young gentleman. This had to be James Junior's bedroom. Emily walked over to his desk. There was a stack of workbooks on it, the old-fashioned kind, multiplication, long division, and reading comprehension. They didn't look like they had been provided by a school. It was extra training for James's son. Extra pressure.

As Emily walked away, all she could think of was that the children, and probably James's wife, were prisoners in their own home. How could they possibly thrive living with a tyrant of a man like James?

Emily trotted down the steps and walked into the office. She stared at Judge Conklin's lifeless body for a moment. His wife and children didn't deserve who he was. Elizabeth Gordon, Tony Rossi, and Ander Sabate didn't deserve what Judge Conklin had done to them either. Judge Conklin wasn't God. He was a man like every other. Sure, he had been trusted to administer justice, but his brand wasn't true justice, it was corrupt.

Emily reached into his safe after pulling on a pair of gloves that she had stashed in her pocket. She pulled out a gun from Judge James Conklin's safe, wrapped his fingers around it and held it up to his temple. The sound of the single shot shattered the silence. To everyone else, it would appear that James had ended his miserable life.

In Emily's mind, James had ended it the first time he killed someone.

Now it was just official.

EPILOGUE

The next morning, the news was on fire with more headlines than they could reasonably handle. Not only had the scandal of the day before — the Eric Atkins affair, been debunked, but the perpetrator, the unlikely character of a sitting Chicago judge, James Conklin, had been exposed.

All of it, of course, had been revealed by an anonymous tech wizard who managed to simultaneously message the three major news channels in the Chicago area with the proof.

Emily watched as she started pulling cabinet doors out of her burned kitchen, Miner sniffing around her heels as she did so. Mike had already salvaged a few things she had discarded in the dumpster. Carl had already been by, delivering sandwiches for lunch and telling Emily that his buddy, who was a contractor, would be over later that afternoon to get her a good price on fixing up the mess. Her former father-in-law, Anthony Tizzano, had called as well, asking Emily if she needed any help. She knew what he was asking. She told him no and thanked him for checking in.

As Mike walked back into her house, he glanced at the

news he was streaming on his computer. He held up his hand. "Here we go!"

The news reader stared at the camera, her face in disbelief. "In stunning news this morning, Chicago is reeling with the realization that a well-known judge was behind the accusations made against Senator Eric Atkins yesterday. The judge, James Conklin, had sat on the bench for ten years. He was well known for his stiff stance on crime and his heavy punishments. But it seems that the judge had an agenda of his own. It was recently revealed that not only did he mastermind the attack on Senator Atkins's character, a smear campaign to prevent him from becoming the Senate President, but he may have been responsible for other crimes." The anchors delivered the news with an excited indifference, their faces professionally nonjudgemental.

The broadcast cut to the police chief, who was standing at a podium, his face ashen. "The Chicago PD takes these accusations very seriously. We will look into all cases of Judge Conklin that are coming into question and will act accordingly in concert with the district attorney's office and federal authorities."

Mike smiled. "That's good, isn't it?"

"I guess. We'll see how it shakes out." Emily wasn't all that optimistic about the CPD.

The newscaster continued. "Despite the attack on Senator Atkins's character this week, he is polling higher than ever. In a stunning shift, we've just gotten word that he is going to leave his senate seat and run for governor."

Emily's eyes widened. *Talk about leveraging a situation.* "How about that?"

Mike shrugged. "He just might win. People are funny that way. They won't like that someone went after him. Mob justice might take over."

Emily didn't have a chance to answer. Her phone rang. Lou. "Did you see the news?"

"I did," Emily said. "Did you hear that my kitchen got burned?"

"I did. Need some help?"

She paused, then sighed. "Yeah, sure. Come on over whenever. I'll be here all day."

"I can do better than that. I'm outside with a box of donuts."

As Lou walked in, Miner gave a bark and then rubbed up against Lou, waiting for his back to be scratched. Lou dropped the box of donuts on the table, studying the damage. "This isn't as bad as I thought it would be."

Emily winced. It was bad enough. "I thought you'd be at work this morning."

He shrugged. "Took the day off."

That seemed strange to Emily. There would be a lot of paperwork to do after discovering what Judge Conklin was up to, a lot of additional investigating and files to look over. "Is your new partner handling that?"

"The FBI is stepping in to take over the investigation since it involves a sitting judge. I guess they are worried about optics or something."

Emily wondered if Cash would be assigned to the case. It wouldn't surprise her. He was one of the senior field agents at Chicago's FBI office. Maybe she'd hear from him, maybe she wouldn't. It was okay either way.

Lou continued. "And, speaking of Courtney, I got a call from Captain Ingram this morning. Apparently, Courtney abruptly quit her job. No notice. No nothing. Supposedly got an amazing job offer in San Diego she just couldn't pass up. Private security gig." Lou raised his eyebrows conspiratorially.

Emily stood up, wiping a sooty hand across her forehead. "Wait. What?"

Lou reached into the box and pulled out a glazed donut. "Yeah. Seems a little strange to me too. My guess is that whoever was feeding information to Judge Conklin is covering their you-know-what. Courtney must have been in on it. Probably doing someone's dirty work. That was probably why she gave me the creeps. Might never know who told her to do it or why, but I got what I wanted. No partner, plus the case is solved."

"Any news on Judge Conklin's wife?" Mike asked.

After Judge Conklin's unfortunate suicide the night before, Emily had left the house immediately. Mysteriously, after an amazing dinner, Janice's card was declined at the Plaza Hotel for their overnight stay, so she and the children had to return home. What they found was horrific, to be sure, but at least it was over.

"I guess the FBI is interviewing them this morning," Lou said.

Emily nodded slowly. While she wanted to believe that the case was over, she wasn't sure. "Who do you think was behind it?"

"The link to CPD?"

Lou shook his head. "No idea, but my guess is it goes to the top?"

"All the way to the chief?"

"Maybe."

Mike made his way over to the box of donuts and took two, one for each fist, shoving one covered in pink frosting in his mouth first. Chewing, he added, "Corruption usually starts at the top, but the chief seems to have his job this morning."

Emily sunk to the floor and started unscrewing another blistered cabinet door to take to the dumpster. Mike was right. The chief still did have his job. The city was running as usual, CPD officers responding to calls, people going to work and taking their kids to school. She shook her head, not sure how to feel. "Some things never change."

Lou bent over and planted a brotherly kiss on the top of her head. "And sometimes that's good."

If you'd like to join my mailing list and be the first to get updates on new books and exclusive sales, giveaways and releases, click here!
I'll send you a prequel to the next series FREE!

Join the KJ Kalis Facebook Reader Group here

Made in the USA
Coppell, TX
15 February 2025